Savage Thunder

Also by Cassie Edwards
in Large Print:

Savage Moon
Savage Obsession
Fire Cloud
Passion's Web

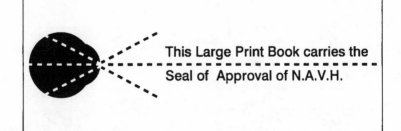

Savage Thunder

Cassie Edwards

Thorndike Press • Waterville, Maine

12\23\02

Published in 2002 by arrangement with Leisure Books,
a division of Dorchester Publishing Co., Inc.

Thorndike Press Large Print Famous Authors Series.

The tree indicium is a trademark of Thorndike Press.

The text of this Large Print edition is unabridged.
Other aspects of the book may vary from the original edition.

Set in 16 pt. Plantin by Myrna S. Raven.

Printed in the United States on permanent paper.

Library of Congress Cataloging-in-Publication Data

Edwards, Cassie.
    Savage thunder / Cassie Edwards.
      p. cm.
    ISBN 0-7862-4783-5 (lg. print : hc : alk. paper)
    1. Mohawk Indians — Fiction. 2. Large type books.
    I. Title.
PS3555.D875 S33 2002
  813'.54—dc21   2002029088

With much affection I dedicate
Savage Thunder
to my friend Harri Garnett of Maine!

Also, in memory of Valerie Ann Taylor,
"Soft Feather"

Acknowledgments

I wish to thank Harriet Lucas Garnett (Harri!), a wonderfully talented poet and friend, for giving me the honor of printing her poetry in *Savage Thunder*. All of the beautiful poetry that you see at the beginning of each of the chapters in this book, as well as Swift Thunder and Moon Song's Song, were written by Harri.

Thunder and Moonlight
(Swift Thunder and Moon Song's Song)

Nothing ever looks the same
After it is bathed in love.
She prayed her silent prayer
To *Tharonhiawakon*, The Creator, above.
Her heart had learned to smile,
They both felt Thunder and Moonlight
  for a while.
Why did he long for her in the night?
Each memory of her sent his heart
  in flight.
He remembered her sighs and her
  cries of delight,
It was then he knew that for her love . . .
  their love . . . he must fight.
The wind blew gently across the land,
She remembered the touch of his hand.
Clouds moved slowly across the
  sky of blue,
She wondered did he dream of her, too?
Moonlight and Thunder have
  "Magic Power,"
She longed for his arms, hour
  after lonely hour.
Her prayers were answered with his
  gentle love,

She knew that their prayers had
   been heard by
Tharonhiawakon above.

— Harriet Lucas Garnett,
   poet and dear friend

Introduction

Savage Thunder is about the *Onkweh-Onweh*, Mohawk Indians, who are one of the oldest of the original five tribes of the "League of the Iroquois." The Iroquois were made up of the league of five nations in upstate New York. These five nations, the Mohawk, Oneida, Cayuga, Seneca, and Onondaga, thought of themselves as an extended family and called themselves the "People of the Longhouse." The five nations became six when in 1722 the Tuscaroras were accepted into the league. Every individual belonged to a clan — the Mohawk clans were the Turtle, Wolf, and Bear.

In *Savage Thunder*, my Mohawk hero, Swift Thunder, belongs to the Bear Clan, which exemplified the teaching of gentleness and strength; they believed it takes more strength to restrain violence than to use it.

Moon Song, the heroine of *Savage Thunder*, is of a rival clan. She is Oneida, and born into a blood feud between the Bear Clan of the Mohawk and the Turtle Clan of the Oneida that had begun before either she or my hero were born.

In most of my Native American books I have written about villages. In *Savage Thunder*, the word "castle" is used by the Iroquois when referring to their villages.

The story that follows tells how Moon Song and Swift Thunder meet, knowing they are enemies, but wanting something far beyond that: to be free to love!

Chapter One

I must admit it was early spring,
When all the world is on a merry fling,
I let my heart go and it was new,
And I began loving you.

Upper New York — 1746

The "castle" of the Oneida people was built on an undulating hill above the Mohawk River which flowed through a picturesque valley, emptying into the Hudson.

The village was comprised of an irregular cluster of bark longhouses behind a palisade. A little apart from the other buildings stood a drab, one-room hut where a girl of twelve winters patiently waited for the day she could emerge from it, no longer a *peenchkquaso,* but a *pchanum,* a woman with a woman's responsibilities.

Moon Song had withstood these past four days alone thanks to her stamina and strength. She was known to her people by her firm, quick step, the determined yet beautiful curve of her lips, and the live-

11

coal glow in her widely set eyes.

She was stately and wore her thick, luscious, jet black hair down past her waist.

"My fourth day," she whispered excitedly as she sat with her legs crossed on a rush mat in the shadowy, windowless hut, where a small fire burned in the firepit in the center of the room.

Although smoke curled up through the smoke hole above her, the air was still stifling and choking.

Que, yes, she was sorely tired of being cooped up in the tiny room.

"But I have done it," she said aloud.

She ran a hand along the buckskin fabric of her dress. She would soon wear the softest of doeskin dresses, fringed, beaded, and beautiful, the proper accoutrements of a lady.

She had sat for hours preparing the clothes that she would wear in her new life. Each bead, each tiny shell and porcupine quill had been sewn onto her lovely garments with care and pride.

To be an Oneida woman meant everything to Oneida girls. Life only truly began when a girl stepped over the wondrous threshold of adulthood!

There would be no more girlish games or dolls. Her chin would be lifted proudly as she worked alongside her mother and the other women carrying wood and water. She would feel important as she planted seeds in the garden.

She could hardly wait for her mother's arrival today to end the solitude she had endured these past four days.

She gazed slowly around her and shuddered at the unpleasantness of the hut. The only furniture was a small platform for sleeping, upon which were spread pelts and blankets.

Otherwise, it was bare.

She had brought her hairbrush and four changes of clothes, and had bathed each day from a basin of water that her mother had brought for her each morning, along with the food that would have to last her the whole day.

The sole person she had seen these past four days was her mother, who was the only one allowed to tend to her.

Moon Song had been made to eat sparingly during this time, though that was not too hard. All Oneida boys and girls were taught to eat sparingly and healthfully. They had been taught that gluttony was a sin, that too many corn cakes dripping with maple syrup would bring on the bogeyman.

Oh, yes, Moon Song was proud of this special time in her life. She was eager to be looked upon as a *pchanum,* a woman, and she planned to make her mother proud.

Her mother had been living the life of a widow for six years and had devoted her life to her *n-nitschaan,* her daughter.

"A wild, brave little thing," Moon Song whispered and giggled as she thought about her mother's description of her. Moon Song had always done things beyond what was ordinary for a girl her age, things that even *she* knew were too daring for her own good.

But she loved life. She loved to take from it all she could.

She had seen how quickly life could change, and how quickly women became old before their time.

"Especially my mother," she whispered. Since Moon Song's father's death, her mother, Dove Woman, had aged so much it pained Moon Song sometimes even to look at her.

Her mother had always been so beautiful and full of life; it just didn't seem right to Moon Song that she rarely smiled now. Dove Woman still mourned the man she had loved since she had been a young girl who had just left her own time in the menstrual hut.

Moon Song's mother's and father's love had been so special . . . so enduring.

The life had seemed to have been sucked from her mother that day when news came of Moon Song's father's untimely death in the Mohawk River.

"I have tried so hard to do things to make her smile," Moon Song whispered as she slowly shoved a log into the dying flames of the lodge fire.

But today, even if her mother did not smile as she held her daughter's hand when Moon Song left the menstrual hut, she knew that her mother would be happy for her. Her mother had prepared Moon Song for this special day for as long as Moon Song could remember. In an Oneida woman's life, this day was almost as important as the one when she would speak her vows with the man who would father her children.

The one thing that clouded Moon Song's pride in becoming a woman was the fact that just prior to her father's death in the Mohawk River, he had betrothed Moon Song to a boy but little older than she, the son of their Turtle Clan's *sachem*, chief.

Moon Song had not complained, because she knew that in time she would find her man to love, and surely she would be allowed to marry one of her own choosing.

But, of late, Piercing Eyes, Moon Song's betrothed, was taking his betrothal to Moon Song too seriously, when in fact it was meant only to seal the friendship between two families, rather than be a permanent bond.

Moon Song had always been indifferent to the whole procedure, knowing that it had nothing to do with actual marriage, and she had thought Piercing Eyes was equally unconcerned.

But as her body began developing into a woman's, she had seen Piercing Eyes staring at the way her breasts strained against the bodice of her buckskin dress. He had even whispered shameful references to them into Moon Song's ear.

Recently, he had publicly laid claim to her, saying she *would* be his wife!

Moon Song had dared to openly laugh at Piercing Eyes, who would one day more than likely be a powerful *sachem* like his father. She had openly told him that she would never marry anyone she did not love.

Humiliated by her derision, Piercing Eyes had backed off and now kept his distance.

At least for the time being, he seemed to have forgotten his idea of how their futures should be joined. Instead he had involved himself in the activities of the boys his age who were preparing themselves to become men, who would be labeled warriors and feared by their enemies.

She hoped he would become so caught up in his new status in life that he would put warring ahead of wooing.

When the small door of the menstrual hut started to creak open, Moon Song scurried to her feet. She hurried to the door and opened it the rest of the way.

She smiled broadly when she found her mother standing there and felt the fresh air sweep across her face. The sound of children laughing in the courtyard came to her, sweet and wonderful. Freedom was so near she could almost taste it!

Her very soul cried out for it.

"Daughter, it is time now to leave the hut," Dove Woman said, remaining outside.

She reached her hands out for Moon Song. *"Bi, come,"* she murmured. "You have proven yourself a woman. Come now, Moon Song. Go forth among your people and carry the title of 'woman' proudly."

Filled with happiness, Moon Song flung

herself into her mother's frail arms and hugged her. "Mother, Mother," she murmured, joy warming her through and through. "I *am* a woman. A *woman.*"

Then she stepped away from her mother, her smile fading. "But I feel no different," she murmured. "The only difference is my joy over having achieved my goal, and over being able to leave this horrible, closed-in place."

Her mother nodded in understanding of what her daughter had described. "I, too, expected more than what I felt on the day I first left the menstrual hut," Dove Woman said.

She moved to Moon Song's side and slid an arm around her waist to lead her outside.

She walked her away from the hut toward their longhouse, which sat amid many others.

Moon Song gazed at their longhouse as they approached it and smiled, for she would be home again, not in the drab, small hut.

It was a home that she and her mother were proud of, although smaller than most others in the castle.

The Oneida tribe was one of the five tribes in the league of the Iroquois, who called themselves the "People of the Longhouse."

All longhouses were rectangular structures of poles and bark. Their high roofs were arched. Each longhouse had almost the same furnishings, which usually were scarce.

A firepit for both cooking and warmth was built in the center of each lodge, dug into the earthen floor, which was then surrounded by rock.

An opening in the roof served as both window and chimney with overlapping pieces of bark to keep out the rain.

Moon Song and her mother had separate rooms where each slept on a platform close to the earth, and used part of a shelf that ran the length of the room for storage. Here such items as corn, bowls filled with food, and skin robes were kept.

Beneath the platform, snowshoes, bows, spears, and winnowing baskets were stored.

Rush mats covered the earthen floor throughout, and bearskin curtains were at the windows, ready to be drawn tightly closed with buckskin ties when it rained, or grew blustery in the winter.

Moon Song could identify a variety of smells in her mother's longhouse — kettle soup, sweet grass, and bear grease, as well as the pleasant aromas that came from the braids of corn, strings of dried apples and squash, and bundles of roots that hung on the walls and from the rafters.

"Daughter, on the day I left my own first time in the menstrual hut I discovered that it was not expected of the woman to *feel* older and wiser because of her time spent there," her mother said, interrupting Moon Song's thoughts. "That comes with true aging . . . with performing the duties of a woman."

"And I will, Mother," Moon Song said eagerly. "Although I have been a dutiful daughter who always did my chores willingly, I will do them twice as eagerly now, Mother, to prove my worth as a woman."

"*N-nitschaan, N-nitschaan,* do not be so hasty to promise things that you might regret later," Dove Woman said, laughing softly.

Her mother's laughter was like an elixir to Moon Song, for her mother rarely laughed.

But today she was actually laughing softly as though she too had been transformed into someone different.

Her mood seemed lighter. Her dark eyes even had more life in them. Pride in her daughter seemed to have caused this transformation.

Moon Song vowed she would prove her worth to her mother, time and again. She would not disappoint her.

Moon Song would even try not to be so quick to do things which might raise the eyebrows of the elders.

But even as she was thinking these things, she was eyeing the open gate of the palisade and hungering for the freedom she had been denied these past four days and nights.

Although she had not eaten her morning meal yet, the hunger she felt for freedom was more powerful.

She so ached to get in her canoe and enjoy the beauty that surrounded the Mohawk River on this late spring morning.

She wished to see the fresh new leaves on the limbs of the trees, and the newly budded flowers along the riverbank that the sunshine had beckoned from their long winter's rest.

Even now she heard the call of the bluejay and cardinal in the forest beyond the castle's palisade.

She could even see the yellow finches as they darted above her now, like streaks of golden sunlight, on their way to the trees that grew just inside the castle walls.

Their song pleased Moon Song the most, for their calls announced that spring had finally arrived in the land of the Oneida.

"I sense your restlessness," Dove Woman said. She stopped and drew Moon Song's eyes to her. "I know your love of canoeing and how you must have missed it these past days. Go now, daughter. I understand. But do not stay too long. There will be a council soon with the rest of the girls. You are expected to be there, among them."

Moon Song hugged her mother. "Thank you, Mother," she murmured. "The winter was so long. Now that the river has thrown off its weight of ice, how can I not be eager to travel in my canoe to see what might have changed while the world was isolated in winter's grip?"

"Just do not go far, or stay too long," Dove Woman said, stepping away from Moon Song. She reached a hand to her daughter's hair and brushed a fallen lock back from her brow. "My daughter is now a woman. Ah, but I am so proud."

Then she gave Moon Song a playful slap on her behind. "Hurry now, but do not delay your return for long," she said. She sighed with pride as Moon Song smiled broadly at her over her shoulder, then ran toward the open gate.

After sorting through the canoes that were moored along the riverbank and finding hers, Moon Song slid it into the water, then leaped inside and picked up her paddle.

Her heart raced as she paddled her way out to the middle of the river and began her journey, with the sun making a path of fire in the water.

She was proud of owning her own canoe, which she had painstakingly made with her own hands. The Oneida covered their canoes with elm or spruce bark. Their river craft were sturdy, but she knew they were not as fast or nimble as the birchbark canoes made by her Algonquian neighbors.

The Oneida's canoes possessed other advantages. Because of the thick, rough bark, they could be used as ladders to scale enemy walls, or as shields to block enemy arrows.

Moon Song's small canoe, however, was used only for pleasure. The winter had been long. She had grown sorely tired of looking at the ice that covered the river.

She would never forget the joy that had rushed through her on that day when the ice split in half beneath the steady, warm rays of the sun.

The sound of the ice breaking apart had been like a blast of gunfire, explosive and loud enough to cause the village dogs to howl with fright.

It also seemed to have awakened all of the wild creatures that had slept through the cold days of winter, as well as the birds that knew they would not have to work so hard any longer as they foraged for food to keep them alive until spring brought fresh plants and flowers, and worms to the surface, for them to feast upon.

Today the forest was alive with song on each side of the river. The aroma of blooming flowers came to Moon Song as though great bursts of perfume were filling the air.

Her heart soared at the thought that she was now a woman. She searched for the perfect place to pray to *Tharonhiawakon,* the creator, for guidance in this new life of responsibility.

Although she would never allow the despicable, cold-hearted Piercing Eyes to have her as his wife, she *did* hope to marry. She would have many children, for that was the main goal of all Oneida women.

"Also a grandchild would fill mother's heart with such happiness," she whispered.

She smiled as she envisioned her mother holding a grandchild, her eyes filled with a bliss that her husband's death had robbed from her.

Qua, yes, Moon Song would make it happen, not only for herself, but also for her mother.

But first she had to find someone whom she could love as much as her mother had loved *her* husband.

Moon Song wondered if that could be possible, for she had seen something very special in her father's and mother's love, a dedication that was rarely seen between man and woman.

"I want something as special," Moon Song whispered. "I want something as sweet."

Moon Song started when suddenly the bird song was stilled. Anxiously she hoped she had not traveled too far from the safety of her home.

She stilled her paddle and leaned an ear to the left as she listened to the sound of shouts and cheers coming from somewhere in the forest nearby.

Having been lost in thought, she had not realized just how far she had gone. Her people's enemy, the Bear Clan of the Mohawk, lived not far from the Turtle

Clan of the Oneida.

Therein lay a constant threat to her people, for there had been a blood feud between the Bear Clan and the Turtle Clan that had begun before Moon Song was born.

She always wondered when the Mohawk might continue the blood feud which had been dormant for quite a while now.

But fear was something almost foreign to Moon Song, who was almost too brave sometimes for her own good. Ignoring the warning that was going off inside her brain at this very moment, she let her curiosity get the best of her again. She *had* to see who was shouting and cheering, and to know why.

It sounded like some sort of test was being performed by boys, for it was the voices of boys that could be heard between the cheers.

Her heart pounding with excitement, Moon Song steered her canoe toward shore.

After she had it beached, she hid herself behind trees and tall bushes as she sought the source of the shouts and cheers that sometimes burst into gay laughter.

As she pushed her way onward, the leaves of last autumn lay lightly scattered upon the ground as though no human foot had passed over them, which meant that those she was drawing near to had come from a different direction.

And she had seen no canoes beached anywhere along the shore, which again meant that the boys had not traveled there by water. They had come on foot and surely lived nearby.

She began to suspect that she was near the castle of the Bear clan.

Yet even that suspicion did not slow her steps. She knew that she was too close now not to go on and see who these boys were, and what they were doing.

She would stay hidden. They would never suspect that she was there, watching.

Finally she came to a place in the trees where there was a break up ahead, enough for her to see ten boys.

What she saw them doing made her cringe. She shuddered involuntarily at the blood on some of their bodies and found a shelter close enough to see the ritual this group of boys was performing.

As she knelt behind a thick bush and watched, she concluded that these boys must be around fifteen winters of age. They were taking turns dashing themselves against a wall of rock.

Now that she saw exactly what they were doing, she understood the ritual. It was practiced by all boys of the League of the Iroquois to prove their masculinity.

Noting the roach of hair running down the center of each boy's head, she knew for certain that this group was Mohawk.

Moon Song's eyes were drawn suddenly to one boy in particular. Though he was dressed like the others in a breechclout and moccasins, and his hair and eye color were the same, there were two things that set him apart from his companions.

He had a full head of black hair, and he wore it long to his waist with a headband holding it back from his brow, not in the normal Mohawk fashion.

And then there was the color of his skin. Though it was dark, the color came from having been burned by the sun, not from his heritage.

Also . . . there was something else different about the young man. He had features like those found on the faces of white men and boys.

All the same, he was, oh, so very handsome, so muscled for one his age. Gazing at him almost stole Moon Song's breath away.

She found that she could hardly stop looking at him.

And he was, oh, so courageous, throwing himself over and over again against the hard wall of rock.

When he started to bleed, Moon Song could no longer stand to watch the ritual.

Covering her mouth with a hand to stifle a sob of horror at what these youths were doing to themselves, she ran back toward the river.

When she reached the Mohawk, she stopped panting as she tried to catch her breath.

A lone tree, stately and tall, caught her attention. It hung over the river, its broad, long limbs reaching out like arms, beckoning to the spirits that dwelled in the river, and Moon Song decided to stay there long enough to say her prayers. Then she would be on her way.

After kneeling under the tree, where the grass was cool and soft beneath her knees, Moon Song began giving thanks to *Tharonhiawakon,* but too often found her mind straying to the handsome, intriguing boy who was today becoming a man.

Had she not just become a woman?

And would it not be wonderful to meet that boy face to face?

She quickly reminded herself that this

29

boy was an enemy. Worse, he was a half-breed.

She forced herself to put him from her mind as she resumed her prayers, pleading for guidance. She truly needed it, for she knew better than to look upon anyone of Mohawk blood as anything but an enemy.

Chapter Two

Their love was magic, or so it seemed.
Images filled the night when they dreamed.
In daylight their world was cold.
Only in their dreams could their
    hearts be bold.

Swift Thunder's body was aching from throwing himself against the wall of rock, yet he knew that he must bear the pain and suffering in order to successfully complete his puberty rites.

Now fifteen, it was time to test and prove his masculinity by bashing himself against the wall of rock until he was bruised and bleeding.

When he felt blood on his bare chest, arms, and legs, and he looked down and saw that his breechclout was spotted with it, Swift Thunder stopped and inhaled a quiet breath of relief that he had finally achieved his goal.

One by one his friends, whose bodies were also spotted with blood, stopped and cheered as they took turns hugging and congratulating each other.

Swift Thunder joined them as they stood together discussing the ritual. How proud they were to achieve the status of *nimannau,* men!

As they started to leave for their homes at the Mohawk Castle of the Bear, Swift Thunder remained unmoving.

When they stopped and turned to give him a questioning look, he quickly explained why he would come later to join them in the celebration that was planned for them by their relatives and friends.

"I wish to commune in private with *Tharonhiawakon,* the creator, and also take a swim to cleanse my body. Then I will return home," Swift Thunder said, knowing that he spoke only a half-truth to his friends. He did not want to share with them how he had a strong feeling of a presence besides themselves in the area. He did not feel threatened by this presence, but rather mystically drawn to it.

Showing the blood on his person to his people was not required to prove his success today. Bruises were proof enough that he had gone as far in the rites as was required of him.

"Do not linger long," Winter Rain, Swift Thunder's best friend, advised. "Without you, the celebration will be only halfheartedly felt by me."

Swift Thunder placed a hand on Winter Rain's thin shoulder. "Friend, I promise I will return shortly," he said, smiling.

"I would come and join your prayers, but I know that you prefer to speak with *Tharonhiawakon* alone," Winter Rain said as Swift Thunder lowered his hand to his side. "So, Swift Thunder, I will see you soon?"

"*Qua*, yes, soon," Swift Thunder said.

He bent low and swept his pet baby cougar into his arms as it came to him, mewing.

Swift Thunder had found the tiny creature abandoned and half starved. After much devoted attention from Swift Thunder, and much food, the cougar was now fat, so fat it wobbled as it walked and ran.

Swift Thunder held the cougar in his arms as he began running barefoot toward the river.

"Blue, I know that I am getting blood on you, but a bath in the river with me will soon clean it off," Swift Thunder said, smiling down at his cougar as the kitten gazed up at him with its trusting bluish-green eyes. "And, ah, how beautifully sleek your fur has become now that your diet is rich in oil."

As the sun came down through the leaves of the trees overhead, it made Blue's eyes shine with a mixture of blue and green. Swift Thunder was reminded of why he had named his pet Blue, for sometimes the kitten's eyes looked blue and other times green.

The kitten's soft fur sent a gentle warmth through Swift Thunder's body, almost making him forget how it ached.

But he had not forgotten what had made him decide to take a separate path from his friends', and he now focused his attention on listening for sounds of a possible intruder on his people's land. His eyes, which were almost as keen as an eagle's, scanned the forest around him.

After he went farther still, and neither saw nor heard anyone, Swift Thunder was puzzled as to why he had sensed that someone was there earlier. Surely the intruder had fled elsewhere at Swift Thunder's approach.

"Ah, well, I do need to pray, and I do need to swim," he said, shrugging. He stroked a hand across his cougar's back. "So *bi-yanc,* come, little one, join me, for although Winter Rain is my very best *human* friend, you are the best *animal* friend a man could ever want."

He thought back to when he had found the abandoned baby cougar, and how he had looked far and wide for its mother, yet knew even before he had gone on the hunt that he would not find her.

More than likely, she was dead, or she would not have abandoned her baby. If the kitten had wandered from its home, the mother would surely have searched for it. A baby, whether two- or four-legged, was the heart and soul of a parent.

Anxious to swim, Swift Thunder searched the riverbank for a peaceful place to pray.

Shading the water from the morning sun, trees hung their freshly leafed limbs over the Mohawk River like huge umbrellas. Wild roses rambled along the riverbank, their sweet scent filling the air with soft perfume.

Enjoying nature's gifts, Swift Thunder placed Blue on the ground beside him, then knelt and lifted his eyes heavenward as he gave thanks to the Creator for allowing him to make his entrance into manhood with dignity, and for granting him the courage not to reveal to his friends the true pain it had caused him.

He prayed for guidance as he traveled the road of life as a man.

He prayed that his chieftain grandfather, Fire Wolf, would live forever and ever!

Swift Thunder prayed on, about things close to his heart; then, feeling at peace with himself, he rose to his feet.

Stretching his arms high above his head, he gazed into the water. It had not been so long ago that ice stretched smooth and cold across the top, sealing it. It had not been all that long ago that the river had broken free of the ice as the Mohawk Valley began budding in the April sunshine.

Swift Thunder knew that the water was still cold, but he liked it that way. When he swam in it, it invigorated him — it made him feel like a man!

"Today I *am* a man," he said, smiling down at Blue as his pet rubbed himself back and forth against Swift Thunder's ankles.

He smiled down at the little cougar, then dove with his breechclout still on, head first, into the river.

He stiffened himself against the burst of cold as his body hit the water, wincing when the icy river sent spirals of pain across his bruised body.

When his head broke through the surface and he began swimming, he had to smile. He had heard a splash and knew that his pet had dived in and would soon be swimming beside him.

Although most cats, of all sizes, were loath to be in water, his cougar always swam beside Swift Thunder like a fish.

After Swift Thunder got used to the cold, he found the water soothing to his self-inflicted wounds.

Then remembering those who awaited his arrival at their Castle of the Bear, especially his grandfather who would be proud that his grandson had endured the rites that proved him a man today, Swift Thunder turned and began swimming toward shore, his cougar still beside him.

Swift Thunder stopped swimming suddenly when he saw a young girl standing on the embankment, watching him.

His heart skipped a beat when their eyes met and held.

Then a thought came to Swift Thunder. Surely it had been this maiden who somehow had mystically lured him to the river.

But why?

Why was it meant for them to know one another?

Whatever the reason, he could not help but be glad, for she was the most beautiful girl he had ever seen.

He saw such sweet innocence in her dark eyes.

He saw her tininess, so delicate that were a breeze to come along, she might be whisked away by it.

But most wonderful of all, her voluminous, waist-length dark hair framed a face of perfection.

Shaking himself out of his reverie, the sort he had never experienced before, Swift Thunder swam on to shore.

After scooping Blue into his arms, he went dripping out of the water toward the girl.

Up close, he was even more captivated by her loveliness — by her large brown eyes, her alluring, beautifully shaped lips, and her perfect facial features.

He could tell that she was not the same age as he, but younger. He saw that she was budding into a young lady by the swells that were evident beneath the buckskin of her dress.

Stunned to be face to face with the young brave she had longed to meet, Moon Song found that words were frozen deep inside her. She was silent as he emerged from the water, his deep brown eyes holding hers.

Now that he was out of the water, Moon Song saw that the brave had washed the blood from his body. But the bruises were there, physical proof that he had accomplished his puberty rites today just as she had.

Oh, how he did intrigue her!

She only hoped that she would regain her ability to speak before he tired of her and her silence and turned, leaving her there like the fool she was feeling herself to be.

"Who are you?" Swift Thunder suddenly asked, his eyes moving slowly over her, again familiarizing himself with her loveliness. His eyes met and held hers again. "Where are your people?" he asked. "Of which clan are you? Which people? Mohawk? Or Oneida?"

Wanting to prove to him that she could speak as intelligently as he, and glad that he spoke in a language she understood, which both the Mohawk and Oneida shared, Moon Song cleared her throat nervously.

"I am of the Castle of the Oneida Turtle clan," Moon Song said warily.

Having been afraid that was exactly what she would say, Swift Thunder stiffened.

But when she hurried on to speak her

name, telling him that it was Moon Song in a voice so soft and sweet, he softened toward her.

"I am called Swift Thunder," he said, knowing that he, too, had to reveal which clan and castle were his. He knew that she might become frightened and flee into the forest away from him. Yet he knew it must be said, for she was patiently waiting with wide eyes for him to speak it.

"I am Mohawk, of the Castle of the Bear," he blurted out. He was stunned that she seemed not at all disturbed by the knowledge that he was from the very clan that for many years had had a blood feud with her own people.

Instead, her eyes went to his cougar, as though what he had said had mattered not at all to her.

Seeing her so intrigued by his tiny pet, glad to have something to talk about besides clans and past feuds, Swift Thunder took a step closer to Moon Song.

"My cougar's name is Blue," he said. "I gave him that name because his eyes are sometimes blue."

He ran a hand slowly over his pet's fur, the kitten's purring proof that he relished being pampered.

"I have never seen a cougar kitten before," Moon Song said, dying to hold and pet the lovely thing. "I have never seen *any* cougar that would allow humans near it. How is it that you have this kitten, and you call it your own? Where is its mother?"

"I am its mother, father, and everything else that matters to Blue," Swift Thunder said, shrugging.

He then hurried on to tell her how and why the kitten was in his possession.

"Blue was nearly starved to death when I found him," Swift Thunder said solemnly. "I fed him and nursed him back to health. He is very devoted to me now, as I am to him. But one day he will be like his father, strong, proud, and able to fend for himself."

"What a lovely story," Moon Song murmured. She reached a hand out, and as Swift Thunder removed his hand from Blue's back, Moon Song placed hers there.

She felt a gentle warmth flow through her at the mere touch of the beautiful kitten.

"Do you wish to hold him?" Swift Thunder asked, and was glad that he had offered when he saw Moon Song's eyes light up at the suggestion.

"I would love to," Moon Song said. Nonetheless, her pulse raced with anxiety.

She had been taught to fear cougars.

But she reminded herself that this was a kitten . . . tiny, tame, and beautiful, and her fear faded into the wind as she reached out and took the kitten from Swift Thunder. The cougar responded gently and sweetly as she held him against her bosom.

And when Blue's tongue sought Moon Song's hand and began licking it, she was lost, heart and soul, to the dear animal.

Swift Thunder was touched in his own way as he watched his pet react to Moon Song. Blue seemed utterly content in her arms.

Afraid that he, too, was attracted to this beautiful maiden, and knowing it was not wise, Swift Thunder broke the magic of the moment by saying what he wished he did not have to say.

"You should not be so far from your home," he blurted out. "You should not be talking with the enemy. Your people and mine have chosen different roads. Yours have chosen to be loyal to the French, mine to the English."

"*Qua,* I know these things, but at the moment it does not matter to me," Moon Song murmured, shrugging.

She gazed even more deeply into Swift Thunder's eyes and tilted her head slightly.

"Does it truly matter to you who your people, or mine, are allies with?" she asked softly.

Shaken by her response, and even her question, Swift Thunder was even more captivated by her.

Wanting to be friends with her, yet knowing that it was not meant to be, Swift Thunder said again things he wished he did not have to say.

"Do you forget so easily our peoples' past feuds?" he asked, his voice drawn. "Do you forget how during the height of the feud, cousins killed cousins, and there were battles more horrifying than the man-eating monsters that our people's story-teller describes at night beside the large outdoor fire?"

"How can I forget, even though I wish to?" Moon Song said, wishing he had not pursued this topic.

"Why *are* you so far from your castle?" Swift Thunder asked. "What has brought you to the land of your enemy?"

"Not long ago this land was not your people's," Moon Song pointed out. "Why did your people come and establish your castle so close to ours? Are you here to stir up the old feud? Or is it by accident that you plant your roots so close to people who you know are your enemy?"

"It is not for me to say," Swift Thunder replied, flinching when she suddenly gave the little cougar back to him. She no longer seemed as sweet and friendly as before.

He felt to blame, for he had said things that would rile anyone.

"I had not realized I had traveled so far," Moon Song said, turning to gaze toward the river where her canoe awaited out of sight. "I am only here because I was . . . was . . . searching for the perfect place to pray."

"I, too, came to the river today to pray," Swift Thunder said softly, bringing Moon Song around to gaze at him again. "Also to wash my body clean of blood brought on by my puberty rites."

Moon Song's eyes moved to his bruised body and saw that blood was again seeping from his wounds.

With hardly a thought of what she was doing, just wanting to do something that might ease the tension that had developed between them, Moon Song turned and bent down beside the river and cupped water in her hands.

Gently smiling at Swift Thunder, Moon Song rose to her feet and let the water roll from her hands onto his bloody chest.

When he winced with pain, she took a quick step away from him. "I am sorry," she said, her voice breaking, her eyes wide as she gazed into his again. "I . . . I . . . only wanted to help you feel better, not cause you more pain."

Feeling her sweetness in his very soul, Swift Thunder laid a gentle hand on Moon Song's arm. "You did me no harm," he said, smiling. "Thank you for trying to help."

"I know about the rites you just participated in," she said, nervously clasping her hands together behind her. "You have today proven to be a *nimannau*, a man."

She smiled. "I, too, went through my own rites, but mine took four days," she said. She proudly lifted her chin. "This is the fourth day. I am now a woman."

Swift Thunder wanted to tell her that he had the feelings of a man for her, but because she was an Oneida of the Turtle Clan, he refrained from revealing such intimate emotions to her.

After today, they would know each other no more.

Their time together today, even as short as it would be, never should have happened.

They were forbidden to each other.

"I do want to help heal your wounds," Moon Song suddenly said. "Tomorrow I will bring medicine that will heal your wounds more quickly. The shaman of my village is Black Raven, my cousin. I will bring his medicine to you, if you will allow it."

Having only moments ago concluded that this would be, *should* be, their one and only time meeting, Swift Thunder was at a loss how to answer her.

He wanted nothing more than to see her again.

There was something magical between them, as though a web was being spun around them, binding them together so they might become as one with one another.

He knew it was not wise to allow this relationship to go farther. But his heart was winning over logic. He *did* want to be with her again. How could he give up this sudden friendship with someone as sweet and beautiful as Moon Song?

Making himself forget which tribe and clan she belonged to, he rushed ahead and said what his heart told him to say.

"Yes, I will be here tomorrow," he said thickly.

His heart pounded strangely at the thought of being with her again, learning more about her.

"Tomorrow, shortly after the sun is at the midpoint in the sky, you will find me here at the place where we are standing today," he quickly added.

Giddy with excitement, yet knowing that she had already been gone for too long, Moon Song gave Swift Thunder a last, lingering smile, then ran along the embankment toward her beached canoe.

She looked over her shoulder at him just before reaching the bend in the land. "I shall be here tomorrow!" she shouted. "And, oh, please bring your baby cougar so that I can hold him again!"

"I shall!" Swift Thunder said, giving her a final wave.

After Moon Song got her canoe out into the river and began paddling toward home, she felt eyes on her.

She turned and saw that Swift Thunder had followed her along the riverbank. He was standing there holding his cougar as he watched her.

She felt a warm glow inside, and knew that Swift Thunder was the cause.

She couldn't believe that along with womanhood had come a man who aroused her deepest emotions.

She would not allow herself to consider the fact that he should be her enemy.

There were too many good things about him that erased that ugly fact.

Then she realized she had not asked him why his appearance was different from other boys of his clan.

Well, there was tomorrow.

She would learn things tomorrow that she had not had time to discover today.

She grew cold inside when she thought of Piercing Eyes, who felt that he owned her.

Her upper lip stiffened. Well, she thought, she would show Piercing Eyes who owned whom!

His heart pounding, Swift Thunder watched Moon Song until she and her canoe became only a speck in the water and then were gone.

A smile broad on his face, he held Blue closer in his arms and ran toward his village.

He felt as though he had won two victories today.

One of his body.

One of his heart.

He felt doubly blessed as a man.

And surely Moon Song would come

again tomorrow, as promised, for although she knew that her people and his were enemies, she also must know that his Mohawk people had a reputation for courage and steadfastness. He hoped she had seen those qualities in him and admired him for them.

Looking heavenward, he whispered a big, heartfelt "thank you" to *Tharonhiawakon*, the one who was always there, smiling down at him with his blessings.

"And please lead her back to me tomorrow," Swift Thunder quickly added.

Chapter Three

Sweet and gentle were your smiles,
You never flaunted your womanly wiles.
You let me unbraid your beautiful hair.
You were, oh, so sweet, and oh, so fair.

The river lapped lazily at the riverbank. Birds trilled their beautiful songs in the nearby trees; a red-tailed hawk screeched its own message into the wind as it soared peacefully above the Mohawk River.

The scent of distant cook fires wafted from the Mohawk Castle of the Bear, carrying with it the delicious smells of cooking meat.

Having arrived at their meeting place at almost the same moment, both Swift Thunder and Moon Song were at a loss for words.

Moon Song had wondered whether Swift Thunder would reconsider their plans and decide not to meet her.

But there he was, so handsome and tan in his breechclout and moccasins. His long, thick hair was held in place with a beaded headband. His eyes revealed a silent anxiousness, and Moon Song knew that her own eyes must reveal the same to him.

She was glad that he could not hear her heart pounding like thunder in her breast.

Nor could he look into her soul and know that she had slept hardly a wink all night after the feast and dancing which had celebrated her womanhood.

If he could, he would know that almost her every thought since their meeting had been of him.

She was concerned that he affected her in such a way, for surely their friendship would be short-lived. If either her people or his discovered that they knew one another, they would put a quick stop to it.

So while she was with him today she was going to take full advantage of their time together. She would allow herself to enjoy it instead of worrying about tomorrow.

Her gaze went to the cougar kitten where he lay in a soft, curled ball at Swift Thunder's feet, peacefully slumbering.

Moon Song had thought often of Blue since yesterday; she had never thought that she could feel attached to a wild animal.

But she adored petting him. She loved the feel of Blue's fur against her fingertips. Ah, how she loved the aura of contentment that seemed to surround the kitten.

Moon Song knew that this kitten's contentment was caused by Swift Thunder's devotion to it, and had to conclude that whomever Swift Thunder befriended would find a devotion deep and pure and loyal.

Moon Song wished to elicit such devotion from Swift Thunder, herself. But first she had to find a way to overcome her speechlessness in his presence.

Swift Thunder was so stunned that Moon Song had actually come to meet him that he could not even find the words to greet her.

He was afraid that if he spoke, his words would come out in a jumble, for he had thought of nothing else but her all night, wondering if there was some way they could have a future together.

But he truly knew that even thinking about that was premature. He had to get through *today*.

Making an impression on her now was his first concern.

"*Wigan*, it is good that you came," he blurted out.

His pulse raced as he noted how perfectly beautiful she was.

She wore beautifully cured doeskin

today. Her dress was decorated with tiny pink shells. It clung to her slender body, sweetly revealing her breasts as they pressed against the soft fabric.

And her feet were small and delicate in moccasins decorated with the same pink shells that adorned her dress.

Her hair hung long and luscious down her perfectly straight back, and she wore a crown of tiny pink roses which sent off a heady fragrance.

Her eyes were brilliant — brown and wide and mesmerizing.

Her lips were slightly parted, revealing wonderfully white teeth behind them.

And as she smiled at him, he was truly concerned about how her smile affected him.

He felt dizzy. His knees felt suddenly weak. He was supposed to be a man, and here he was allowing a maiden to take his strength.

It was a first for him, and he could not deny the deliciousness of all the feelings sweeping through him.

"I did not think that *you* would come," Moon Song said.

She nervously clasped her hands behind her as she, too, felt a sweetness that was new to her, a feeling which had begun yesterday when she saw Swift Thunder for the first time.

Through the night this sweetness had grown and grown as she thought of Swift Thunder and anticipated being with him again.

She knew that although she had proved herself a woman yesterday, she was truly still a mere child, and he was yet more boy than man.

Was it fate that brought them together on the special day when each was accepted by the community as an adult?

She noticed that the bruises on his body had turned purple, yellow, and red. She recalled how he had thrown himself against the wall of rock, how the blood had oozed from his flesh.

Surely his wounds hurt as bad as they looked. Strangely, she felt his pain deep inside her heart.

"I am a man of my word, and when I say I will do something, I do it," Swift Thunder said, enjoying the sound of the word "man" as it passed across his lips.

He felt he was very much a man with this beautiful creature standing before him, looking so concerned even though they had only met yesterday.

Swift Thunder felt as though he had

known Moon Song a lifetime and knew that even if they were torn apart by circumstances not under their control, he would never forget her.

"I am also a person of my word," Moon Song said, glancing at her beached canoe. Then she looked quickly back at Swift Thunder. "I have not only brought medicine for your bruises, but I have also brought your kitten a gift of food."

"You did not have to bring medicine from your shaman, for my village has its own, but I do appreciate your kindness," Swift Thunder said.

His gaze moved to Moon Song's canoe as he wondered what she had brought for his pet.

"And I am truly grateful that you brought something for Blue," he said, smiling at her.

"Blue is special, is he not?" Moon Song said. She gazed again at the kitten as it lay peacefully sleeping at Swift Thunder's moccasined feet. "I have never had a pet. You are lucky, especially since your pet is a cougar that will some day be powerful enough to frighten other predators."

She smiled softly as she looked up at Swift Thunder. "I, too, might be afraid of him then, for I have been taught to avoid such large forest creatures," she murmured.

Again she glanced down at Blue. The kitten slowly opened his eyes and looked up at Moon Song as though he knew that she was talking about him.

"Do you not believe that when Blue grows into adulthood you might, also, be somewhat afraid of him?" she asked.

Swift Thunder reached down and swept Blue into his arms. He held the kitten out away from him so that their eyes could meet and hold. "Blue will be his own powerful self when he grows up. He may be large and threatening to most, but to those who have befriended him, he will be always like a kitten," he said. "Moon Song, *you* will never have cause to fear him, for he has known your kindness and gentleness toward him."

"Will you set him free in the forest when he is of an age to feel the cry of freedom?" Moon Song asked.

She stepped closer to Swift Thunder.

She reached a hand out and ran her fingers across Blue's sleek back. "Or will you tie him up to make sure he does not ever leave you?" she asked.

"No ropes will ever imprison Blue," Swift Thunder said thickly. "He will be free to choose. If a time comes when he feels the need to join his kind, or if he longs for a mate, then I will say good-bye and wish him well. But I hope he will always return from time to time to his friends."

"Let me get my gift for Blue, and the medicine I have brought for you," Moon Song murmured. "I must not be gone long from my castle. I would not want anyone to begin wondering where I am."

She started for the canoe, then stopped and turned to look at Swift Thunder again. "Do you wish to meet again from time to time?" she blurted out. "Do . . . do . . . you think we can set up a time and meet . . . meet . . . each day? Or do you feel that your hours should be spent with braves instead of a mere *peenchkquaso?*" she asked meekly, feeling more like a girl than a woman.

"Mere girl . . . ?" Swift Thunder said, taken aback at the way she described herself.

To him she was far from being a "mere girl."

He stepped closer to her, then placed Blue on the ground. He reached a hand out and gently touched Moon Song's soft, copper cheek.

"When I look at you, when I am near you, I see you as the woman your rites proved you to be," he said thickly. "And although I fear I should not share my feelings so openly with you, I cannot help but say that I felt something for you the moment I saw you standing on the riverbank. It was as though you had appeared magically, as though you came from the heavens and . . ."

He caught himself before revealing any more of his feelings for her. He was making himself vulnerable to deep hurt if she treated him like a fool.

Surely to her he was still only a brave who had many years left before he could call himself a warrior.

Yet in her eyes he saw that his fears were unfounded. The tone of her voice said that her feelings matched his.

They were both emotionally older than their years, more mature than the companions they spent their days with.

"Do you truly feel those things about me?" Moon Song asked, touched deeply that he would reveal so much to her.

"I feel that you are more than . . . what is your age?" he asked, his eyebrows lifting. "You have not said, yet I have concluded that you are but twelve winters of age. Am I right?"

"Yes, twelve winters is my age," Moon Song said, smiling brightly that he seemed to know so much about her in such a short time. "And you?"

"Fifteen," Swift Thunder said, puffing out his chest proudly.

"You are so much older than I," Moon Song said, her eyes widening. "Three winters is —"

"Is not a lifetime," Swift Thunder said, chuckling. He lowered his hand. "Let us go to your canoe and see what you have brought Blue."

When he saw what it was, and learned that she had caught the rabbit and baked it herself, Swift Thunder's feelings for Moon Song deepened.

He watched as she knelt down before Blue and gave his kitten the gift of food.

He chuckled when the little cougar began gobbling it up as though he had not eaten in days, whereas in truth he had eaten a huge morning meal.

"He truly likes it," Moon Song said, clasping her hands together before her.

"He will remember always who gave him such a hearty meal of rabbit," Swift Thunder said.

"I am happy that he likes it, and in turn, likes me," Moon Song replied, smiling at Swift Thunder.

Her smile waned as she again noted the bruises on his chest. "Now let me take care of you," she murmured, grabbing a bag of medicinal supplies from her canoe.

"Come and we will sit beneath that tree over there," Swift Thunder said, nodding toward a beautiful weeping willow, whose limbs were filled with fresh leaves waving softly in the breeze.

Beneath the tree was a bed of fallen leaves from last winter's strong winds' pruning. The leaves were dried, yet soft.

Carrying her bag for her, Swift Thunder went with Moon Song. When he sat down, she moved to her knees before him.

As she took one vial of herbs and then another from her bag, she saw his eyes watching what she chose.

She guessed that he had been treated earlier by his shaman. Had he washed those poultices from his wounds before meeting with her today, so that she would feel free to use whatever she had brought?

Swift Thunder sat square-shouldered as her tiny, soft fingers began applying lotion across his worst contusions.

"Tell me if I hurt you," Moon Song said, gently applying the medicine to his muscled chest.

"You could never hurt me," Swift Thunder said.

Feeling wonderfully free and at ease with Swift Thunder, and feeling as though she could ask him anything, she blurted out a question that had puzzled her since the day before.

"I see a difference between you and your friends," she said, her eyes suddenly meeting and holding his, while her fingers still actively spread the herbal medicines. "It is in your facial features, your skin color, and . . ."

"My father was an Englishman," Swift Thunder said when he saw her hesitate.

"He was English?" Moon Song said, her eyes widening in wonder.

She picked up a doeskin cloth and wiped her fingers clean on it, then sat down before Swift Thunder and listened.

"Yes, my father was an Englishman of Irish descent," Swift Thunder said, drawing his legs up before him and hugging them with his arms. "My father came to America as a land speculator and trader. He became a good friend of the Mohawk. He admired my people's character. He was always fair in his business dealings with the Mohawk and began participating in our ceremonies as he was invited to join them.

He met and eventually married a Mohawk woman. She was the chief's daughter. They had one son. That son was Swift Thunder. In me, everyone could see a part of both my parents. My facial features and skin color resemble my father. My black hair and eyes come from my mother."

"You wear your hair different from the way the Mohawk braves and warriors wear theirs," Moon Song said.

"*Esta,* no, I do not wear the typical hair roach because my mother and father compromised about things after I was born," Swift Thunder said. He stretched his legs out before him and allowed Blue to crawl onto his lap and roll up into a contented ball.

"I was to be named an Indian name which was my mother's choice, but my father got his wish that I would never wear the roach, but instead wear my hair long, like his," Swift Thunder said. "My mother was happy to oblige since she loved her husband so much."

"And so your father and mother live now at the Castle of the Bear?" Moon Song asked.

She saw that she had said the wrong thing, for a haunted look came to Swift Thunder's eyes.

"My parents never joined the Mohawk at the Castle of the Bear, for my father had a thriving trading post," Swift Thunder said. "The trading post was upriver from where the Clan of the Bear's castle was established at that time. One day, when I was quite small, my chieftain grandfather, Fire Wolf, saw flames from the wall of his castle. The fire was in the direction of his daughter's and son-in-law's lodge. Chief Fire Wolf and several of his warriors hurried there. They discovered that the trading post had been burned to the ground, yet the cabin behind it had not been disturbed, except. . . ."

He paused and took a deep breath, sighed, then continued the tale he had not told for so long. It was like reliving that day all over again.

"My mother's body was there," he said, swallowing hard. "My mother was killed by a hatchet blow to the skull. My father . . . he . . . was missing."

"And you?" Moon Song said, horrified by what Swift Thunder had lived through.

"When my mother heard the commotion at the trading post, she hurried me, a young brave of four winters, into a crawl space beneath the cabin," Swift Thunder said thickly. "She had just gotten the trapdoor hidden beneath furniture when those who set my father's trading post on fire came and . . . and . . ."

"You do not have to say it," Moon Song said. She crawled over to him and twined her arms around his neck. "Say no more. I can tell that it pains you to relive what happened."

Feeling her arms around his neck and smelling the sweetness of Moon Song's skin was what saved Swift Thunder from feeling the depths of pain.

It was like a miracle that he and Moon Song had found one another.

He had to believe this was how his mother and father had felt when they'd fallen in love.

He had to refrain, though, from returning her hug, for he felt as though it might not be appropriate. She was much younger than he, and vulnerable in her sweet innocence.

When she eased away from him, their eyes looking deeply into each other's, he knew that it had been their destiny to meet.

Now they would grow into true adulthood knowing one another.

Despite what might be considered wrong or right by their people, when he and she were of marrying age, he would have her as his wife!

"My grandfather, my mother's chieftain father, and my grandmother adopted me," Swift Thunder said, feeling as though he should finish his story so that she would understand who he was and why. "A widespread search was made for my father, but he was never seen or heard from again."

"I am so sorry," Moon Song said.

She settled back down on the ground and tried not to let him see how his nearness made her cheeks flush, her heart pound.

"Tell me about *your* parents," Swift Thunder said, recognizing the blush, and understanding what had caused it.

Moon Song's eyes lowered, for as he had known sorrow in the past, so had she. It still pained her to think about it, much less talk about it. But she wanted to be absolutely open with Swift Thunder.

"My father died in the Mohawk River some time ago. Like you, my age numbered four winters when I lost him," she murmured.

Slowly she looked up again at him. "That was when our castle was farther upriver than it is now. My mother has since been both mother and father to me," she said softly.

She wanted to tell him about the betrothal to Piercing Eyes, but felt that was best left unsaid. She didn't want him to think she was already taken.

"We have much in common," Swift Thunder said, daring to take one of her hands.

When she twined her fingers through his, his heart soared. "I am sorry about your father," he said. "I am sure life has not been easy for you or your mother without a man in the family."

"We have survived well enough," Moon Song murmured. "And I love my mother so much."

Then she took her hand from his, gathered the vials, and placed them back in the bag. "I truly cannot stay any longer," she murmured. "Speaking of my mother reminds me that she might be missing me and wondering what is keeping me so long. I told her I was going canoeing. She allows it, yet because of the way my father died, she never stops worrying about me until she has me home again safely with her."

"I understand," Swift Thunder said. He took her bag and carried it for her as she walked beside him to her canoe.

Moon Song looked over her shoulder at Blue, who was leaping and playing in the tall grass.

"I shall miss Blue," she said, smiling at Swift Thunder. "If I could sneak him beneath my skirt and take him home, I would enjoy it so much."

"He is yours to pet and play with each time we meet," Swift Thunder said, setting the bag in her canoe. He took her hands. Their eyes met and held. "Will you come the same time tomorrow?"

Overwhelmed by her feelings for him, Moon Song could only nod a silent "yes."

Then she did something completely spontaneous.

She flung herself into his arms, hugged him, then pushed her canoe out into the river and boarded it.

As she paddled away from Swift Thunder, she smiled.

"Tomorrow!" he shouted at her.

"*Qua*, tomorrow!" she shouted back.

Feeling as though the river was made of clouds instead of water, Moon Song took herself home in her canoe. But as she came in sight of the riverbank, she stopped paddling in astonishment.

People were bringing their belongings to the river and placing them in a long convoy of canoes. As her eyes sorted through the crowd, she saw that everyone was readying themselves for travel in the river. And she could tell that it was not any ordinary travel. They were placing all of their household belongings in their large, personal canoes.

Half stumbling up the riverbank, Moon Song rushed onward until she reached her own lodge.

When she stepped inside and found all of her mother's belongings sitting in a pile in the center of the lodge, as well as Moon Song's own personal things, she was speechless.

Her mother came to her and drew her into her arms. "We are moving on, Moon Song," she murmured. "Help me take our things to the river."

Moon Song yanked herself free of her mother's arms. "I do not understand!" she cried. "How could this be happening? You never told me about any move. How can we be moving? Where? Why?"

"I was told only moments ago that our people must travel where they will be closer to the fort of French soldiers who are our allies. The soldiers need the assistance of our warriors," Dove Woman said, her voice drawn and sad.

"No!" Moon Song cried. "We cannot do this. *This* is our home now! We cannot move again." Visions of Swift Thunder's face, and even Blue's, came to Moon Song's mind. "*Esta,* mother. We cannot leave. Not now!"

When her mother reached out for her, Moon Song ignored the gesture and left the longhouse in a mad run.

When she came to the chief's lodge, she did not stop to announce her arrival. She rushed on inside and found herself suddenly looking up at him, all muscle and brawn, his eyes angry because of her disrespectful behavior.

"Chief Charging Crow, how can you take our people from their homes so suddenly?" Moon Song cried as tears flooded her eyes. "*This* is our *home!* Everyone is happy here. Why would we abandon our castle? Why so suddenly?"

"This is not a sudden decision," he said in a low, deep growl. "It has been discussed in council for many sunrises now. You are a mere girl who is not brought into council and told such important plans."

"But, Chief Charging Crow, I am a *woman* now," Moon Song said, quickly wiping the tears of a child from her eyes. "I should have been allowed to sit in council."

"No woman joined our councils," he growled out. "That is why no women knew of the plan until today."

"That is unfair," Moon Song sobbed. "None of this is fair."

"You call yourself a woman, yet you are acting like a child," Chief Charging Crow chided.

"But I am a woman," Moon Song said, even knowing that she was growing close to a disobedience to her chief that could get her in terrible trouble. "Do you forget our people's celebration after . . . after . . . I spent my four days in the menstrual hut?"

"*Que,* I remember, and yes, you *are* now recognized as a woman," Chief Charging Crow said, deeply sighing. He leaned down into her face. "Go, then, and do a woman's work. Help your mother load her supplies, then help the elderly into canoes."

Knowing that she had no choice but to obey, Moon Song felt as though her heart was being torn in shreds. She would never see Swift Thunder again, for she had no time to go and tell him that she was leaving, or why.

They would never see one another again.

He would think that she had not come to their meeting place because she'd changed her mind about him.

Returning slowly to her mother's longhouse, Moon Song felt eyes on her.

When she saw Piercing Eyes leering at her, his narrow, piercing eyes mentally undressing her, she shivered uncontrollably.

Needing to get away from him, Moon Song broke into a frenzied run.

When she got to her longhouse she hurried inside and ran into her mother's arms.

Sobbing, she clung to her.

"It is going to be all right," Dove Woman murmured, stroking her fingers through Moon Song's long, thick hair.

As she did this, she did not even notice when Moon Song's crown of roses fell to the floor.

Chapter Four

He closed his eyes against the pain.
Nothing would ever be the same.
His heart was torn from duty's call.
He rode away from his everything, his all.

Clouds were building overhead.

Flashes of lightning zigzagged in lurid streaks across the darkening sky.

The wind was strangely still, which Swift Thunder knew was a bad sign. The storm would soon erupt, yet it was the least of his worries.

He stood on the riverbank, gazing down at the calm waters of the Mohawk, and still he saw no sign of Moon Song approaching in her canoe. He was filled with mixed emotions — confusion over why Moon Song had failed to come now to their meeting place for three days, disappointment at not being able to see her, and fear that someone had discovered Moon Song's escapade and had put a stop to her meeting with Swift Thunder.

That she might have been punished for being with someone who truly cared for her filled his heart with resentment. He could no longer just stand there and watch and wait to see if Moon Song was going to show up today.

He wanted to go to the Oneida Castle of the Turtle and see if Moon Song was all right. But he knew that was impossible.

The Oneida would not allow Swift Thunder to get near the gate, much less go inside their castle and question them about one of their beautiful maidens.

"But I have to at least go and observe what is happening there," he said, hurrying toward his beached canoe.

He had left Blue at home, for Swift Thunder had planned to travel upriver to spy on the Oneida if Moon Song did not come today.

Swift Thunder had not wanted to involve his pet in the danger. If Swift Thunder was caught, he might even be taken captive.

But except for placing his cougar in danger, Swift Thunder would chance anything to get one glimpse of Moon Song. He had to make certain she was safe.

His jaw set tightly, Swift Thunder gave his canoe a shove and sent it into the water, then waded out and climbed in.

He determinedly lifted the paddle and

guided his canoe out to the center of the river.

He was proud of this canoe; he'd just finished making it the day before his puberty rites. It was a dugout canoe shaped from a single tree trunk, made by charring and scraping.

He had decided to undertake this task alone, instead of allowing his best friend, Winter Rain, to help him, and he had worked strenuously day in and day out.

Even Swift Thunder's chieftain grandfather had praised him for a job well done.

If grandfather knew what I was doing now, he would have his doubts about my being chief one day, Swift Thunder thought.

Seeing his grandfather frowning at him in his mind's eye, Swift Thunder almost swung the canoe around.

But nothing would dissuade him from the task at hand, not even the great claps of savage thunder that echoed all around him as one lightning flash was followed by another.

He gazed at the trees whose limbs hung over the water. No breeze stirred their leaves.

Even the water was strangely calm and glassy.

He knew from experience that this was

the calm before the storm, and was very aware of the danger he was putting himself in by being on the water.

If the lightning did not claim him, then the furious winds that would soon come with the storm might.

This knowledge made him paddle much harder.

He made himself ignore how much darker the sky was now than moments earlier.

He must be brave now, for he was too far from home to turn back and beat the storm that would soon ravage the river. If he could make it safely to the shore opposite the Castle of the Turtle, then he would seek shelter until the storm was past.

When it was over, he would seek answers about Moon Song. He would never forget her smile, her dancing eyes, or how sweet she smelled.

Most of all, he would never forget the softness of her skin when she had accidentally brushed her hand against his chest while applying the medicinal herbs.

He did not understand how she could be so loving to him and then break her promise to meet him.

"There has to be a reason," he whispered.

He winced when a flash of lightning lit the whole world around him.

He paddled even harder.

Just as he got his first glimpse of the Castle of the Turtle as he rounded a bend in the river, all hell broke loose. The wind hit at almost the same moment the rain began falling in torrents.

Swift Thunder worked against the wind until the muscles of his arms ached. Despite his efforts, the waves lashed the canoe back and forth, as though it weighed no more than a feather.

Soaked to the bone, his hair blowing in wet strands around his face, Swift Thunder leaped from the canoe and dragged it to shore.

He then went and huddled in a clump of thick bushes beneath tall trees. Shivering from the cold, he hugged himself with his arms.

He tried to see the great wall that protected those who lived in the Castle of the Turtle. But the rain was too heavy, falling in thick, gray sheets from the heavens. Swift Thunder winced with each new flash of lightning and clap of thunder.

He eyed his canoe, which had slid back closer to the water. He prayed to *Tharonhiawakon* that his canoe would not be taken from him.

He prayed, too, that *Tharonhiawakon* did not look down at him and see him as a foolish young man whose priorities had become mixed up after meeting the most beautiful maiden in the world.

He hung his head in an effort to keep the rain from stinging his face. He tried to ignore the savage thunder that shook the very ground beneath his moccasined feet.

Finally the rain lessened to a fine spray. The winds calmed. The clouds overhead began to part to reveal a blue sky, where only moments ago it was black.

Swift Thunder pushed himself up from the ground. He stretched his aching, cold back and watched the rolling, black clouds disappear along the horizon.

Then he gazed intently across the river at the Castle of the Turtle. He was not surprised that the walls were deserted; he assumed the storm had sent everyone for cover.

But one thing *did* make his eyebrows lift in wonder. There were no canoes beached anywhere near the great wall.

Even if the Oneida had thought to protect their canoes against the ravaging winds, they would not have taken them away from the river area. Certainly the canoes would not have been carried inside the walls of their Castle. They would have been tied down along the beach.

He looked back at the wall and still saw no activity.

It puzzled him that the large gate was wide open, but still he saw no one coming or going from the castle. He felt that something was terribly wrong, yet he knew it was still best not to allow anyone to see him.

Quickly formulating a plan, he decided he would carry his canoe through the forest on this side of the river, and when he came to a place far enough away where he would not be seen crossing the river, he would board his canoe and paddle to the Castle of the Turtle.

He would hide his canoe and go the rest of the way on foot. He would go close enough to climb a tree and get a good look down into the castle.

Huffing and puffing, he dragged his canoe through the forest. He wished now that he had not made it so large.

Finally, when he felt it was safe enough to cross the river, he shoved his canoe into the water and paddled to the other side.

Once there, he moored his canoe in a safe, hidden place, then ran through the forest until he saw the walls of the castle through a break in the trees a short distance away.

He slowed his pace and began searching for a tree that would bring him higher than the top of the walls.

And when he did see one that had limbs almost like steps high into the tree, he hurried to it and climbed up, stopping when he finally could see down inside the palisade.

He gasped when he saw no signs of occupation, not even smoke rising from the chimneys of the many longhouses, or dogs running in the courtyard. Where there was usually a constantly burning central fire, there now lay only wet, deep ashes.

His gaze swept around the walls of the castle, where usually guards were posted to keep an eye out for the enemy, but he saw no one there.

He remembered the absence of canoes outside. He saw that they had not been brought past the wide gate into the courtyard. Nothing at all was there, except for racks that stood empty where drying meat usually hung.

"They are gone," Swift Thunder suddenly said aloud, realizing that whispers were no longer required, for there was no one within hearing distance.

A keen despair washed over him to realize that for some reason the Oneida had uprooted themselves and abandoned their castle. And along with them had gone the beautiful maiden he would never forget!

Thinking he might be able to figure out why they had left, Swift Thunder scampered down the tree and ran to the open gate.

He hesitated before going inside where his enemies had made their homes. It was as though he could feel their presence now, leering, weapons drawn, hate for him even worse than the storm he had just endured.

An involuntary shiver raced across his flesh as he looked slowly around him, and then up at the tall walls, but still heard only a strange sort of silence and saw nothing but empty dwellings.

Suddenly memories of Moon Song flooded him, and he was surprised when a sob leapt from his throat.

Shaken by his reaction to the knowledge that he would never see Moon Song again, Swift Thunder almost turned and ran. But, still hoping to find some clue as to why they had left so quickly, he decided to investigate.

He moved cautiously into the courtyard,

in case someone was still there, hiding.

He felt somewhat foolish for having come this close to his enemy without any sort of weapon. He had not taken the time this morning to strap his sheathed knife to his waist, nor to bring his bow and arrow.

Moving stealthily onward, his eyes darting everywhere, Swift Thunder moved from longhouse to longhouse, then stopped abruptly when he entered one and saw something that made his heart ache.

He knelt on the earthen floor where a crown of tiny rosebuds lay, dried up and dejected looking.

In a flash he saw the rosebuds in Moon Song's hair, and how they had made her look like a princess in her loveliness!

His fingers trembled as he reached for the rosebuds and touched one of them. "Moon Song," he whispered, realizing that he was surely in her home.

He wondered why the roses had fallen from her hair.

Had it been because she had been made to leave her home in haste?

"Why?" he whispered, slowly rising to his feet to look around him, seeing Moon Song everywhere his eyes lingered.

When he saw a tiny beaded bag that seemed to have been overlooked when

Moon Song and her mother had fled their home, Swift Thunder grabbed it.

As he studied it, he wondered if Moon Song had been the one to have sewn the beads on the buckskin.

But even if she hadn't, he would pretend that she had, for he would take the bag and keep it with him forever.

Carrying the bag as though it were a precious thing, he went back out to the main room and again stared down at the fallen, dried rosebuds.

He gazed at the bag, and then again at the roses, then smiled as he bent and gingerly picked up the crown and placed it delicately inside the bag.

Now he definitely had a part of Moon Song to keep with him, for he knew those were the rosebuds that she had worn. He would like to believe that she had purposely left them there for him to find, but that would be wishing for too much.

But surely when she'd been told that she had to leave with her people, she had thought at least for a moment about him. Their moments together had been special and unforgettable to him. Surely they were the same for her.

Taking his prize, he ran from the lodge, and then from the castle. Paddling his canoe quickly, he was soon home again, yet he could not shake Moon Song's memory.

He could not help wondering, over and over again, where a whole clan of people might disappear.

And again, he was troubled about why they would leave a castle that seemed suited to them so well.

He was so deep in thought as he sat beside the lodge fire in his grandfather's longhouse that he did not hear Fire Wolf enter.

He did not know his grandfather was there until he laid a heavy hand on Swift Thunder's shoulder, startling him out of his thoughts.

"Grandson, where is Winter Rain?" Fire Wolf asked as his eyes met and held Swift Thunder's.

"Grandson, why are you alone? The rains have come and gone. It is now a beautiful day for young warriors to be outside, not inside. You have all winter to linger beside the lodge fire."

As Fire Wolf lifted his hand away from Swift Thunder's shoulder, Swift Thunder rose to his feet and stood in his grandfather's tall shadow.

"I will go now and find Winter Rain,"

Swift Thunder said, trying hard not to let his grandfather see how despondent he was.

"Grandson, I sense there is something troubling you," Fire Wolf said, now scrutinizing Swift Thunder even more closely. "You seem dispirited. Why?"

Swift Thunder could not find a way to tell his grandfather about the Oneida maiden who had made him more aware of his manhood with her beguiling ways than any puberty rites could ever have done.

He even wondered now if he could ever get Moon Song off his mind, so that another woman could enter his heart.

Swift Thunder had always aspired to have a wife as soon as he was of an age when it was normal for a warrior to take a wife to his bed.

He had hoped to have many sons.

But now?

He would just concentrate on making himself a better man for his people. The threat of war was always in the air like the steady, threatening buzz of a giant bumblebee. Even with one enemy now gone from the area, there remained others who would enjoy taking down the Mohawk.

"Grandfather, I did not mean to worry you," Swift Thunder finally said. "Since

84

grandmother's death, I have tried to fill the vacant place her absence has left in your heart."

"I see that whatever is troubling you is something that you do not wish to talk about," Fire Wolf said, drawing Swift Thunder into his arms. "It is enough that you are with me, my grandson. You *have* filled the vacancy in my life left by your mother's and your grandmother's deaths. You know that I am always here for you, should there be anything you need to talk over."

"Yes, I know," Swift Thunder said, reveling in this closeness with his grandfather. "I love you so, Grandfather."

"One day, Swift Thunder, you will take my place as chief," Fire Wolf said thickly. "Our people will be proud, as will I, even though I walk the road to the hereafter. I shall be with you even then, my grandson, in spirit."

"As Grandmother and Mother are with us now," Swift Thunder said, gazing up and seeing his grandfather smile.

"Yes, they are here; they are with us always," Fire Wolf said.

He released Swift Thunder. "Now go," he said, motioning with a hand toward the door. "Be the young man you are now, for

too soon you will be a man with many responsibilities. You will be chief."

Smiling, Swift Thunder nodded. But as
soon as he left the longhouse, he was once
more overwhelmed by thoughts of Moon
Song. He could not shake his memory of
her.

He went to stand beside the river and
gazed with longing toward the spot where
they had once stood together, enemies
turned friends.

"Where are you?" he whispered. "Are
you thinking of me?"

Yes, he had wanted more than friendship
with her. He had wanted to grow up with
her until they were old enough to marry.

He had envisioned her already as that
grown woman who would be a beautiful,
caring wife.

Chapter Five

Inside his heart a battle raged.
The pain left him almost dazed.
Who he wanted he could not love.
His anguish he sent to Tharonhiawakon,
    above.

Ten years later — 1756

Concluding his solitary hunt by packing his string of birds in a bundle on his back beside his quiver of arrows and placing his large bow in his canoe, Swift Thunder turned to Blue and clapped his hands.

Grown up now, and understanding Swift Thunder's command, Blue leapt gracefully into the canoe and sat down, waiting for Swift Thunder to follow.

But Swift Thunder paused before stepping into the canoe. He was lost in thought, recalling that time ten years ago when he had first seen Moon Song standing on the riverbank on this exact spot as she watched Swift Thunder leaving the river after his brief swim.

Through the years, Swift Thunder had

relived that moment over and over again, even knowing that it was wasted energy, for he knew that Moon Song was gone from his life forever.

But how could anyone forget the face of an angel whose voice matched the sweetness of birdsong?

He purposely came to this place in the river often, to think of her.

This must stop, Swift Thunder scolded himself. *Why? Why must she continue to haunt me?*

But he knew that even while thinking these things, he would not change the direction in which he was guiding his canoe. As he had many times before, he felt a strong urge to travel to where the Castle of the Turtle still stood, undisturbed, except for creeping vines, since it had been abandoned so many years ago.

He kept thinking that the Turtle might return one day, yet each time he went there and saw that nothing had changed, that no one was there, he vowed never to go there again.

His jaw tight, his heart instead of logic guiding him today, Swift Thunder placed his pack of birds in his canoe, shoved his canoe out into deeper water, then boarded it.

Pausing only long enough to give the cougar a fond stroke with his hand, Swift Thunder then lifted his paddle and sent his canoe in the direction of the abandoned Castle of the Turtle.

As he took each stroke with his paddle, he kept recalling that day when he realized that the sweet and innocent Moon Song was gone from his life.

"But never from my heart," he whispered, still paddling determinedly where he knew he should not be going.

His thoughts strayed to his ailing grandfather and how Fire Wolf would disapprove of Swift Thunder's inability to banish his lost love from his mind. His grandfather had tried hard to persuade Swift Thunder to take a wife and form a family, but Swift Thunder had refused, for Moon Song was still too strong a force in his soul to consider taking another woman into his lodge.

Although he had only known Moon Song for a short time, and they were both very young, it had been clear to them both that fate had brought them together for a purpose. But why had fate been so cruel as to tear them apart?

Over the years he had learned more about why Moon Song had been taken from him. Rumors of war had sent the

Oneida closer to the forts of the Frenchmen, to whom they gave their loyalty.

Although he had made discreet inquiries, he had never discovered the location of the Oneida's new castle, or the French fort with whom the Oneida had aligned themselves. He had only met the Oneida and French enemy on the battlefield, not during a raid on an Oneida castle or French fort.

The "French and Indian War," as it had been called, was behind all of them, at least for now, and Swift Thunder was proud to say that he had assisted the British in gaining a victory over the Oneida and the French in the Battle of Lake George the prior year.

As Swift Thunder paddled at a steady pace through the water, his cougar now resting at his feet asleep, he continued to think about the outcome of the war.

He smiled proudly as he thought of receiving a knighthood from the King of England for his and his warriors' triumph in battle over the French.

Because of that honor, and because of his grandfather's worsening health, Swift Thunder was now *sachem,* acting chief.

Swift Thunder never ignored his grandfather's advice, for his grandfather was the wisest of all men, and beloved by his people.

One thing, though, that Swift Thunder had never discussed with his grandfather was his secret love for a woman whom he doubted he would ever see again.

When his grandfather asked if he had found that "special woman" yet, Swift Thunder would shake his head. It was not a lie, for he had *not* found Moon Song through the years. But despite that disappointment, his ears were ever alert for that name, his eyes alert for that face.

Yes, she would be older now, but surely he would still recognize her.

With maturity she would have blossomed into someone even more intriguingly beautiful than she had been those ten long summers ago.

As Swift Thunder drew closer to where he could see the Castle of the Turtle from the river, he was no more anxious than the last several times he had paddled past it in hopes of seeing Moon Song on the riverbank.

Suddenly his eyes widened and his body tightened. He paused in his paddling and listened intently as he heard the sound of trees being felled. He could also hear the thump, thump of hammering. His heart skipped a beat when he heard the drone of voices.

His hand trembling, his heart thudding, he resumed his paddling. He was too close to the Castle of the Turtle to believe that the sounds were coming from anywhere but there.

Could that mean . . . ?

He swallowed hard as he made the turn in the river that would give him a full view of what once was the Castle of the Turtle.

He could see warriors carrying wood through the wide gate of the castle, and he began to believe the Oneida had, indeed, returned to what had been theirs.

Not wanting to be seen, Swift Thunder made a sharp turn to the right and hid his canoe behind tall scrub plants along the embankment.

Swift Thunder's heart raced when among those men coming and going through the opened gate he recognized Piercing Eyes, the Oneida chief's son. Piercing Eyes had been among the Oneida who led forces combined with the French against the Bear Clan of Mohawk and the English soldiers.

Swift Thunder had gained a private victory over Piercing Eyes by wounding him in battle. The hated son of Chief Charging Crow was now one-armed, and even more vile-tempered and bitter because of it.

But that no longer concerned Swift Thunder. Warring was behind them all, and it was obvious that Piercing Eye's chieftain father had felt that it was safe enough to return to their castle on the Mohawk. Although the French and their Oneida allies had lost the war, only the French had been ordered from the area.

What *did* matter to Swift Thunder was Moon Song's whereabouts.

Through those troubled years had she forgotten Swift Thunder?

Had another man stolen her heart?

Was she . . . a . . . mother?

He could not envision Moon Song any other way than in his arms.

Yet he knew it was foolish to hope for so much. Their time together had been short-lived, and possibly was not even important to her now. Swift Thunder made himself turn his canoe back in the direction of his home.

His strokes through the water were dispirited now.

He had dreamed of the day when he might be reunited with Moon Song, yet today, when that possibility was closer than he would have ever imagined, he felt that all of his dreams were in vain.

After all, the Oneida had reclaimed their original castle, but Moon Song had not sought Swift Thunder out to tell him she was home again.

That had to mean she had forgotten Swift Thunder and made her life with someone else.

Surely she had heard about his victory over her people, and saw him as her true enemy now.

If she did not despise him, why then had she not found a way to let Swift Thunder know that she had returned to the area?

He had been foolish to allow her to remain in his heart through the years.

He had been foolish to paddle past the abandoned castle time and again and dream of seeing her.

He glanced down at the medicine bundle where he kept some of her rosebuds and had a strong urge to yank it off and pitch it into the river.

Yet he had to hang on to the possibility that his conclusions were wrong. He had to give it more time. He had to give *her* more time.

Surely he could not have wasted so many

years dreaming an impossible dream.

He had always felt that, even though they had been separated, it was their destiny to meet again.

Chapter Six

Lessons are learned sometimes with pain.
Nothing is more blessed than something
* we gain,*
Our own strife aside and hard work
* each day*
Can in the end be our sweetest pay.

Moon Song's excitement at returning to the castle on the Mohawk River had quickly turned to fear, and then a quiet rebellion when she was forced to stand before Chief Charging Crow and was told that the time had come for her betrothal to his son to be finalized by marriage vows.

As Moon Song's lovely, soft-spoken mother stood at her side, visibly trembling beneath the glower and harsh voice of the chief, Moon Song set aside her teaching of respect for elders to speak her mind.

She had decided earlier that no matter what was done to her, she was not going to marry this man's loathsome son.

She had hated Piercing Eyes since they were children. There was no way she would marry him.

And she wanted to go see Swift Thunder. She would have gone earlier except there had been too much activity for her to sneak out without being seen.

She wanted so badly to learn if Swift Thunder was married. She knew that he was alive, and was even now chief of his clan of Mohawk. She knew of his success in the war against her own people and the French, and how the King of England had honored him in some way for his dedicated service to the English people.

Oh, just to get one look at Swift Thunder would thrill Moon Song.

Her shoulders squared, her chin lifted, Moon Song looked Chief Charging Crow square in the eye as he sat on a pelt-covered platform in his private longhouse.

"Chief Charging Crow, you know that I never, *ever* promised myself to your son," Moon Song said. She was glad that she had found the courage to say what she had carried in her heart for too many years now. "You know that it was planned for me by my father."

She inhaled a quavering, nervous breath, then again spoke her mind. "I am now an adult and know my own heart," she said.

She was trying to keep her voice steady and strong, even though her heart was thundering in her chest as if many drums were pounding there.

"Chief Charging Crow, I do not love Piercing Eyes," she quickly added. "I never have. How can I marry a man I do not love? I cannot do this thing that would make my life pure misery."

His face a furrow of wrinkles, gaunt with age and the failures that plagued him deep in his soul, Chief Charging Crow drew a blanket more tightly around his thin, frail shoulders.

He purposely glared at Moon Song in an effort to make her cower like a scared puppy in his presence.

Yet he saw that she still stood strong and straight, her jaw set with determination.

"Moon Song, you have been taught that the most important of an Oneida woman's responsibilities is to bear children, thus assuring the future of our tribe," Chief Charging Crow said in a low growl. "Since our losses during the recent war, when so many of our valued Oneida warriors died, the need to bring forth children is more important than ever."

"I am very well aware of that, and I want to fulfill the duty of womanhood, but I also want to marry someone I want to marry, not someone appointed for me," Moon

Song responded. "Must I remind you that long ago, when I was betrothed to your son, it was not anyone's intent for us to marry? It was only meant to seal the friendship between our families, rather than be a permanent bond."

The old chief's eyes narrowed as he glared at Moon Song. "You have not even kept *that* promise," he said flatly. "You have always shunned my son as though he were no more than a fly that a person swats away."

He placed a hand on one knee and leaned closer to Moon Song.

A slow, mocking smile tugged at his lips. "Well, Moon Song, things are going to change," he said. "You *will* marry my son, for it is my son's deepest desire that it should be so."

He yanked on the corners of his blanket again and drew it more closely around him. "And my son suffered much at the hands of our enemies, the Bear Clan," he said, his voice drawn. "My son deserves something now that will give him a reason to smile. That is *you*, Moon Song. He has earned the right to have what he asks for. He was one of our people's most valiant warriors during the long fight. He must forever carry the visible signs of failure that the war brought our people, for he lost one arm. You *will* marry him. You will bring sunshine into my son's eyes again. You will give him children."

Shaken to the core by the determination in her chief's voice, Moon Song reached over and took one of her mother's hands for reassurance.

Against all odds, her mother had kept Moon Song safe, healthy, and happy.

But now?

Had that come to an end?

When Moon Song felt the cold clamminess of her mother's trembling hand, she wondered if she should stop the battle with her chief and accept her fate.

Moon Song was afraid that she might be bringing hardship to her mother by continuing to oppose their chief.

But no, she *must* stand firm in her decision. She could not bear one minute alone with Piercing Eyes.

Moon Song eased her hand from her mother's and dared to take a step closer to the chief. "Chief Charging Crow, I understand how you feel, and I sympathize with Piercing Eyes, yet I also have my own feelings, my own future, to protect," she said, her voice filled with strength. "I cannot marry a man I do not love, not for any reason. I do not love Piercing Eyes. Never could I learn to. He and I have always been in conflict through the years, and I know that most of his anger toward me was because he knew that I had sworn to him that I would never marry him, not even if you tried to force me into it. I cannot be forced into something that would make my entire life a mockery. I cannot share a bed with your son, nor can I bear children to a man I . . . I . . . ."

She made herself stop short of saying the word "loathe." She was already treading on dangerous ground.

Chief Charging Crow shook a fist at Moon Song. "How dare you defy your chief?" he shouted, the threat and anger in his voice causing Moon Song and her mother to hold each other's hands in a fiercer grip than before.

Yet Moon Song would not allow herself to cower as she had seen other women, even men, do when their chief demanded this or that of them.

She would die before she spent one minute in Piercing Eyes' lodge!

"You, Moon Song, are insulting your forebears, your traditions, and the customs of your tribe by refusing to marry the choice of your chief," Charging Crow said, his voice now lower and more controlled. "Every Indian girl must marry when the time comes, or she is a disgrace to herself and her people. If not for the war delaying marriages among our warriors and maidens, you would have wed Piercing Eyes long ago."

Moon Song knew that what he said was partially true, that the time for her to have married had passed. The war had changed so many people's habits and lives.

Yes, she craved a man's arms and body at night while she lay alone in her bed. Yet no matter what her chief said, and no matter how lonesome she felt at night, she would not marry just anyone, especially not Piercing Eyes.

"Chief Charging Crow, it is not my intent to offend you, or anyone," she murmured. She slipped her hand from her mother's. "I will continue to serve you gladly, but I cannot marry Piercing Eyes."

She sighed heavily. "Please, oh, please, release me from this duty you ask of me," she pleaded. "Please leave me the freedom to choose."

Chief Charging Crow glared at Moon Song, yet in a sense he was proud of her, for she was proving to be as indomitable as he.

He was proud to see that she could stand her ground, that she could fight for her rights, for that indicated strength and courage in a woman!

"I will give you time to come to your senses," he blurted out.

Surprised almost speechless that the chief had given in at least for a while, Moon Song swallowed hard as she gazed into his faded brown eyes.

Then she smiled and thanked him, and hurriedly left the lodge with her mother.

Moon Song and her mother didn't speak of what had just happened in the chief's lodge until they reached the privacy of their own and had closed the door between them and the outside world.

Then Dove Woman drew Moon Song into her arms and hugged her. "My daughter, my daughter," she cried, clinging to her. "I cannot scold you for standing firm against our *sachem,* for I could not bear to see you married to such a cold and scheming man as Piercing Eyes."

She stepped away from Moon Song, then reached for her hands and held them as they gazed into each other's eyes. "Do you know that it was Piercing Eyes' suggestion that our people side with the French?" she said, her voice tight with anger.

"Yes, I know this, yet the chief treats his son as if he is some sort of hero," Moon Song said, sighing heavily.

"He must do this because Piercing Eyes is his son, his *only* son, even though deep inside our chief's heart he is ashamed of everything Piercing Eyes stands for," Dove Woman said, dropping her hands from Moon Song's.

She went to the firepit, put more wood into the glowing coals, and watched the flames leap upward.

"Yes, our chief would ruin my daughter's life for a son who truly should be banished for the disgrace he has brought to his people," Dove Woman said solemnly.

She turned to Moon Song. "I must rest now," she murmured. "Things like what we were just forced to endure tire me so."

"Yes. And, Mother, I am so sorry," Moon Song said, moving into her mother's arms.

They hugged for a moment; then Moon Song watched her mother leave the room for her bedroom.

Going over the chief's threats in her mind, Moon Song paced the floor nervously.

"I must do something," she whispered.

She glanced toward the window and saw

that the afternoon sun was waning in the sky.

She stopped when a thought came to her, as though *Tharonhiawakon* had reached down from the heavens and placed his comforting hand on her shoulder.

Yes, she knew what her next move must be. Under cover of darkness, while her mother slept tonight, Moon Song would go in her canoe to Swift Thunder's village. She must know whether or not he was married.

Did he even remember Moon Song?

If so, if he did not belong to another woman, might he find a way to solve Moon Song's problem?

There was no doubt in her heart that the chief would see her married to his son. He was only biding his time.

Yet by giving her this time, he might have given her the chance to change the course of her life forever.

But that all depended on Swift Thunder.

Chapter Seven

Sometimes the effort of merely trying.
Is all there is to hold back the crying.
Her face was forever inside his heart.
He didn't want them to have to part.

Unable to stop thinking of Moon Song, Swift Thunder paced back and forth in his longhouse.

The moon cast a soft glow through the windows. The ground outside was white with moonlight, yet the moon was at an angle in the sky instead of straight above in the heavens.

This reminded him that night had fallen long ago, and that soon daylight would be creeping in along the horizon.

He glanced at the door, then at the darkness outside the window again.

His jaw tightened with a sudden determination not to stay there any longer, wondering about Moon Song, when he should be seeking ways to know the truth.

All sorts of plans had troubled Swift Thunder's mind since he had seen that the Oneida castle was occupied again.

Now the time had finally come for him to make a final decision. There was no way on this earth that he could sleep tonight while knowing that Moon Song was nearby.

He would not even allow himself to think that she might be married now. He would not allow himself to envision her in someone else's arms, in someone else's blankets, belonging to someone else's heart!

Qua, he must carry out the plan that he had decided upon.

He must go and spend the night across the river from the Castle of the Turtle and watch those who would go to the river in the morning to get water or to bathe.

If Moon Song was among the women, he would study her well, to see whether or not she was heavy with child, or whether or not children were with her, and if so, he would forget her.

He gazed into the leaping flames of his lodge fire. Would he even know her now?

Ten winters and summers had passed since they had experienced those special days together by the river.

As Swift Thunder looked into the river on bright and sunny days and studied his reflection, he could see what the years had done to his appearance.

His was the face of a mature man, his body that of an adult.

He had ofttimes placed Moon Song in his mind's eye as he envisioned how she might now look.

That was all he had to go on. But that was enough.

Surely anyone as beautiful as Moon Song had been could only be more ravishing and heart-stopping now.

Qua, he truly did believe that he would know her, as she would know him if she saw him. Theirs was a magical sort of bonding that had begun on a magical day of youth.

Determined, he grabbed up his quiver of arrows and positioned it on his bare back, then slid his powerful bow over a shoulder.

He gazed down at his sleeping cougar and thought it was best that Blue did not accompany him on his journey. He was not sure how long he would be gone.

Blue would be better off at home where he would be fed, should Swift Thunder spend more than one night in the forest observing the Oneida castle.

Having one faithful confidant with whom he shared everything, especially his memories of Moon Song, Swift Thunder went to Winter Rain's lodge and gently knocked on the door.

As he waited, he looked warily around him, checking whether anyone lingered at this late hour outside their lodges. He did not want anyone to see him leaving his castle, and was glad when he saw no one.

Winter Rain, who also had not yet chosen a mate, came to the door and opened it. The fire's glow from the hearth behind him revealed to Swift Thunder the sleep in his friend's eyes.

"My friend, the time has come," Swift Thunder said. "I can no longer just sit and wait. I must go and see."

"The woman again?" Winter Rain said, frowning. Swift Thunder knew that his friend still could not accept Swift Thunder's endless infatuation with a woman who should be his enemy, yet out of respect Winter Rain did not voice his feelings.

"*Qua*, the woman again," Swift Thunder said, raking his fingers through his long, black hair in frustration. "Now that I know her people have returned to their castle, how can I not wonder if she returned with them?"

"What is your plan?" Winter Rain asked, stepping outside to stand with Swift

Thunder, his body bare, his muscles rippling beneath the moon's glow.

Swift Thunder hurried through his plan, then awaited his friend's response.

Winter Rain slid an arm around Swift Thunder's neck and hugged him, then stepped away from him again. "Go," he said thickly. "Follow your heart. Winter Rain will keep things safe and in order at our castle in your absence."

"Feed Blue tomorrow morning and see that he is able to run and stretch his legs?" Swift Thunder said, feeling guilty over leaving his cougar at home, when normally his pet accompanied him everywhere.

"Blue and I will enjoy one another's company," Winter Rain said, gently patting Swift Thunder on the shoulder. "Go. But be wary of the Oneida who might have sentries posted on the other side of the river where you are planning to go for your spying."

Swift Thunder nodded, gave Winter Rain a quick hug, then ran to his canoe and boarded it.

Soon he was traveling down the moon-splashed avenue of the Mohawk River, his arms not able to move the paddle quickly enough to satisfy his eagerness to reach his planned observation post.

The night would soon be over, and then would come the morning and his chance to study the women.

He looked heavenward. "Please let her be among them," he prayed aloud to *Tharonhiawakon.*

He traveled onward, but did not get much farther before he saw by the light of the moon that a canoe was skimming up the river toward him. His eyes told him that the canoe was carrying only one passenger.

A warning shot through him. It might be an Oneida warrior coming to snoop on the Mohawk.

He started to make a quick turn to the right, to get into hiding along the riverbank, but stopped and stared when he realized that the lone person in the canoe was a woman.

He sat unmoving in his canoe as he waited for the other craft to get closer, stunned that this woman did not flee upon her first discovery of a warrior on the river with her.

He knew that she must have seen him. The moon left nothing untouched tonight.

Scarcely breathing, his eyes narrowed as he gazed at the person in the approaching canoe. He gasped and almost dropped his paddle in the river when the moon's glow revealed the woman's face to him.

She was the woman of his dreams!

Although she was grown now instead of a maiden of twelve winters, it *was* Moon Song!

After all those weary, aching years of missing her, there she was, as though she had heard the beckoning of his heart!

"Moon Song . . ." he whispered, dizzy with the joy that came with seeing her again. "My . . . Moon Song!"

Moon Song had seen the approaching canoe and was aware that it had suddenly stopped. She had almost turned and fled in fright.

But there had been something about the warrior that gave her the courage to continue.

She had invented in her mind how Swift Thunder would look now that he was twenty-five, and tonight, beneath the moon and the stars, she knew that her mental picture of him was correct. For this man, who was looking so intently at her from his canoe, had all of the features she had imagined.

And the closer she came to the man in the canoe, the more certain she was that her dreams had come true.

She had found Swift Thunder!

And . . . he . . . had found her!

It was a miracle.

It was magical.

Passion filled her in sweet, rolling waves as she saw just how handsome he was, and how muscular.

Qua, after all these years, the long nights of wondering and thinking about Swift Thunder, now he was here, as though she had willed him to join her.

She could hardly control the beat of her heart as he began paddling his canoe toward her; she now paddled harder and harder toward him.

When their canoes came side by side, Swift Thunder reached out and grabbed Moon Song's craft and held it next to his.

"Swift Thunder?" Moon Song said, her own voice sounding strange and haunted to her.

"Moon Song?" Swift Thunder said, his eyes taking in her loveliness, his heart soaring at the sweetness of her voice.

"I . . . I . . . was on my way to find you," Moon Song said, thrilled that he was actually there, so close she could reach out and touch him.

But she dared not be that bold.

She still knew nothing about him, except

that he was now his people's chief.

If there were children and a wife, her world would tumble down around her, for she had purposely saved herself for him.

"My heart must have heard you, for I am on the river tonight because of you," Swift Thunder said, his voice sounding strange and thick to him. "When I discovered that you were in the area again, I wanted to see you . . . to talk with you."

"How had you planned to do this?" Moon Song asked softly. "You are headed toward my people's castle. Were you going to go there and announce that you wished to see me?"

"Your people hate me, for I was the one who led the victory against them," Swift Thunder said, sorry to remind her, yet knowing that it was necessary. "So, no, I would not have been foolish enough to knock on your gate. I was going to observe from across the river. I was going to watch for you."

"But I am older," Moon Song said, almost shyly. "How would you know me? How did you recognize me tonight?"

"How could I not?" Swift Thunder said, wanting to take her into his arms right away.

Oh, how badly he needed to hold her!

"How . . . did . . . you know me?" he asked guardedly.

She smiled the sweet smile that he remembered, the smile that he had taken with him to bed at night.

"How could I not know *you?*" she murmured.

Caught in her own rapture, Moon Song reached out for Swift Thunder's face, melting inside when she felt the warmth of his flesh against her fingertips.

"How could I not know you, when I have seen you every night in my dreams?" she murmured.

He reached up and took her hand in his. He kissed its palm, then eased his hand away. "I was there, truly I was there, for my thoughts transported me into your mind as my dreams combined with yours and brought us together," he said.

"Follow me?" he asked, lifting his paddle and pointing it toward shore.

She smiled, thrilled, and nodded, then paddled her canoe next to his until they reached the shore.

Once there, they got out of their canoes and beached them side by side.

Slowly they turned to one another.

Their eyes met and held.

They were then mystically drawn into

each other's arms.

Their bodies strained together as their lips met and exploded into fiery kisses, one after another. Swift Thunder's hands moved over Moon Song, familiarizing himself with her body in case fate again drew them apart for many years.

Breathing hard, they broke apart.

Moon Song gazed into Swift Thunder's eyes. She loved him more than she had ever thought possible.

"Come and sit with me?" Swift Thunder said, breaking the spell.

"Yes, I would love to sit with you," Moon Song said, so filled with joy she felt that surely she glowed from it.

Quietly they sat down on the soft grass by the riverbank.

Beneath the sweet splash of the moon's glow, Moon Song blurted out how she had thought of him through the years, and why she had never been able to keep their planned rendezvous.

She told him that she knew about his role in the war, and how proud she was of him, even though she knew that he was responsible for her people's loss.

"I never cast any blame on you, because I knew that you had no choice but to fight my people, as I had no choice but to go where they felt they had the better advantage," Moon Song said, swallowing hard.

She reached over and gently touched Swift Thunder's face again. "During the heat of the war, I would lie in my bed at night and wonder if an arrow or hatchet had downed you," she said, her voice breaking. "I prayed often to *Tharonhiawakon* for your safety. When the war was over, and I heard the news that you were alive, and that you were even honored in some way by the King of England, you do not know how happy I was. I knew that you were deserving of all good things, as Piercing Eyes was deserving of all bad."

"Piercing Eyes?" Swift Thunder said, wondering if she knew that it was Swift Thunder who was responsible for Piercing Eyes' missing arm.

Moon Song dropped her hand away from him and hung her head. "If you only knew what my chief is asking of me," she said, a sob lodging in her throat.

Hearing how distraught she was, Swift Thunder placed a gentle hand beneath Moon Song's chin and lifted her face so that he could look into her eyes.

"What is Chief Charging Crow asking of you?" Swift Thunder asked thickly, almost afraid to know. "It must be something terrible."

"Marrying Piercing Eyes would be the worst of all things for me, and —" Moon Song did not get the chance to say the rest, for that had been enough for Swift Thunder to guess what the problem was.

"Your chief is asking a beautiful, sweet woman like you to marry his loathsome, despicable son?" Swift Thunder gasped out.

He found what she had just revealed to him so hard to fathom, it seemed impossible.

To lose her to such a man?

No.

Never!

"I was promised to Piercing Eyes long ago, but the war and other things got in the way," Moon Song said softly. "But now the war is behind us."

Her eyes suddenly filled with desperation. "I cannot marry him," she cried. "I despise him. I . . . I . . . was coming tonight in hopes of somehow finding you. Please, oh, please save me from this marriage that I deplore."

She flung herself into his arms. "Although some would wonder how, I know that I have always loved *you*," she cried.

"Those times with you were all that I needed to know that I could never love another. Although truly still a child, I had the feelings of a woman!"

"As I had the feelings of a man when I was with you," Swift Thunder said, relishing the feel of her in his arms. He held her tightly. "I have always loved you, and . . . always will."

Again their lips met in a frenzied kiss.

Again Swift Thunder's hands moved over her, loving the way her body fit against his, as though they were one.

He ached to have her, yet he knew that had to wait. For now, she had a crucial problem and she had come to him for help.

He couldn't even imagine someone as precious and sweet as she married to a man like Piercing Eyes.

He could not . . . he *would* not allow it to happen.

Although it was hard to give up the moment of blissful kissing, Swift Thunder stepped away from Moon Song.

He held her hands as he gazed into her eyes. "I will do everything humanly possible to keep you from being forced to marry Piercing Eyes," he said, hearing her heavy sigh of relief. "But you must return home. For now, pretend all is well. Give me time to prepare a place to hide for you. I cannot arouse your people's anger by taking you to my castle. You *will* be taken there later, but for now, everything must be done in secrecy."

"I knew you would help me," Moon Song sobbed as she flung herself into his arms and desperately hugged him. "Thank you. Oh, thank you."

"Wait two sunrises, then come and meet me where we first met long ago," Swift Thunder said. He slowly caressed her back as she clung to him. "If you discover that the chief is going to force a wedding on you before the day of our planned meeting, then come on to my castle. Under those circumstances, I will go to war with your people if that is what is required to keep you safe."

She crept from his arms and gazed questioningly into his eyes. "You would do that for me?" she gasped out. "Truly? You would go to war . . . for . . . me?"

"I would do *any*thing for you," Swift Thunder said huskily. "I have waited a lifetime for you. Nothing or no one will ever separate us again."

"When you discovered me gone when my people abandoned their castle, did you realize that I had failed you because I had no control over my destiny at that time?"

Moon Song asked softly.

"I was stunned to see the abandoned castle," Swift Thunder said. "When I saw that no one was there, I entered the castle. I went from longhouse to longhouse to see if there were any clues as to why you were gone."

He untied his medicine bundle from his waist and opened it.

As she watched, her eyes wide, he shook some dried rosebuds into his hand, then smiled at her.

"That day? I found rosebuds on the floor of one of the longhouses," he said. "Recalling those you wore in your hair, I was sure they were yours. I found a beaded bag that was also left behind in that longhouse. I used it to carry away the rosebuds; then when I arrived at my home, I placed them in my medicine bundle. I have since carried them and your scent with me everywhere I have gone."

"I am so touched to know that," Moon Song said, swallowing hard.

She was so in love. How could she leave him again? Yet she must.

"And the bag?" she asked, purposely delaying their good-bye tonight. "It is one I accidentally left behind. I am so glad you found it."

"Did you sew the beads onto the bag yourself?" Swift Thunder asked, recalling how often he had taken out that bag from hiding and had run his fingers over the beads as he thought of her.

"The bag was one of the first things my mother taught me to make when I was a mere girl of four winters," Moon Song said, smiling proudly. "I am so glad I accidentally left it behind for you to find."

She looked at his canoe, then at Swift Thunder. "I recall your baby cougar so well," she murmured. "He was so beautiful. Blue. That was his name, was it not?"

"Blue is his name, yes, and Blue is now grown and still my companion," Swift Thunder said, smiling broadly that she remembered his pet.

"Where is he?" Moon Song asked softly. "I thought he was your constant companion."

"He is in my lodge, where I felt he would be safer than with me while I was searching for you," Swift Thunder explained. "When you and I meet again, Blue will be with me. He will enjoy your touch and sweetness as he did when he was only a kitten."

"I shall eagerly anticipate seeing him again, but now I must be gone, Swift

Thunder," Moon Song said, truly hating to say good-bye, for the last time they had shared farewells, it had been too long a good-bye!

Swift Thunder twined his arms around her waist and drew her against his hard body. He kissed her deeply and passionately.

He then reluctantly let her go and watched her paddle away from him. He was reminded of another time when he had watched her, and then how long it had been since he had seen her again.

He circled his hands into tight fists at his sides, swearing to himself that he would never allow so much time to pass again before holding her and kissing her . . . before claiming her as his!

Chapter Eight

Never forget what price love must cost,
Many are always forever lost.
When the chance is shown to you,
Take it and use it or be forever blue.

After Swift Thunder had talked everything over with Winter Rain, explaining Moon Song's predicament and their feelings for one another, Winter Rain had agreed to help Swift Thunder in every way possible.

Swift Thunder sat now on a blanket spread on the floor in his grandfather's lodge. There was no sound but the crackling of the fire in the fireplace made of stone.

Fire Wolf was puffing on his pipe, blowing smoke rings into the air as he quietly went over in his mind what his grandson had just told him on this early morn . . . about a woman whom Fire Wolf could not approve of for his chieftain grandson.

Tense, waiting for his grandfather to say something, Swift Thunder gazed with much pride at his grandfather and knew that he was thinking now with his heart, not his logic.

Swift Thunder knew that his grandfather would never want to approve of his grandson marrying into the enemy clan, yet Fire Wolf understood just how much Swift Thunder loved Moon Song.

As Swift Thunder waited for his grandfather to speak the words he hoped to hear, he thought about this wonderful old man.

Though no war paint had slashed his face for many moons now, in his prime Fire Wolf had been a war chief.

But since the recent victory, they all hoped that warring was behind them.

Peace was a wondrous thing to behold, when warriors became husbands and fathers again instead of men who awakened each morning wondering if that day would be their last.

Now, as his people awakened to a new dawn each day, the plans were for hunting, planting, celebrating, and all of the wonderful things that came with a peaceful existence.

There was one thing, though, that might change their lives again: Swift Thunder's love for Moon Song, and what might happen between enemy clans because of it!

His thoughts returned to the moment

when he saw his grandfather take his pipe stem from his lips and rest the bowl on his knee where his legs were crossed before him and covered loosely with a blanket.

Swift Thunder's pulse raced as he waited for his grandfather to speak. He even leaned forward in anticipation when Fire Wolf turned his old, faded eyes toward him.

When his grandfather did not smile, Swift Thunder knew that Fire Wolf had not completely accepted his grandson's decision to help an enemy maiden and eventually make her his wife.

Swift Thunder's heart pounded hard as he patiently waited for his grandfather to speak. When he did, he felt no relief, for his grandfather's words were not what Swift Thunder wanted to hear.

"I have heard you speak from your heart, and I have sorted through your words and your feelings. I feel wary of this that you ask of me and our people," Fire Wolf said, his voice low and throaty with age. "I must warn you against the folly of loving someone of an enemy tribe and clan . . . especially a woman who is promised to an enemy chief's son. If she was promised as a child, it should be no different now that she is grown."

Swift Thunder's jaw tightened, and he knew that what he was going to say was bordering on disobedience to his grandfather, yet it had to be said. "Grandfather, no woman should be forced to marry someone she loathes," he said, his voice tight and drawn. "You know that if a woman of our clan came to me, her *sachem*, and voiced aloud her unwillingness to marry someone she was betrothed to as a child, I would not give her request a second thought. I would release her of that duty and gladly see her wed the man of her heart. How can Charging Crow not be as generous with the women of his clan?"

"You know why Charging Crow is not as generous with this particular woman," Fire Wolf grumbled. "She has been promised to his *son* since their childhood days. Do you not see how both the chief and son might lose face were the chief to agree to set Moon Song free of her promise? Both Charging Crow and Piercing Eyes would lose face among their people."

"As I see it, they would lose face if they forced an innocent woman to marry a man she does not want, especially if this man is someone like Piercing Eyes, whom, as I have heard it told, even his own people despise," Swift Thunder said dryly. "Did he

127

not lead them into a war they lost? Is he not ridiculed every time he walks among his people?"

He ran his fingers through his long hair. "We must help Moon Song," he said thickly. "I cannot stand by and see her life ruined."

"Two clans might be pulled into war again," Fire Wolf said, his voice drawn. "My grandson, is this woman worth it?"

"Grandfather, if you could meet and know Moon Song, you would not even ask a question such as that," Swift Thunder said. "Even a few minutes with her would prove to you her worth, and you would make the sacrifices necessary to protect her from marriage to a man such as Piercing Eyes."

Fire Wolf reached for his small bundle of tobacco and shook more leaves into the bowl of his pipe, lit the tobacco with a burning twig from the fireplace, then sat for a moment quietly thinking as he gazed into the flames of the lodge fire.

Swift Thunder's patience was running thin, for he had a full day ahead. He had made his plans before coming to his grandfather's lodge to seek his approval.

He watched the smoke rings from the pipe being sucked up the tall stone chimney of the fireplace.

He listened to his grandfather sucking on the pipe.

When Fire Wolf lowered the pipe from his lips and gazed at Swift Thunder, Swift Thunder knew by his easy, slow smile that Fire Wolf's trust in his grandson had helped him make his decision.

"Grandson, tell me your plans, for I will not stand in the way of anything you wish to do," Fire Wolf said. He placed his pipe on the hearth and folded his arms beneath his blanket, for he was now ready to truly listen.

"Thank you, Grandfather," Swift Thunder said, smiling broadly. "Here is what I feel is my best plan. It is . . ."

As Swift Thunder explained things to his grandfather, Fire Wolf occasionally nodded, then sat quietly awhile, then nodded again, for he knew that his grandson had left nothing to chance.

Chapter Nine

Thoughts of his love filled her days.
She wondered would they ever find
their way?

Thunder rumbled savagely in the distance, making Moon Song even more restless. It was hard to wait for her meeting with Swift Thunder. She was not sure how long Chief Charging Crow would wait before announcing to everyone the marriage date of his son and Moon Song. She knew that he still planned for them to wed.

That knowledge ate at Moon Song like a sore. If by chance Swift Thunder could not come up with a plan that would save her, she had already decided to run far away, so that no one would ever be able to find her.

Not even Swift Thunder, for she knew that if Swift Thunder did not help her, it would be because he had decided that it might cause too many problems for his people, and she would never do anything to place him in such an awkward position. If he did not meet with her as planned, she would know then that their dream of being together was an impossible one.

She fought the tears that burned at the corners of her eyes as she sat with her mother in their longhouse beside the lodge fire, sharing chores.

Today Moon Song was glad to have something to busy her hands, which helped to distract her mind. Her people grew hemp from which twine, nets, and cloth were produced. Today her mother was working on a basket.

Moon Song was plaiting corn leaves into a pair of shoes.

"*N-nitschaan*, daughter, I listened with an open heart as you confided in me about Swift Thunder, and even though I see much danger in Swift Thunder helping you, I will also do everything within my power to get you away from Piercing Eyes," Dove Woman murmured.

"But, *woakkimuk*, mother, what if my escape places *you* in danger?" Moon Song said, laying aside the half-made shoes.

She reached a hand out for her mother.

Her mother rested her work on her lap, then twined her fingers through Moon Song's.

"Daughter, since you were born, and especially since your father's death, you have been my life," Dove Woman murmured.

"Your happiness is my only reason for living. So, daughter, if Swift Thunder is what will make you happy, it does not matter to me if he is of the enemy clan and tribe. True love comes only once in a woman's life. It would not be fair for anyone to deny you this love."

"He is such a special man," Moon Song said, easing her hand from her mother's and resuming the plaiting of the corn leaves. "And you should see his pet cougar."

She paused and gazed into the lodge fire. "I am so anxious to see Blue now as a grown cougar," she murmured. "When I last saw him he was such a sweet, beautiful kitten."

Dove Woman shivered. "You must be careful around that animal," she warned. "Although tamed as a kitten, it still has the instincts of a wild cougar."

"Blue could never be wild and dangerous," Moon Song said.

She smiled as she recalled Blue licking her hand, then curling into a ball on her lap. "Oh, I do hope I get the chance to be his friend again," she said, sighing.

Moon Song flinched when the glow of lightning danced through the windows of the longhouse, followed by a loud, almost deafening clap of thunder.

And before Dove Woman could go and lower the buckskin flaps at the windows, rain began to fall in torrents.

Moon Song rushed to her feet and helped tie down the flaps at the windows, then sat back down and resumed work on the pair of shoes she hoped never to finish, for if things worked out, she would be gone with Swift Thunder tomorrow.

She would take nothing with her.

She would start life anew with Swift Thunder.

As the rain continued to fall in heavy sheets, the savage thunder was like giant drums being beaten in the heavens. Moon Song wondered if the sudden storm might be a bad omen.

She focused on better things . . . on those last moments with Swift Thunder and how they had found such passion in one another's arms.

And it was not just one of those dreams that had kept her sane through the years, but reality.

It gave her hope that if she could have a life with Swift Thunder, it would be something precious.

"Things will work out," Dove Woman murmured, bringing Moon Song's eyes quickly to her. "I have done everything within my power to make life good for you; I will not let it turn sour now."

Moon Song laid her things aside and went to her mother, who also laid her sewing beside her.

Feeling like a small child who sought comfort in her mother's arms, Moon Song clung to Dove Woman.

"Please help make it happen, Mother," she pleaded, tears streaming from her eyes. "Please?"

Then Moon Song clung even more tightly. "But if things do work out for me, I will miss *you* so," she sobbed.

"I will always be with you," Dove Woman reassured her. "In your heart, daughter. You will carry me around in your heart, as you will be with me in mine."

"Like Father is always with us," Moon Song murmured.

"Yes, like Father," Dove Woman murmured, caressing Moon Song's back. "Now close your eyes. Rest yourself in my arms. Let me hold you now, Moon Song, for soon you will be far from me."

Moon Song slowly closed her eyes and listened to her mother humming a song that she had sung to Moon Song since she was a small child.

Tonight it seemed important to be that small child again, if only for a while, for who ever knew what tomorrow would bring?

Chapter Ten

The sunset brought the day's sweet end,
And they could be together again.

After the storm which had temporarily kept him from putting his plan into action, Swift Thunder now sat in a comfortable over-stuffed chair in a dark, high-ceilinged room, before a roaring fire in the presence of many black-robed white men, sharing bitter tea and small cakes with them.

Upon his arrival this early evening at the monastery on the Hudson River, which was called a "Praying Castle" by the Mohawk, Swift Thunder had presented the priests with lavish gifts of beaver furs, then had gone with them into council in a room that always astounded Swift Thunder.

It was the many shelves of books that put him in such awe, yet it was from those books that he had learned to read after having made the acquaintance of the priests.

Swift Thunder's people saw the "Black Robes," as they were called, as kind and caring people, whereas the Oneida's Turtle

Clan thought them fanatics who lured the Iroquois into Christianity.

Thus far the priests had not interfered in Swift Thunder's people's lives. They had dedicated themselves to the English settlers in the area, bringing their religion to America.

Having fought for the English in the recent war, and having been given the special honor of knight by the English king, Swift Thunder enjoyed being with the priests. One of them, Brother John, had become a close friend.

Swift Thunder had an understanding with the priests: leave his people and children to practice their own religion, and the Mohawk would leave the priests to theirs.

Swift Thunder knew that the Black Robes' castle was used as a refuge — a place of safety for whites.

Since Swift Thunder was in part white, he felt he had a right to come to them, to seek their help, to seek refuge, not for himself but for his woman, an Oneida.

"And so you wish to bring Moon Song to our castle soon?" Brother John asked as he gazed through thick-lensed glasses at Swift Thunder. His long, gray hair was not a true reflection of his age, for Brother John was not elderly. He had told Swift

Thunder that an ailment back in England had not only almost entirely claimed his eyesight, but had turned his hair snow white and had caused him to lose weight, which gave him the gaunt features of a much older man.

But inside his heart was what mattered, he had told Swift Thunder.

There he was still a "young" man of fifty.

Swift Thunder watched Father John petting a cat that was a recent addition at the Praying Castle. Seeing the cat made Swift Thunder think of Blue. His cougar had disappeared from the longhouse last night while Swift Thunder was out. Blue had never done such a thing before and Swift Thunder was worried.

"Swift Thunder, didn't you hear my question?" Father John asked, slowly stroking his cat. "Do you want to bring Moon Song to the monastery soon?"

Swift Thunder looked quickly up at Father John, smiling awkwardly when he realized that his mind had been sidetracked by the cat.

"Yes, that is my request, if you will honor it," he said, setting his tiny porcelain cup in its saucer, with only a few tea leaves left at the bottom.

"But, Swift Thunder, you said that she is

of your enemy clan, the Turtle Clan of Oneida," Father John said, watching his cat leap from his lap and go lie closer to the fire.

Father John flicked fur from the skirt of his black robe, then arranged its folds more snugly around his legs as the fire warmed him through and through.

"Yes, she would be considered my enemy, but we do not think of ourselves in that way," Swift Thunder said.

His gaze moved slowly around the half circle of priests who sat in chairs on each side of him, all of them facing the blazing fire.

When the fire snapped, crackled, and popped, the sound carried to the high ceiling, then bounced back again in a strange sort of hollow echo.

"You said that ten years separated you and then fate brought you together again," Father John said, twining his fingers together, then resting his hands on his lap.

"As war changes the course of so many's lives, so did it change ours for a while," Swift Thunder said. "But now that we have come together again in our hearts, we neither one want anything to come between us again, for we knew from that very first day, when we were so young, that we were meant for one another."

"It is good that you have found a woman so that you can marry and have children, for I know that your grandfather aches to hold a grandchild in his arms," Father John said, nodding as he recalled his pleasant meetings with Fire Wolf.

The first time Father John had met Fire Wolf, the priest knew that he was in the presence of someone special. Their friendship had grown, and now Fire Wolf came to the Praying Castle for tea and cake even more often than Swift Thunder. Swift Thunder was now their people's leader, which gave Fire Wolf time to relax and contemplate what was, what had been, and how it would be when he met his loved ones in the hereafter.

Those were the things discussed between Father John and Fire Wolf.

"Yes, Grandfather had only one daughter and one grandson to hold on his lap and share his life with," Swift Thunder said. He passed a hand over his breechclout, smoothing it out across his muscled thighs. "But even then, his daughter was taken from him too soon in life."

"But he still had you, and you have filled those empty spaces in his heart with much pride and love," Father John said, smiling. "And I will do what I can to keep your Moon Song safe."

Then Father John leaned closer to Swift Thunder, so that their eyes were level. "But there is one thing that I cannot help wondering about," he said, his voice drawn.

"What is that?" Swift Thunder asked, raising an eyebrow.

"Do you think this woman will actually come if you tell her the plan?" Father John asked, leaning even closer to Swift Thunder, his voice lowered.

Swift Thunder was very aware of the other robed men leaning closer, too, in an effort not to miss anything that was being said, for there were no secrets in this Praying Castle.

He smiled as the cat came and brushed against his legs, purring. He reached down and stroked the cat's thick fur, but drew his hand away when the cat sauntered off to one of the priests and leapt on his lap.

Swift Thunder's gaze swept past the seated men. A mysterious cloaked figure had slipped quietly into the room and stood in the dark shadows.

Swift Thunder could not tell if this mysterious figure was looking at him or not, for a hood was drawn down over his brow which shadowed his face and eyes.

From the strange sense of foreboding that came with the man's presence, and the way he stood apart from the other priests, in the shadows, Swift Thunder believed that the cloaked figure was looking at him.

Could it be because he did not want Swift Thunder to know who he was? Surely so, or why would he be standing away from everyone, only observing instead of participating?

But Swift Thunder didn't want to show a lack of faith in Father John's sincerity by asking him about the dark, foreboding figure. It might show a lack of trust to point out to Father John that someone was standing just inside the room, hiding his identity behind a hooded cloak.

Yes, his questions were best left unvoiced.

Yet Swift Thunder was uneasy; was he bringing Moon Song to a place where a mysterious cloaked figure might prove dangerous to her?

He forced himself to look away from the cloaked figure, yet knew that it must be a man, for Swift Thunder had never seen any women at the Praying Castle. The priests even did their own cooking.

Yes, he *must* trust Father John to watch out for Moon Song once she was there, for where else could Swift Thunder keep her in hiding while he returned home to his duties as chief?

"Swift Thunder, again you did not hear my question," Father John said, drawing Swift Thunder out of his troubled thoughts.

"The question?" Swift Thunder asked, feeling a rush of heat to his cheeks, for he didn't remember what Father John had asked him.

He glanced over at the mysterious cloaked figure, stunned that he was no longer there, as though Swift Thunder had only imagined seeing him.

He looked quickly at Father John again. "You must forgive me," he said. "My mind wandered again. Please tell me your question once more."

"I asked you if Moon Song will come for refuge here when her clan despises white holy men," Father John said softly. "Will she remain once she knows that you cannot stay with her, but instead return to the duties of your people?"

"Moon Song is not like any Oneida that I have ever known," Swift Thunder said, his eyes lighting up as he envisioned her loveliness, her sweetness. "She is tender-hearted, sweet, innocent, and —"

"Bring her soon," Father John said, smiling as he interrupted Swift Thunder. "She will be safe. I will see to it that she is happy."

"Thank you, Father John," Swift Thunder said, rising from the chair. "You mentioned how Moon Song's people despise white holy men. That is why Moon Song will be safe here. Her people will have no reason to suspect that Moon Song is here."

Father John moved shakily to his feet, and Swift Thunder was reminded of the ailment that had almost destroyed his friend's life. While standing, Father John's body trembled. His bony, weak knees barely held him up.

And when Father John embraced Swift Thunder, Swift Thunder felt the bones of his friend's body through the cotton fabric of the black robe.

Swift Thunder returned the embrace, expressing his fondness for the holy man. Father John had become a link to Swift Thunder's other life . . . the life that had been stolen from him on the day of his mother's murder and his father's disappearance.

But Swift Thunder had lived a full, happy, productive life as a Mohawk, and could not see himself in any other setting than as chief of a powerful people.

He felt blessed to have been so loved by his grandfather, and then in turn by his grandfather's people.

"Come with the woman when it is convenient for you," Father John said, stepping shakily away from Swift Thunder. He smiled and picked up the cat as it came to him, meowing. "And next time bring Blue. I have not seen your pet cougar for some time now."

A sadness swept over Swift Thunder's face. "Last night Blue disappeared and has not yet returned home," he said, his voice breaking. "He has never done that before. I fear he has answered the call of the wild."

"He will return when the time is right for him to come back into your life," Father John said, running his fingers through his cat's fur. "Until then, come and enjoy my cat. It loves being petted."

Swift Thunder reached over and stroked the cat's fur, enjoying the way it purred so contentedly.

"He is a pretty, gentle thing," Swift Thunder said. "What is his name?"

"*Her* name is Josephine," Father John

said, chuckling. "Josephine was my mother's name."

Swift Thunder turned and smiled at another priest as he came with a napkin-covered basket of sweet cakes that were a gift for his grandfather. He took the basket and sniffed the aroma of freshly baked cakes, hungry again for them even though he had filled his stomach with several only moments ago.

"My grandfather thanks you for these," Swift Thunder said as he walked with Father John toward the huge oak front door.

"Tell your grandfather to come soon for a long visit," Father John said, opening the door just as a huge bridge was being lowered by chains across a small channel of water.

Father John had instituted this idea of a bridge and moat in case he might come under attack some day by renegade Indians.

Then Father John frowned. "But perhaps it would not be wise for your grandfather to come while the woman is here."

"Yes, you are right," Swift Thunder agreed. "Even though Grandfather knows my plan, he cannot fully agree with it, for he finds it hard to understand a grandson whose heart has been captured by an Oneida."

"Who can say what your love for Moon Song will bring both your people?" Father John said, stepping out onto the bridge with Swift Thunder. "Perhaps it might make enemies friends."

Swift Thunder laughed. "I cannot imagine that happening, yet it does not hurt to wish for it," he said, walking over the bridge with Father John, then down a slope of land toward the Hudson River.

"I pray that all will go well for you and your woman, and also Blue," Father John said as Swift Thunder placed the basket of cakes in his canoe.

He turned to give Father John a farewell embrace, then stopped short when he saw a figure in a window on the fourth floor of the Praying Castle, the mysterious cloaked person who had stood in the dark corner for a moment.

He was now standing at the window staring at Swift Thunder.

Wondering what this man's interest in him might be, Swift Thunder turned quickly toward Father John.

"Is something wrong?" Father John asked, giving Swift Thunder a questioning look.

When Father John saw Swift Thunder glance at the Praying Castle, he, too, looked, but he saw nothing out of the ordinary.

"It is nothing," Swift Thunder said, deciding not to pursue the mystery. "I will come soon with Moon Song."

"I will prepare her a room," Father John said, waving at Swift Thunder as he leapt into his canoe and began paddling out to the middle of the river.

Chapter Eleven

Burning alive one flame at a time,
In those moments you were mine.
When we heard our sighs and cries
of delight,
It was then we knew we must
for our love fight.

It was a sweet time of remembrance as Swift Thunder and Moon Song sat holding hands where they had met as children fresh from rites which proved she was worthy of being called a woman, and Swift Thunder a man.

There were no signs of the recent storm, except that all of the leaves on the trees seemed a brighter green, and more wild-flowers had opened up to perfume the air.

Moon Song felt renewed herself. She was relieved she had been able to escape her castle without being seen, to be with the man she had been born to love.

Today, as the warriors of her castle had gone into council shortly after the noon meal was eaten, Moon Song had taken the opportunity to slip through the wide gate, waiting for the moment when the one posted sentry had turned his back to gaze heavenward at a pair of eagles that soared overhead.

When Moon Song saw the eagles, goose bumps rose on her flesh, for she felt as though they had been sent there by *Tharonhiawakon* to draw attention from Moon Song's escape.

She *had* prayed to *Tharonhiawakon* to help her find a way to go to Swift Thunder today so they could complete their plans for her escape.

Tharonhiawakon knew Piercing Eyes' evil ways and would not put this burden on Moon Song. She took the soaring eagles as proof of it.

"I could not sleep last night for fear you would not come," Swift Thunder suddenly said, taking Moon Song from her thoughts to him.

"I made certain that only my mother knows that I am gone," Moon Song murmured. The breeze lifted her hair from her shoulders and flung a long strand across her lips.

Swift Thunder brushed the hair away.

He tried to control the trembling of his fingers as he placed them on her lips and slowly traced their outline.

Her sensual shudder proved that his

mere touch caused her pleasure; she gasped lightly and slowly closed her eyes.

Swift Thunder removed his fingers from her lips, then placed his lips there and gently kissed her.

Shaken by the intensity of the passion that was overwhelming her, Moon Song twined her arms around Swift Thunder's neck. Without even thinking about what she was doing, she moved onto his lap facing him, her legs straddling him.

Moon Song's sweet body awakened fires within Swift Thunder that he had not known were there. He enfolded her in his arms and kissed her more deeply, more heatedly.

While they kissed, their bodies straining together, Swift Thunder lifted Moon Song from his lap and gently laid her on the thick bed of grass beside the Mohawk River.

As his hands swept over her body, feeling the heat of her flesh through the doeskin of her dress, he reveled in her response to him. She arched up into his seeking fingers, then sucked in a wild breath of ecstasy as he slid a hand up inside the skirt of her dress, and made a slow path along the silken flesh of her inner thigh.

When he got to that wondrous place

where the secrets of Moon Song's womanhood lay beneath soft fronds of hair, he
knew that he must stop now, or he would
not be able to.

Yet everything within him, every fiber of
his being, wanted Moon Song. He had
waited so long for her, how could he stop
now?

He could tell that she was feeling the
same things, and as intensely as he. She,
too, was breathless at the realization of
where his hand rested.

Swift Thunder wanted so badly to reach
onward and cover her secret place with his
hand, to touch her fronds of hair, to delve
into them where her womanhood awaited
the sweet caresses of the man who loved
her.

Yet he knew he must go no further with
this seduction. He respected Moon Song.
He did not want her to feel he had taken
advantage of her.

He wanted their first time together to be
filled with wonder, not apprehension.

Moon Song was very aware of how torn
Swift Thunder was at this moment.

She was also aware of her own aching
need. It was a feeling that his fingers, that
he alone, had aroused.

She felt as though she would die if he

did not give her completeness, for she was a woman who had waited a lifetime for this man.

Yet she did not want to make him feel wrong about what they might do. She wanted their moment of coming together to remain in his heart as a wonderful memory, not something he would feel guilty about.

She slid her lips from his.

She placed her hands gently on each side of his face and smiled into his eyes as he looked at her with a deep, hot passion.

"I love you," she murmured, her voice breaking with the emotion she felt. "And I know you love me. I know you want me."

She leaned forward and brushed his lips with a trembling kiss, then gazed into his eyes again. "I want you as much as you want me," she said, tears warm in the corners of her eyes, tears of her happiness.

"I do not want to take advantage of your innocence," Swift Thunder said huskily. "But, Moon Song, how can I deny that I want to make love with you? I cannot say I have saved myself for this moment with you, for I am a man, with a man's needs. There *have* been women, but none I loved as I have always loved you. I had always hoped I would find someone to share my heart with forever, for I truly did not think that you and I would meet again. But no one ever compared with you."

"I understand how a man's needs must be fed, and a woman also has such needs, but I never gave into such hungers. Truthfully, I knew them not until you held me in your arms and kissed me again after all those empty years without you," Moon Song murmured.

"But I . . . did . . . break down in the face of temptation," Swift Thunder said, his eyes full of apology as he gazed deeply into hers.

"And I understand that it was because you are a man with the hungers of a man's body," Moon Song said, smiling sweetly at him. "A woman is not that needy of sexual release. At least *this* woman isn't."

She lowered her hands to his chest.

Slowly she swept her fingers over the powerful muscles there; then her fingers circled his nipples.

She moved her hands slowly downward and saw that she was causing his body to tremble and his breath to quicken.

"Or shall I say this woman *wasn't?*" she said, her voice sounding strangely husky to her. "I now feel needs that make me dizzy with such sweet passion. My body, it . . ."

"Your body . . . *you* . . . need this man whose mind is reeling from his own need," Swift Thunder said, sucking in a wild breath of rapture when Moon Song moved her fingers inside the waist of his breechclout.

He knew that she had only a short way to go before realizing the true extent of his arousal, for his manhood was stretched tight and throbbing from its own need, as though it were a separate entity, a being of its own, with its own heartbeat.

"Swift Thunder, in body I am a *wuskochquau,* a virgin," Moon Song said, stopping herself from being so brazen as to actually touch his manhood. She could see its full outline pressed against his breechclout.

She had never seen a man undressed, so she was not exactly sure what to expect, except that she knew this part of a man's anatomy was supposed to fulfill all a woman's sexual longings.

She could recall hearing her mother and father making love so many years ago. From those recollections she knew what to expect with Swift Thunder, for she loved him as deeply as her mother had loved her father.

"For that reason alone I feel we must

stop what we are tempted to do," Swift Thunder said, taking her hand from his body, gently holding it down at his side.

"Swift Thunder, please let me finish what I was going to say," Moon Song murmured. "I was saying that I am a virgin, but so often through the years, in my heart, I have made love with you. After those dreams I would wake up feeling strangely fulfilled, as though you were there, truly having made love with me. My body felt it. My very soul felt it."

"That is because I *was* there, for surely at those very moments when you were feeling those things, I had made love to you in my own dream," Swift Thunder said huskily.

"Let us make it real today, Swift Thunder, and then even if you have not found a way to hide me, to save me, at least I will have these precious moments with you to remember," Moon Song said. She took her hand from his and again slid it slowly down his muscled chest toward his waistband. "Let me remove your breechclout. Then you can take off my dress. We are in our secret place where we are well hidden. No one will see, not even if they ride past in a canoe."

"But I *have* found a way to keep you

hidden until I feel it is safe to take you to my home as my future bride," Swift Thunder said. He swallowed hard when she moved her hand still lower, her eyes widening in wonder at what he had said.

He closed his eyes and let his head fall back as her fingers finally found his aching manhood.

He could hardly hold back a cry of ecstasy as the softness of her fingers closed around his heat and began moving on him as though she had done this many times before. Yet he knew without a doubt that this was completely new to her.

"I will tell you later where I will take you," Swift Thunder managed to say between gasps as her lips left a heated path of kisses across his chest, then lower down across his stomach.

Although he knew she was a virgin, because she had said so, he was amazed at her skill to please him.

No woman he had bedded had touched him in such a way, yet he knew that was because none of those women truly loved him and wanted to make his heart soar with the passion that was overwhelming him at this moment.

He knew that he was now beyond coherent thought, that nothing could stop what had begun. He would finally have this woman as he had dreamed so often of having her.

His body ached and cried out for completion, yet he would not allow that to happen until he gave her the pleasuring that she had saved herself for.

His heart thudding as though someone were hammering inside his chest, Swift Thunder reached for Moon Song's hands and held them away from himself.

"To make this a perfect moment for both of us, we must enter that realm of bliss together," he said, their eyes meeting and holding. "And I feel that we must move farther away from the river to be better hidden from anyone who might pass by. Your canoe is hidden well enough amid the bushes. Let us take ourselves to a cave I found that is hollowed into the wall of rock where I proved myself to be a man."

"I shall never forget that day," Moon Song said, her breath catching as Swift Thunder grabbed her up into his arms.

"Nor shall I," Swift Thunder said huskily as he carried her away from the river. "As fate would have it, that day began our love affair, which will be sealed today when we join our bodies and our hearts as one."

"Yes, our destiny was fulfilled that day,"

Moon Song said, gently laying her cheek on his bare, muscled chest.

"No, today it is finally being fulfilled," Swift Thunder said, smiling into her eyes. "Today we truly become man and woman, and soon we will be husband and wife."

"And then there will be children born of our love," Moon Song said, sighing with blissful joy. "Can you imagine it, Swift Thunder? Our . . . very . . . own children?"

"It will happen," Swift Thunder said, brushing a kiss across her brow. "Perhaps even today I shall plant the seed that will give us our first child."

"I so want that. Swift Thunder, do you truly feel that you have a place to take me where I will be safe from Piercing Eyes?" Moon Song asked, not wanting to show her doubts.

"There *is* a place where I know you will be safe, if you will agree to go there," Swift Thunder said, stopping to gaze into her eyes to judge her reaction.

"Tell me," Moon Song said, her eyes searching his.

He hurriedly told her his plan to take her to the Praying Castle. He explained that once her people gave up their search for her, she could then go to Swift Thunder's castle, where he would marry her. And pity

159

anyone who tried to come for her then, especially Piercing Eyes!

He was so relieved when she said she trusted him in every way and in whatever decision he made for her.

"*Qua,* I will go and stay in seclusion at the Praying Castle for as long as you deem it necessary," she said, as he bent low and carried her into the cave, where she was surprised to see a small burning fire amid a circle of rocks, a basket of food, and thick pelts spread around the fire.

"You prepared this place for us before I came to meet with you?" Moon Song asked as he gently set her on the pelts beside the fire.

"Do not look at me as though I planned to seduce you here," Swift Thunder said. "I knew that we would be safer talking here than out in the open. No one saw me leave with the pelts or the food, for I placed them in my canoe in the middle of the night when everyone else was asleep."

"It was such a lovely thing for you to do," Moon Song said as she gazed around at the preparations.

She gasped when she saw roses lying close to the pelts and knew they were for her, surely as a reminder of those roses she wore in her hair so long ago.

160

She reached her arms out for Swift Thunder as he sat down beside her. "Hug me," she murmured. "Please hold me, for I have never felt as special as now."

He drew her into his embrace and held her close.

"It will be wonderful to go with you to your castle," she murmured. "I have dreamed of nothing but being yours from the moment we met."

She wouldn't allow herself to worry about her mother at this time; her mother wanted Moon Song to be happy and knew that Swift Thunder held the secret to that happiness.

Her mother had already accepted that she must lose Moon Song, as mothers must do when their daughters got to the marrying age.

But in this case her mother had had Moon Song much longer than usual, for the war had intervened.

Suddenly a thought came to Moon Song. She leaned away from Swift Thunder and gazed at him. "Where is Blue?" she asked. "I am so anxious to see him."

When sadness filled Swift Thunder's eyes, she wished she had not mentioned Blue.

"He is gone," Swift Thunder said, his

voice breaking. He swept a fallen lock of hair back from Moon Song's face. "But I understand his absence. He is a male, such as I, seeking a mate."

"Will he return to you?" Moon Song asked, hoping to see and pet Blue again even though she knew he was no longer a kitten.

"In time," Swift Thunder said, then reached his hands to the fringed hem of Moon Song's dress and slowly began drawing it up her body. He pulled it over her head and tossed it aside.

When he saw her body, so slim, so perfect, her breasts round and full, he sucked in a wild breath of pleasure.

Thrilled by his pleasure, Moon Song reached for one of his hands and took it to her breast, trembling with passion as his fingers kneaded, his thumb slowly, teasingly circling her nipple.

When he leaned down and swept his tongue over one of her nipples, Moon Song was struck to the core of her being with rapture.

She closed her eyes and let him take charge as he laid her down on the soft pelts.

She wasn't even aware of when he removed his breechclout, only of when she

162

felt his manhood probing at the juncture of her thighs.

As though she had done this countless times before, as though she knew what to do to make this lovemaking as magical as she had always imagined it to be, she parted her legs and gave Swift Thunder better access to her body.

He twined his fingers through her hair and brought her lips to his, and as he kissed her feverishly, his hands moving seductively all over her body, lingering at her more sensitive places, she felt him slowly shoving himself into her.

When he thrust even more deeply and she felt an instant of pain, his kiss deepened, robbing her of all memory of that pain, especially since an intense rapture took its place inside her heart.

They rocked and tangled, their kisses becoming frenzied, their bodies moving rhythmically together as that moment of wondrous rapture grew nearer and nearer.

And then they both cried out their fulfillment as they found that ultimate completeness at almost the same moment.

Slowly they came down from their cloud of pleasure, yet still they clung and kissed, their bodies locked in a sweet embrace.

Then Swift Thunder rolled off her and

stretched out on his back.

Stunned by the total ecstasy of the moment, Moon Song lay there, reliving it, then turned toward Swift Thunder.

"When do I go to the Praying Castle?" she blurted out. "I am so anxious to begin our true life, which can happen only when I am able to go with you to your home and be your wife."

"Tomorrow," Swift Thunder said. He turned on his side and faced her. He reached a hand to her cheek. "My woman, I just made you my wife, for no ceremony could ever make it more real than it is today."

"My *wachia,* my husband," Moon Song murmured, truly feeling married to Swift Thunder. It did not seem wrong to make love with him since her heart had been his for so long.

It was the first time Moon Song had been with a man sexually, and her joy confirmed her decision to defy everything and everyone to be with Swift Thunder, the only man she would ever love.

She cuddled closer to him, and as they watched the flames of the fire caress the logs, they spoke of their future . . . a future they would share together.

Nothing would be allowed to stand in their way ever again!

Chapter Twelve

Sorrow, heartache, and pain,
They visit each one both the same.
These words both had heard before,
Still it hurt to close love's door.

Dove Woman could not help smiling even though she knew she was going to lose her daughter, and more than likely never see her again.

Once Moon Song left the castle of the Oneida and married Swift Thunder, Moon Song's life would be centered around her husband and *his* people, for Swift Thunder was a Mohawk *sachem*.

Nonetheless, it made Dove Woman smile, because finally her daughter had found the happiness that Dove Woman had known. It was in Moon Song's eyes as she talked about Swift Thunder and their plans. It was in her daughter's voice.

"I must do all I can to make it possible for her to marry Swift Thunder," Dove Woman whispered as she cut more wild carrots into the venison stew she was preparing over her fire.

The aroma of the venison had already begun to waft up from the simmering water, filling Dove Woman's lodge with the scent of perhaps the last meal she would share with her daughter.

She truly believed that when Moon Song arrived home today, she would have plans that would set her free from her bonds with Piercing Eyes.

"Bless that young Mohawk *sachem* for loving my daughter so much," Dove Woman whispered as she continued to think about Swift Thunder. Humming contentedly, forcing all traces of sadness from her heart, Dove Woman began adding wild onions to the stew.

She flinched when the strong smell made her eyes smart. Closing her eyes, she rubbed them with the back of her left hand.

When she opened her eyes again she jumped and gasped with horror at the discovery that she was no longer alone. During that one moment when she had closed her eyes, Piercing Eyes had entered her lodge. He now stood over her, glaring.

"What do you want here?" Dove Woman managed in a voice hardly stronger than a whisper. Her fear was keen inside her heart . . . a fear born of knowing that Piercing

Eyes was there because of Moon Song.

"Where is Moon Song?" Piercing Eyes growled out.

He looked lopsided and off center to Dove Woman because of the vacant place where one arm should be.

Worst of all, she knew who had caused the loss of his arm. The very man her daughter was in love with!

She had tried to protect Moon Song from this knowledge, yet knew that Piercing Eyes would make an issue of it when he discovered Moon Song's relationship with the Mohawk *sachem.*

But even if this man had both arms, he would be no more attractive than he was now. He always wore a bitter scowl across his long face. His nose was narrow and strangely flat on the top, as though someone had hit him in the face with a board.

His shoulders were narrow. His stomach protruded over the waistband of his breechclout, proving his laziness. Indeed, he lay around most of the time stuffing his mouth with food instead of doing something worthwhile for his people.

He always complained about his arm, saying the lack of it made it impossible to do the normal day's activities of a man.

With only one arm he could not hunt, nor fight off an enemy if he came face to face with one.

Yes, he took advantage of his weaknesses and did not worry that it made him look lazy and shiftless to everyone who saw him.

"Where . . . is . . . your daughter?" Piercing Eyes demanded, his narrow lips pursed. The dark pupils of his eyes were even more piercing today as he stood over a helpless woman.

When Dove Woman gathered her courage to stand up to this weasel of a man, she laid her knife aside although she was tempted to use it on this man she loathed.

But instead she stood up and held her chin proudly as she stared defiantly into his eyes.

"And so you choose the silent treatment on your chief's son today, do you?" Piercing Eyes said, his voice rising in pitch with each word.

Enjoying his frustration, Dove Woman could not help but smile.

Yet deep in her heart she was afraid for her daughter.

This evil man would soon conclude that Moon Song was no longer at the Oneida castle and would send warriors far and wide to search for her.

If she was found with Swift Thunder, her lover would die a quick death, and then Moon Song would be brought back to her people's castle and put on display to be ridiculed for having consorted with the enemy . . . the enemy who was responsible for the Oneida having lost the recent war.

She prayed to herself that the search would not uncover Moon Song's whereabouts, that she would not return, that somehow Swift Thunder had thought it best to take her into hiding today instead of allowing her to return to her home.

"And so you refuse to speak, do you?" Piercing Eyes said, his rage evident in his face and voice.

Dove Woman stood her ground, silent, hoping that this man could not feel her fear, for she wasn't sure how she might be punished because of her silence.

And she knew that she *would* be punished, to make an example to anyone else who might wish to escape from this life that was no longer as good as it had been before the Oneida had sided with the French.

She held her arms stiffly at her sides, waiting for Piercing Eyes' next move. She was stunned when he just turned around and left.

Yet she knew that was not the last she would hear from him. Her fingers trembled as she picked up the knife and began slicing wild potatoes into her stew.

When all of the ingredients were finally in the pot, she picked up a wooden spoon and began slowly stirring the stew, then jumped with alarm at the sound of loud footsteps. She did not even have time to turn to see who it was. Powerful hands were on both of her arms, yanking her up from the floor.

Her heart pounded with fear, but Dove Woman did not give the warriors who were dragging her from her lodge even a slight glance.

She didn't want to know who was following Piercing Eyes' orders. It would hurt her deeply if they were men whom she had watched grow up from young braves to powerful warriors.

Robbed of her dignity, her heart aching for her daughter who would surely be the next to suffer such mistreatment, Dove Woman kept her eyes lowered to the ground so that she could not see those who were watching her being dragged into the stockade where the enemies of their people were usually locked away.

Her breath caught in her throat when the rough hands shoved her so hard that she fell to her knees on the hard earthen floor.

Tears spilling from her eyes, she cringed when she heard the large bolt lock slide into place and knew that she was a prisoner of her very own people.

Remaining on her knees, she lifted her eyes heavenward and began praying for her beloved daughter's safety.

She did not know that Piercing Eyes was at this very moment standing in the shadows of her longhouse, waiting.

Chapter Thirteen

The wisest heart can sometimes break,
This was so evil could take,
The rainbows and moonlight,
She would not give up without a fight.

Still walking on clouds of rapture, Moon Song felt relieved that she had not been questioned when she had arrived at the tall gate of the Oneida castle. She had had no choice but to return in full view of those who stood at the river's edge, unloading their catch of fish from their canoes. She knew that if she had waited until no one was there, it would be late at night.

She was anxious to talk to her mother, to tell her the plan, and even to share with her the precious moments when she had discovered how it truly felt to be a woman.

As she had beached her canoe she had been aware of some half glances, but she shrugged off her anxiety when those same warriors resumed their activities as though she weren't there.

As she walked through the village toward her longhouse she felt eyes on her again, as though people were watching her, but again shrugged off her uneasiness when she looked around and saw no one acting peculiar.

When she reached her house, the smell of her mother's stew wafted through the open door. It was her favorite. She would recognize its smell anywhere.

She was so anxious to share all that had happened with her mother. Yet she was sad that this would be their last day together.

"Mother!" Moon Song cried excitedly. "*Woakkimuk*, I am home."

When her mother didn't meet her at the door, as she usually did, Moon Song stopped and gazed questioningly at the open door.

Surely her mother was even now walking toward the door to greet her. Shrugging again, Moon Song ran on into the house, then gasped when she found Piercing Eyes standing in the shadows, his beady eyes glaring at her.

A warning shot through her as she looked frantically around her for her mother. Fear grabbed her when she still didn't see Dove Woman.

Turning quick, angry eyes to her tormenter, Moon Song doubled her hands into tight fists at her sides.

"Where . . . is . . . my mother?" she asked, growing cold inside when that question caused a slow, mocking smile to quiver across Piercing Eyes' lips.

Moon Song covered a gasp behind her hand. She knew that Piercing Eyes had done something to her mother.

"Where have you been?" Piercing Eyes asked, taking a slow, stiff step toward her.

"I demand to know where my mother is," Moon Song said defiantly.

Piercing Eyes hurried to Moon Song and grabbed her by the back of the hair with his one hand. He yanked it, yet his eyes remained steadily fixed on hers. "I am the son of your chief, and your betrothed, and I get answers when I ask *you* a question," he growled out. "Where . . . have . . . you been? Who were you with?"

Knowing that no matter what she said or did, nothing would ever be the same again for her or her mother, Moon Song said nothing, only defied Piercing Eyes with a narrow, angry stare.

She flinched when a warrior she knew well hurried into the longhouse and stopped next to her and Piercing Eyes. It was Piercing Eyes' warrior Four Toes. He was the one who did all of Piercing Eyes' dirty work, for he was the only one who still gave Piercing Eyes the loyalty he asked of all Oneida warriors.

Four Toes gave Moon Song a quick, strange sort of look, then kept his eyes straight ahead as he shuffled his moccasined feet nervously on the earthen floor.

"I have done as you ordered me to do," Four Toes said excitedly. He gave Moon Song another quick look, then again gazed at Piercing Eyes. "I followed Moon Song."

As Four Toes proceeded to tell Piercing Eyes exactly what he had seen, how Moon Song had met with Swift Thunder, and how she had gone into a cave with Swift Thunder and surely made love with him there, in private, Moon Song's hopes of ever again seeing Swift Thunder sank.

Tears came to her eyes as she imagined this sneaky warrior spying on her and Swift Thunder as they made such sweet love. Yet surely he would not admit to having done anything so shameful.

But the fact was that she had been caught, and surely her mother was even now paying for what her people would call a sin. Moon Song wanted to lash out at Piercing Eyes and pummel his chest and shout at him, but knew that none of that would achieve anything.

Piercing Eyes' fingers were still tight in her hair, so Moon Song could not step away from him when he leaned his face into hers, his foul breath making her recoil.

"You have been disloyal to me, your betrothed, and even to your *sachem,* by going to the enemy and consorting with him," Piercing Eyes hissed out. "You . . . will . . . pay!"

He suddenly yanked his hand away from her hair, then rubbed it briskly against his breechclout as though he meant to cleanse her filth away.

Free of his grip, Moon Song took a slow step away from him, but knew that she was trapped. She wondered what he would do next.

"I do not want you now, not since you have been with the enemy," Piercing Eyes said, his eyes flashing angrily. "But no Mohawk, especially not Swift Thunder, will have you, either."

He idly shrugged and flipped his long, black hair back from his shoulders. "But first things first," he said, chuckling ominously. "Yes, first things first. I must send your Mohawk lover a message."

Dying a slow death inside at what this evil, conniving man might be planning, Moon Song asked guardedly, "What . . .

sort . . . of message?"

Wild, mocking laughter was his only reply. He left the longhouse, his laughter loud and ominous.

"My mother," she whispered. "He did not tell me where Mother is!"

She started to run after him, but she did not get across the threshold, for Four Toes was suddenly there blocking her way.

"Please, Four Toes, let me go and find my mother," Moon Song pleaded, her heart torn between worry over her mother and Swift Thunder. As fiendish as Piercing Eyes was when it came to his hatred for the Mohawk, surely he would devise the most terrible way to kill Swift Thunder.

And her mother?

Oh, what was he going to do with her?

Her breath was knocked away when Four Toes gave her a hard shove, causing her to fall backward. She steadied herself, then pleaded with her jailer.

"Four Toes, we played together as children," she murmured. "We have always been friends. How can you treat me like this? Please do not let Piercing Eyes turn you into someone like him."

"He is our chief's son, and what he commands, I do," Four Toes said; then his eyes wavered as he took a step closer to Moon

Song. "Your mother? She has been taken to the stockade. Moon Song, do as you are told, or you will be thrown into the stockade with your mother."

Moon Song grew cold inside to know where her mother was being held. She knew that she must guard against being put there herself, for if she was locked away, how could she devise a way to set her mother free?

Something told her that Piercing Eyes was going to use her mother as a pawn to make Moon Song pay for her disobedience.

And then again, there was Swift Thunder. She must find a way to warn him.

Praying that the next warrior sent to guard her was someone she could convince to help her, Moon Song backed into her house, then flinched as though she had been shot when the door was slammed closed.

She was glad that there were no locks on the longhouses. At least in that respect she wasn't locked in, but she knew that she would be carefully guarded, not only at the front of the house, but also at the back where she could have found escape through windows.

"What am I to do?" she sobbed as she began a nervous pacing. She had to find a way to escape so that she could go and free her mother, as well.

She only hoped she was not too late.

She had no idea how far Piercing Eyes would go in his scheming madness to have complete control of Moon Song's destiny.

"And what sort of message is he going to send to Swift Thunder?" she whispered aloud, shivering at the knowledge that whatever Piercing Eyes chose to do, it would be something cruel and degrading.

"Please, my love, oh, Swift Thunder, keep yourself safe," Moon Song whispered, a sob in the depths of her throat almost choking her.

She had no choice now but to wait for that perfect moment when she could make her escape.

Then she would do everything within her power to save the two most precious people in her life . . . her mother . . . her lover!

Chapter Fourteen

A tiny flutter near her heart
Brought tears and wishes they would
*   never part.*
She crept away into the night.
She was not there when he reached
*   to hold her tight.*

The night seemed endless for Moon Song as she lay wakeful upon mats before her lodge fire, the fire's glow the only light in the longhouse. She felt a wild longing for freedom within her soul.

It was a cry now, also, for her mother, for Moon Song felt distraught that she could not do anything to free her mother.

Sighing, flipping her waist-length hair across her shoulders as she rose from the mats, Moon Song knew that daybreak would soon arrive, and with it her last chance to free her mother and slip away under the cover of darkness.

"I cannot just sit and wait any longer for something to happen," she whispered, staring at the closed door. "I must make it happen. I must do what I can *now*, not later."

Her pulse racing, knowing she had little chance of convincing Four Toes to open the door, no matter what ploy she used, Moon Song went to the door and spoke through it.

"Four Toes, are you awake?" she asked.

"I was ordered to stay awake, so I am awake," Four Toes grumbled. "Moon Song, what do you want of Four Toes?"

She wondered if the other sentries were awake, too. She was going to have to take a chance that Four Toes was more devoted than the others.

"Four Toes, I cannot sleep because I am thirsty," Moon Song said. "And I am out of water. It is hot and close in here tonight, Four Toes. My throat is parched dry. Please have mercy and give me some water."

For a moment he did not respond in any way, and she thought he must see right through her ploy.

Then when he replied in the easy tone of voice that she had grown to know when they were children enjoying one another's company, she smiled devilishly and reached out for a stool that she had purposely slid closer to the door.

"I will share my water with you," Four Toes said as he opened the door.

Moon Song slipped into the darker shadows, picked up the stool, and as Four Toes stepped inside the longhouse, she brought it down on his head.

When she heard a strange sort of cracking sound when the stool came in contact with Four Toes' skull, she cringed, for she had not wanted to hurt her old friend, but only temporarily knock him unconscious.

As he crumpled to the floor, obviously unconscious, guilt made Moon Song stay long enough to check on Four Toes.

As she put her fingers on the vein in his neck, and felt a steady pulse, she sighed with relief that she had not killed him.

But as she brushed her hand against his arm and felt wetness, she knew that it was blood.

"I am sorry," she whispered, truly regretting having harmed Four Toes in any way. He was not a bad man, only dutiful to his chief and chief's son. He did not deserve an injury that in truth should have been Piercing Eyes'; Piercing Eyes was the one responsible for Moon Song's problems.

"And what of Swift Thunder?" she whispered as she tiptoed outside the lodge.

"What has Piercing Eyes done to Swift Thunder?"

She stopped and looked slowly about, relieved that none of the assigned warriors were where they could see her.

They were surely around at the back, and she hoped they were asleep.

If they had been awake they would have heard Four Toes' loud grunt of pain as he lurched forward.

Hoping that the guards and everyone else at the castle would stay sound asleep for a while longer, Moon Song broke into a hard run toward the stockade.

When it came into view and Moon Song saw no warrior standing guard, she stopped in her tracks. The door of the stockade stood wide open.

Afraid to think what might have happened to her mother, Moon Song ran to the stockade and rushed inside.

It was empty, but a pool of fresh blood on the earthen floor caused Moon Song's heart to sink and her knees to grow weak. What if her mother had been killed?

But Moon Song could not believe that Piercing Eyes was that evil, that he could be responsible for such a horrendous act.

Her mother had done nothing wrong!

Realizing how quickly time was passing,

and that her escape could be discovered at any moment, Moon Song saw no choice but to leave.

Praying that the blood was not her mother's, Moon Song ran behind the lodges.

She stayed in the shadows until she came to a place where she felt it was safe to risk climbing the palisade. She struggled as she tried to climb over the wall, using a length of rope she had brought along for that purpose.

When she finally achieved her goal, she fled into the darkness of the forest.

Chapter Fifteen

He longed for her deep in the night,
She'd bewitched his heart, gave it flight.

Swift Thunder left his lodge early to go to the river for his morning bath before anyone else awakened. He wanted a private time for his morning prayers to *Tharonhiawakon.*

Taking a shortcut through the forest to get to the place in the river where he usually bathed, Swift Thunder was suddenly aware that the forest seemed abnormally still.

He missed the call of a loon that swam most nights on the river, singing its haunting refrain.

He missed the occasional yapping of a coyote from a nearby bluff.

He most certainly was aware that no frogs or crickets serenaded him.

The strange silence seemed foreboding to Swift Thunder. He slowed his pace and took notice of everything around him, for the forest was never silent unless there was an intruder.

His eyes and ears alert, Swift Thunder

could detect no sign of danger, however, so he ran on toward his destination.

Morning was just beginning its soft glow along the horizon, but the moon was still bright enough to cast its sheen on the river. When Swift Thunder got close enough to the water to see the river's full width, something he saw on the shore made him stop, startled.

Taking slow, stealthy steps onward, he stared at the figure of a woman sitting in a canoe beached on the rocky shore. An involuntary shiver raced through him. He knew that something was wrong . . . there was something very strange about how the canoe was positioned in such an upright position on the shore, whereas a beached canoe usually rested on its side, or upside down.

And the woman in the canoe was sitting so still, so stiff! It even looked as though something was supporting her back to keep her sitting upright.

He walked guardedly now, his pulse racing when he realized that the woman had not moved a muscle.

He wondered if he cried out to her, whether she would show that she was alive, for Swift Thunder was beginning to believe that she wasn't.

He stepped a little closer, moved to his right so that he could see her face, then stopped again.

The moon gave him a full view of the woman, but the wind whipped her long black hair across her face, impeding Swift Thunder's ability to see her features.

Something grabbed at his heart when he saw a splash of blood on the front of the woman's dress and concluded that she had died from a knife wound in the belly. He could not imagine how anyone could commit such a vicious act against a woman. It most certainly was the work of a coward!

He looked quickly away from the wound. The more he studied the woman — her build, her size, the length and color of her hair, the beaded dress she wore — the more he felt an emptiness deep inside his soul. He could not believe this was anyone but Moon Song!

Filled with an anguish so deep that he could hardly take the steps required to confirm his belief, he forced his feet onward. Just as he reached the canoe, the wind whipped the hair away from the face.

Shaken to the very core of his being when he saw the full features of the woman, Swift Thunder took a quick step away and gasped. It was not Moon Song, but someone who looked so much like her it could be no one other than Moon Song's mother.

He could not believe the cruelty of whoever had done this, and knew it had to be the work of Piercing Eyes. The Oneida chief's son had surely discovered Moon Song's plan and taken his vengeance out on her mother, while at the same time sending a warning message to Swift Thunder.

A sickening thought came to him. What of Moon Song? Had something also happened to her?

Would her body be planted soon for Swift Thunder to find, as well?

Swift Thunder could not wait for that to happen. He had to find out now, today, if Moon Song was still alive, and make sure that she had not been harmed by the Oneida maniac.

He had to find a way to rescue her if she was still alive.

He gazed with deep sadness at the woman who still sat so strangely in the beached canoe, her hair constantly whipping around her face.

It was indecent of Piercing Eyes to have treated this woman in such a way, and he

188

knew that it *had* been Piercing Eyes, for who else would have a reason to end this lovely woman's life, and in such a terrible way?

No doubt Piercing Eyes was holding Moon Song captive; her mother's body had been used to send a message to Swift Thunder . . . a message saying, "I dare you to come and get Moon Song!"

Swift Thunder circled his hands into tight fists at his sides, for he would take that dare. He would save the woman of his desire.

And he would kill anyone who tried to stop him.

He was filled with deep, gnawing regret, wishing now that he had finished the job when he had the chance during the war instead of only wounding the chief's demented son.

Swift Thunder knew now that as long as Piercing Eyes was alive, he would be a thorn in not only Swift Thunder's side, but also Moon Song's.

Had he known his enemy's plan to marry Moon Song, or to what length Piercing Eyes would go to have her, he would not have been so lenient with Piercing Eyes.

He would have killed him!

Suddenly Swift Thunder heard the

splash of a canoe approaching.

He had come for his bath and prayer without a weapon. Had he stepped into a trap?

He glanced at the woman sitting so oddly quiet in the beached canoe. His heart sank. Yes, she had been planted there purposely as part of a trap that he might not be able to save himself from.

Chapter Sixteen

He closed his eyes, but try as he might,
He couldn't erase her face from his sight.

Swift Thunder looked up the moon-splashed avenue of the river in hopes of getting his first visible sign of whoever was approaching.

As he waited he realized that the splash he heard was the sound of only one paddle dipping rhythmically into the water.

That had to mean that it was only one canoe, and perhaps one person.

Swift Thunder bent low behind the canoe in which Moon Song's mother sat so quietly. As he hunkered low, he craned his head around one end of the canoe and waited for the other canoe to get close enough for him to see who was manning it.

His breath caught in his throat when the moon's glow revealed Moon Song as she rounded the slight bend in the river.

Swift Thunder looked up at Moon Song's mother, and then he looked at Moon Song, who was getting closer and closer, who would at any moment see —

Before he could jump from behind the canoe to warn Moon Song, a scream that sounded like glass shattering broke through the early morning air, and Swift Thunder knew that Moon Song had seen . . . she now knew. . . .

Swift Thunder leapt up and ran into the river, splashing through the water toward Moon Song's canoe. Just before he reached it, Moon Song collapsed in a faint.

"Moon Song," Swift Thunder gasped out.

A sob caught in his throat as he dragged the canoe closer to shore, then reached inside and lifted her into his arms.

Holding her close, he carried her ashore.

As he gazed down at her, the moon's glow revealed her sweet innocence, and tears streaming from her closed eyes. He carried her beneath an elm tree, then sat down.

He held her on his lap, cradling her close and slowly rocking her as he waited for her to awaken. He gazed at her for a moment, then looked at her mother, then down at Moon Song again.

He was uncertain what to do.

He felt that he and Moon Song were vulnerable sitting there. He wanted to carry Moon Song quickly into hiding, yet he hated leaving her mother's body there, un-attended.

He waited awhile longer.

But when Moon Song showed no sign of coming to, Swift Thunder knew he had to take her to his lodge and send Winter Rain and others back to the river to get her mother.

Once Moon Song was awake, he could help her through the moments of despair as she recollected what had happened.

And then they must make quick joint decisions about her mother's burial, so that he could get Moon Song to safety at the Praying Castle.

Holding Moon Song close to his heart, knowing how painful this was going to be for her once she was awake, Swift Thunder rose to his feet, gave her mother one last look, then ran with Moon Song in his arms in the direction of his castle.

When he entered the wide gate, the scent of cook fires proved that some of the women were awake, readying themselves for the day.

His people knew what the day held for them, the habitual tasks they would undertake.

But for Moon Song, nothing would ever be the same again. Her mother had been taken from her in a most cruel fashion. And Moon Song was also in danger; whoever had killed her mother might even this moment be planning how Moon Song was going to die.

Swift Thunder vowed he would never allow that to happen.

Aware of some of the women coming to the doors of their longhouses to stare questioningly at him and the woman he was carrying, Swift Thunder still thought of no one but Moon Song. He knew that once she awakened, she would be in torment.

And she would also be aware of the danger she herself was in. She would realize that there was no time for mourning just yet.

She would realize that she must get to safety at the Praying Castle. Whoever had killed her mother and placed her so close to the Castle of the Bear knew Moon Song was involved with Swift Thunder.

He did not want to think about how this might put his own people in danger.

Yet surely everyone knew the strength of the Mohawk warriors. Had the Mohawk not proved that during the recent war?

The crime that had been committed today had all the earmarks of Piercing Eyes' work.

He did not see things with the logic of an intelligent man; he would do something as fiendish as this to prove to the woman who scorned him that he would stop at nothing to have her.

Or was he now intent on destroying her instead of possessing her as his wife?

Piercing Eyes' humiliation in the eyes of his people might make him hate Moon Song more than he could ever want or love her.

Swift Thunder carried Moon Song into his longhouse, then down the long corridor and into his bedroom. Before placing her on his bed of pelts and blankets, he gazed down at her with eyes full of love and sympathy.

He wanted to be there when she awakened, so that he could hold her and comfort her as she relived that dreadful moment when she'd seen her mother sitting lifelessly in the canoe.

Yet he had to leave, at least for a moment.

He had to alert his people to what had happened. He had to send warriors to the river to get Moon Song's mother's body.

"My love, I shall not be long," Swift Thunder whispered, knowing that he had no choice but to leave her, to make sure no

more wrong was done to her mother. She
had already suffered the worst dishonor by
being put on display in such a morbid way.

He had to make sure she was given the
respect she deserved . . . and had been denied.

He brushed a soft kiss across Moon
Song's brow, then gently laid her on his bed
and covered her with a soft white pelt made
of the fur of many snow-white rabbits.

Swift Thunder waited a moment longer,
watching the thick veil of lashes as they lay
across Moon Song's cheeks, hoping they
would show some sign of her awakening.

But when Moon Song continued to lie
unconscious, Swift Thunder turned and
hurried from his longhouse.

He ran to Winter Rain's longhouse and
knocked on the door.

Winter Rain slowly opened the door, his
eyes heavy with sleep. Swift Thunder
brushed past him and went inside.

After Winter Rain closed the door, he
turned to Swift Thunder. "What has happened?" he asked, seeing that Swift
Thunder was tense and worried. "Why
have you come and awakened Winter
Rain?"

Swift Thunder quickly explained everything.

"Winter Rain, again I need your help," Swift Thunder said. He placed a gentle hand on Winter Rain's bare shoulder. "Go now and awaken those warriors who are not yet out of their blankets. Make haste, my friend. Take many with you to the river. Get Moon Song's mother's body. Hide her canoe. Then take her to our burial preparation lodge."

Stunned at what he had heard, Winter Rain stared, wide-eyed, at Swift Thunder.

Then he saw the demand in his chief's eyes and shook himself from his thoughts.

"I will do all of those things. What then, my chief?" Winter Rain said as Swift Thunder lowered his hand to his side, giving Winter Rain the freedom to hurry into his clothes.

"What happens then depends on my woman," Swift Thunder said, his voice drawn. "Moon Song must say where her mother will be buried."

"I understand," Winter Rain said. He gave Swift Thunder a quick hug, then stepped outside with him.

Swift Thunder stood there long enough to see Winter Rain go to the first lodge to awaken the first warrior.

When this warrior came to the door and listened to what Winter Rain had to say, then gave Swift Thunder a quick glance and a nod, proving that he was willing to do whatever his chief wanted of him, Swift Thunder returned the nod, then hurried homeward.

As he entered his bedroom he saw that Moon Song was just now stirring herself awake. He hurried to her and fell to his knees on the floor beside the bed.

Swift Thunder took one of her hands and held it, hoping to offer comfort when she fully awakened and relived the horror of discovering her mother's body.

His pulse raced as he watched her thick lashes fluttering slowly open.

And when she was finally awake and looked around, he could see that she was taken aback when she saw him kneeling beside the bed, his eyes filled with an anxiety she seemed not to understand.

"Swift Thunder, why. . . ."

Then she stopped, gasped, and tears flooded her eyes. He knew she was recalling a memory that would surely haunt her until her dying day.

"No!" she cried. She jerked her hand away from Swift Thunder and covered her eyes with both hands. "No! No!"

Swift Thunder had never felt so helpless as he did watching Moon Song suffer.

He vowed that never again would she be put in this position. Pity anyone who tried to harm Moon Song anew.

Chapter Seventeen

She hugged him tight and through her tears,
She pledged her love for all her years.

Loving Moon Song so much that he felt her pain deep inside his very soul, Swift Thunder gently took her hands down from her face.

He eased her back onto his bed, then placed his hands at her waist and lifted her onto his lap.

He then engulfed her in his loving arms.

"Cry," he said softly. Slowly he caressed her back with gentle strokes of his hand. "Cry away as much pain as you can, and then let Swift Thunder help with the rest."

Tears gushing from her eyes, Moon Song desperately clung to Swift Thunder.

She could not get past that moment when she had seen her mother sitting lifelessly in the canoe with blood on her doeskin dress and knew that her mother was dead.

She felt even now the same anguish that had caused her to faint.

"Swift Thunder, it feels as though my

heart is being torn into shreds," she cried. She leaned away and gazed through her tears at Swift Thunder. "How could he have done this to my mother? He hated *me*. Why take it out on someone else . . . especially someone as sweet and kind as my mother? All she wanted was my happiness. She . . . died . . . because of my new-found happiness with you!"

A sob caught in her throat as she reached a hand to his face. "My love," she said, gazing into his dark, sad eyes. "I recall not only seeing my mother before I fainted, but also *you*, rushing toward me in the water. Thank you, oh, thank you for taking me safely from my canoe after I fainted. Thank you for bringing me where I am safe."

She turned her head and looked slowly around her, and then into Swift Thunder's eyes once again. "I am not at the Praying Castle," she said softly.

"No, you are not at the Praying Castle," Swift Thunder said. He moved his hands to her face and gently framed it. "I could not take you there until you told me what to do about your mother . . . where she should be buried."

Fresh tears splashed from her eyes. "Buried?" she said, her voice catching.

She began crying again, so hard that her whole body shook with the pain of remembering.

Feeling helpless to ease this pain that came with such a loss, Swift Thunder knew that for now there was only one thing to do. He drew her into his comforting, warm arms again and held her until her crying subsided to soft sobs and whimpers.

"I know that it hurts to talk about it, but we must," Swift Thunder said thickly. "Know that your mother's body is safe now, in a lodge not far from mine. Do you wish to go to her now? Or would you rather wait until you are stronger?"

Knowing that she must gather courage inside her heart, Moon Song eased herself from Swift Thunder's arms.

"I will be all right," she said softly, and she knew that she would. Even though she had no parents now to guide her, she had Swift Thunder. In such a short time, he had become everything to her.

Swift Thunder would help her get past the pain that came with losing someone as precious as a mother.

"I knew you would be," Swift Thunder said, smiling at her. "You are a strong woman, but even strong women feel pain such as you are now experiencing."

"I . . . I . . . am ready to go to my mother," Moon Song said, but just as she started to leave Swift Thunder's lap, her courage deserted her again.

She flung herself into Swift Thunder's arms and clung to him. "It is so unfair!" she cried. "She had so much life ahead of her. She was content in her own little world! She was in nobody's way. How could she have died in such a way? How?"

She reached deep inside herself and found enough strength to stop crying, but she still could not leave the comfort of Swift Thunder's arms.

She rested her cheek against his powerful bare chest and relived out loud what she had found when she had returned from those precious moments with Swift Thunder.

"I still cannot believe that this has really happened," she said when she had told him everything. "What did my mother's death gain anyone?"

"I believe that your mother was used as a ploy to send *me* a message," Swift Thunder growled. "This was a way to get back at you, Moon Song, for humiliating Piercing Eyes and breaking your childhood vow to marry him. By bringing your mother close to the Castle of the Bear, leaving her there purposely to be found, Piercing Eyes hoped to lure me to your castle to save *you* from the same fate as your mother."

Moon Song felt the color drain from her face. "Piercing Eyes told me he was going to send you a message," she gulped out. She placed her hands to her throat and gasped. "Oh, how could he have done this horrible thing for such a reason? Only a madman could be capable of this."

"*Qua*, a madman," Swift Thunder said thickly. "That is exactly the sort of man we are dealing with."

Moon Song grabbed Swift Thunder's hands and held them. "Why couldn't Piercing Eyes understand that it was not *my* vow, but something planned between my father and Chief Charging Crow?" she said, searching Swift Thunder's eyes with hers. "We were betrothed before Father knew the sort of man Piercing Eyes would grow up to be. Father wanted me to marry the chief's son who would one day be chief himself. I . . . I . . . was going to be a princess!"

"You *are* a princess," Swift Thunder said, smiling at her. "*Mine.*"

"You do make me feel so special," Moon Song said. "But please believe me when I say that it was never my wish to be a princess, or have a position above the other women of our clan. I wanted to just be *me*, not some person that most women might hate because of the special treatment a princess is given. *I am an ordinary woman.*"

"Ordinary is *not* a word I would use to describe you," Swift Thunder said, chuckling. Then he grew serious again. "Although you do not wish to see yourself as special, Moon Song, you are, in every way."

Moon Song blushed; then she thought again of the wrong that had been done her mother.

"Piercing Eyes knew I would never marry him, no matter what tactic he used to coerce me," Moon Song said, a bitter edge to her voice. "So all of this, especially my mother's death, was for naught. It gained Piercing Eyes only my wrath . . . my intense hatred forever and ever."

"I will avenge what has been done to you and your mother," Swift Thunder said tightly. "I will attack the Castle of the Turtle in full force to avenge your mother's death and the humiliation and disgrace visited upon you at the hands of Piercing Eyes."

A quick panic grabbed Moon Song. "No," she said quickly. "Please do not do that. I would not wish harm to come to my people because of one evil, heartless, deranged man." She flung herself into Swift Thunder's arms again. He held her and comforted her.

Then he placed his hands at her shoulders and gently held her away from him so that their eyes could meet. "I will do nothing that you do not agree to," he said thickly. "Let us now concentrate only on your mother's burial. Where do you wish her to be buried? Will her spirit rest buried away from her people . . . her husband?"

Moon Song thought about his question for a moment, then slowly nodded. "*Qua,* I believe she could," she murmured. "Although the Turtle Clan of the Oneida have long been enemies of the Bear Clan of the Mohawk, are they not both of the Iroquois nation, whose customs and beliefs are the same? Our burials are alike, and no matter where my mother is laid to rest, here in your people's burial grounds or in mine, my mother will be among the Iroquois nation's ancestors. Her spirit will soar upward into the heavens to join her ancestors — her husband, parents, cousins, aunts, uncles . . ."

Her voice trailed off, and then she nodded again. "Yes, my mother will be at peace here, but we must make haste, for I still believe that I am not safe in your castle," she said. "My escape will humiliate Piercing Eyes and Charging Crow. Because a mere woman got the best of them, they will look weak."

"Yes, we must hurry and get you to safety," Swift Thunder said. "I do not think it is wise for you to stay long enough for your mother's burial."

His eyes narrowed. "Since Piercing Eyes is working with a crazed mind, he might try to find a way to come into my village to find you," he said. "If he should, he will not live long enough to regret it. But I still feel it is best that you are not here. The Praying Castle is still the best place for you at this time."

Moon Song moved into his arms again and clung to him. "How can I ever thank you for what you are doing for me?" she murmured. "And for my mother. My love is all that I have to give you in payment."

"That is enough, for always," Swift Thunder said huskily. "Now come, my love. It is time for you to say your final good-bye to your mother." He searched her eyes. "Are you ready?"

She swallowed hard, smiled weakly, then nodded.

Hand in hand, they left Swift Thunder's longhouse.

Swift Thunder walked Moon Song to the lodge where her mother lay in repose, then upon her request he left her there to say her good-bye in private.

Swift Thunder went on to the castle's council house, where his warriors and his grandfather waited for him.

While Moon Song had her last moments with her mother, promising that she would see her again one day, and when she did they could laugh and sing and hold hands as they walked amid the clouds in the here-after, Swift Thunder came to an under-standing with his people about Moon Song's mother being buried there, and about Moon Song soon coming to their castle as his wife.

Winter Rain was given the duty of over-seeing the burial in Swift Thunder's ab-sence.

Swift Thunder and Moon Song then left in haste, paddling down the river toward the Praying Castle. He was awed by her courage, strength, and bravery. He could never love her any more than at this mo-ment.

As Moon Song sat in the canoe behind Swift Thunder, she gazed at him proudly and smiled. She saw him as her knight in shining armor, a legend she had heard as a child when a British trader was taken captive at her people's castle.

He had been held in the stockade, and she and the other children had taken him food and water. She had grown to like the white man.

She had become fond of the stories he told her, explaining to her that such stories could be found in the pages of books. He had made her hunger to learn more about reading and about numbers.

He had seen her interest and had used a stick to draw the letters of the alphabet and numbers in the earthen floor of his cell. She had eagerly learned, absorbing it all like a sponge sucks up water.

She had been stunned speechless and horrified when she saw him hanging dead one day on a stake in the courtyard of her people's castle.

Sick to her stomach at the sight, she had sought refuge behind her longhouse to retch. For days she had not been able to eat, for the memory would not leave her.

Even after the man's body had been taken away, she could not get him off her mind.

It was then that she began seeing the

dark side of her clan's leader, as well as his son's, for she never forgot how Piercing Eyes had stood, smiling mockingly at the dead man's limp, severely abused body after she discovered the bloody remains.

When Piercing Eyes had come later to Moon Song and said she would never see the white man's writing in the dirt anymore, she knew that he had discovered how the white man had taken time to teach her things that she would have never known otherwise. She had wondered if Piercing Eyes was responsible for what had happened to the white man because Moon Song had grown too fond of him and his teachings.

She tried now to recall the white man's name and could not, for time had robbed her memory of that. White people's names were sometimes too strange to remember!

She again thought of Piercing Eyes and his evil ways. She knew that when Piercing Eyes became chief, her people's future would be in jeopardy, for she did not see how a people governed by such a heartless man could thrive.

She wished there was a way to stop Piercing Eyes without bringing her people into danger. For now, it was enough that she was not in danger from Piercing Eyes' cruelty.

It was enough that she had made peace with her mother, and that her mother might even now be holding hands with her husband in the hereafter.

The thought made Moon Song smile. She only wished she could be there with them for at least a brief moment to share the wondrous reunion.

Her thoughts were stilled when she suddenly saw the towering Praying Castle in the distance. She could not help being somewhat wary about going there, for it was known by everyone that the black-robed holy men and the Turtle Clan of the Oneida had never been friends.

"We are almost there," Swift Thunder said as he looked over his shoulder at Moon Song.

She gave him a weak smile.

Chapter Eighteen

She said the words that made him shudder.
She was woman like no other.

Awakened abruptly by a knock on the door of his longhouse, Piercing Eyes rose clumsily from his bed.

Still not able to accept that he had only one arm, he was filled with rage every time he was reminded of his loss. Now, as he tried to wriggle into a robe made of the pelt of a bear, one side of the robe, where there was no arm to anchor it to his body, kept falling away.

Cursing, feeling only half a man, he threw the robe across the room.

Grabbing a blanket and managing to get it around his shoulders, he lumbered in his bare feet to the door and opened it with a hard jerk.

It was light enough for him to see who was there, and also to see the bloody, purplish contusion on Four Toes' forehead. He also saw a look of uneasiness and apology in Four Toes' deepset dark eyes.

Disgustedly suspecting what had caused

his favored warrior to act so sheepishly, and to have such bruises on his person, Piercing Eyes did not even have to be told why Four Toes was there. Moon Song had surely found a way to escape.

"Four Toes, tell me it is not so," Piercing Eyes said, leaning his face into his warrior's. "She did this to you, did she not?" he growled. "You allowed yourself to be tricked by a mere maiden? She is gone?"

"She said she was thirsty, so I opened the door to . . ." Four Toes began, but stopped and took an unsteady step away when Piercing Eyes waved his fist in Four Toes' face.

"How could you be so stupid? Moon Song would use *any* tactic to get free," Piercing Eyes stormed.

Then realizing that his voice might be carrying to his people's ears, he stopped, cleared his throat nervously, and momentarily hung his head in silence. It was so hard for him to accept what was happening to him, and all because of a *woman*.

Although he no longer wanted Moon Song as he had all of his life, he wanted more than ever to be the ruler of her destiny.

He should have been the one to set her free, when he was through using her as an example to others of his people who might try crossing him. He had wanted to tie Moon Song to stakes in the center of the castle's courtyard and watch her being ridiculed by her own people.

Now because of the stupidity of a warrior whom Piercing Eyes had always depended on, none of this would be possible. Instead, it would be Piercing Eyes, and possibly his father, who would be ridiculed when word spread about how Moon Song had escaped.

Now, because of a careless sentry, Moon Song was able to choose her own destiny, no doubt with Swift Thunder. That thought made bitterness rise into Piercing Eyes' throat. It seemed that Swift Thunder would never stop altering Piercing Eyes' life plan.

He wondered just how much more embarrassment his father could take. Piercing Eyes had disappointed him over and over again. If it was anyone else who had brought disgrace time and again to their people, he would have been banished long ago.

Piercing Eyes had to watch his every move now to ensure that his father did not forget that Piercing Eyes was his son, and banish him.

"I apologize for my foolishness," Four Toes said meekly. "But Moon Song has been a friend since we were children. I did not think she would take advantage of such friendship by . . . by . . . tricking me." He reached a hand to his brow, touched the wound, and winced. "I never would have thought she could do this to me."

"How could you not know that your friendship ended the moment you were given the order to guard her?" Piercing Eyes said, his voice mocking. "How could you even want her as a friend, knowing that she has sided with the enemy of our people? She deserves our people's public ridicule. Now it can never happen."

He doubled his hand into a tight fist at his side. "And do you not see?" he said, his voice drawn. "We killed an innocent woman tonight for naught. You had better pray to *Tharonhiawakon* that news does not spread back to our castle that Dove Woman was slain, for it was you who thrust the knife into her belly."

"It was you who ordered me to do it," Four Toes stammered. "It was for you I have done all of these things that my heart did not want me to do."

"You are groveling like a wounded pup," Piercing Eyes grumbled. "You sicken me."

215

With that, Piercing Eyes slammed the door in Four Toes' face.

Dispirited, Piercing Eyes stood before the slow-burning embers of his fire as he wrestled over what to do next about Moon Song. It was so hard to know that she had bested him again, as had Swift Thunder.

And what of her mother? he thought, wincing.

What was Moon Song going to do when she learned that her mother had been murdered?

Surely she would want her mother buried among her ancestors, and if so, would she not then bring her mother to the Castle of the Turtle for burial?

That could go two ways for Piercing Eyes.

If she brought her mother to the Castle of the Turtle and accused him of murder, he would be condemned in the eyes of his people.

But if he set a trap for her, he might get her in his power again.

He would keep sentries posted who would be ordered to keep an eye out for Moon Song's return. And when she was seen, she would be abducted before she reached the castle. This time she would have no chance to escape the wrath of Piercing Eyes.

But what if Moon Song decided not to bring her mother home? What if she asked Swift Thunder to retaliate for her . . . to avenge her mother's death by attacking her own people?

That thought seemed the most logical to Piercing Eyes and filled him with a dread that had only become familiar since his defeat in the recent war.

His mind went back to that fateful day when he'd lost his arm. Swift Thunder had gotten the best of Piercing Eyes, yet had at least spared his life.

Well, Piercing Eyes would not be so generous should he have the opportunity to slam an arrow, or knife, in Swift Thunder's belly! He only hoped *Swift Thunder's death* would be the true answer, a death that would come before Moon Song's.

Yes, he wanted to see Moon Song's face when she lost the man she had chosen over Piercing Eyes!

That thought made him smile.

Chapter Nineteen

Her prayers went drifting into the night,
Her beauty awed him, what a sight.

As Moon Song stood just inside the Praying Castle, gazing at the staircase that led to the upper floors, she felt apprehensive at being left there without Swift Thunder. The huge place was forbidding, and this was the first time she had been around whites since the death of the British trader she had known as a child.

"Father John will be here soon," Swift Thunder said as he squeezed Moon Song's hand. "He has been summoned."

"Please tell me about Father John," Moon Song asked, wishing her voice would not tremble. She wanted to be brave in this new environment.

But she was already so upset about her mother's death, how could she be expected to react bravely? If she didn't have Swift Thunder's support, she knew she would fall apart. She felt like that little girl of long ago when her father had died and she had felt threatened by life's ugly twists and turns.

"He is the priest who is in charge of this Praying Castle," Swift Thunder said softly. "And he is my friend."

He smiled at her, glad when she responded with one of her own sweet smiles.

"Moon Song, he will also be your friend," Swift Thunder said reassuringly. "When you meet him face to face, you will see how I know that you will be able to accept him quickly as a friend . . . as a confidant in your time of trouble."

"He will allow me to mourn for my mother in his castle?" Moon Song asked, her voice breaking as she thought about her mother and the burial rites that she had been forced to miss.

In her mind's eye she could picture the ceremony as she would have arranged it.

The light from a pine torch would be burning low in the lodge. Her mother would be stretched upon a beaver skin laid out on a braided mat of interlaced twigs of maple and oak, woven by Moon Song's own caring hands.

Her mother would be clothed in snow white doeskin and would wear new white moccasins for her journey. Her face would be oiled and her black hair would be loose around her face and shining with bear grease.

"Swift Thunder, I see you have brought your friend to my castle," Father John said as he stepped up to Swift Thunder and Moon Song, drawing Moon Song away from her thoughts.

Father John, dressed in his immaculate black robe, his eyes friendly behind the thick lenses of his eyeglasses, took Moon Song's free hand. "Sweet maiden, know that you can seek a safe haven in the House of the Lord for as long as you wish to stay here."

Moon Song winced somewhat at the phrase "House of the Lord." She was reminded of how Piercing Eyes and his chieftain father had spoken of their hatred for these priests.

She had wanted to understand why, but had never asked. Now she would finally learn the difference between her religion and theirs.

And she *did* feel comfortable in this particular priest's presence. His kindness was so real, how could she not feel welcome?

"Thank you for offering me a safe place to stay," Moon Song said, smiling as the lean, white-haired priest stepped closer to her and gave her a warm hug.

"Always, my dear," Father John murmured. "You are always welcome here."

He stepped back and clasped his hands behind him as he gazed from Moon Song to Swift Thunder, then let his eyes rest on Moon Song. "Now would you like to have some refreshment? Or would you rather go directly to your room?" he asked softly. "If you need to rest, I shall send food to your room later. If you do not wish to join us in the dining hall at meal time, I would understand. But please know that you will be made to feel welcome by everyone who lives here."

"I so appreciate your kindness," Moon Song murmured. She lowered her eyes, then looked up again at the priest. "I do need some moments alone. I would like to go to the room you have assigned me."

"I understand," Father John said, nodding.

Then Swift Thunder reached a hand to Father John's shoulder. "No, you do not entirely understand," he said thickly. "Since my visit with you, much more sadness has come into my woman's life."

Father John's face softened with sympathy as he listened to Swift Thunder explain what had happened to Dove Woman.

When Swift Thunder was through, the priest drew Moon Song into his arms and gave her a loving, comforting embrace. She was deeply touched that a stranger should show her such kindness.

Fighting back tears, she returned the hug, and then stepped away and smiled. She knew now that while she was among such caring people, she would be able to relax and mourn the death of her beloved mother.

"Your privacy will be assured as you seek solace in prayer to your *Tharonhiawakon*," Father John said. "Until you are ready to leave your room, food and drink will be placed outside your door. Then when you wish to sit among us, to share meals with us, know that you are welcome."

"Thank you," Moon Song murmured. "I will always remember your kindness. . . . your understanding."

"Come now with me. I shall show you your room," Father John said, walking toward the stairs. "Your room is on the fourth floor, where you can see the wonders of nature for miles from the window." He stopped and smiled at her before he started up the stairs. "Nature's beauty has a way of calming the troubled heart."

"Yes, I know," Moon Song said, returning his smile.

She welcomed Swift Thunder's arm around her waist as he walked up the stairs with her behind Father John. Her eyes strayed to huge paintings of other priests that hung along the wall of the staircase. Candles were burning in wall sconces beside these paintings, casting dancing light over the dark stairs.

Finally they reached the fourth floor, where a window at the end of the corridor let in a great burst of sunshine revealing closed doors that must lead into many rooms.

They walked past the doors, then came to one where Father John paused, his hand already on the latch. At that moment, a movement at the far end of the corridor attracted Moon Song's attention.

Swift Thunder saw Moon Song look quickly down the corridor. He stiffened when he saw what Moon Song was staring at.

It was the same cloaked figure that Swift Thunder had seen the last time he was at the Praying Castle. As before, the man's hood was drawn over his eyes, shadowing his face.

Swift Thunder started to reach out for Father John, to ask about the hooded figure, but just as he did, the person in question rushed away out of sight.

Swift Thunder was uneasy about the

hooded figure's presence, but as before, he felt that if he questioned Father John, it might show some mistrust on his part. And at this moment he did not want to cause any strain between himself and the priests. Moon Song needed them and their understanding, at least until Swift Thunder could take her home with him.

Moon Song gasped when the hooded figure swept on down the corridor. She gazed up at Swift Thunder and knew that he, also, had seen the cloaked figure. She waited for him to question Father John about who it might be.

When Swift Thunder said nothing, she realized it would be difficult to describe the mysterious person to Father John when he was just another man who wore black robes. The only difference between him and the others was the way his hood was worn lower over his eyes, shadowing his facial features.

Feeling that she might be making too much of the hooded figure watching them, Moon Song made herself forget that she had seen him and went into the room with Father John and Swift Thunder.

She sighed when she found a comfortable room awaiting her. There was a bed with a beautiful patchwork quilt spread across it. There were even lace-trimmed pillows at the head of the bed.

On the tables on each side of the bed were two vases of flowers sending a sweet fragrance throughout the room.

The wooden floor was bare, yet was shiny as though someone had spread bear grease across it.

And the lone window in the room sent shafts of golden sunlight into the room, warming it and giving it a pleasant glow.

"Will you be comfortable here?" Father John asked, as Moon Song spotted another table with a basin and a pitcher of water. She also saw a bar of soap and a neatly folded towel beside it.

She looked quickly at the priest and smiled. "Yes, I will be very comfortable," she murmured. "It is a lovely room. Thank you."

"The flowers were brought by one of my priests only moments ago," Father John said, glancing toward the open door. "I saw Father Jacob just before we came into the room. He was at the far end of the corridor. You might have seen him also."

Moon Song and Swift Thunder shared a quick look, then smiled softly.

Moon Song felt foolish now for having been concerned about the cloaked figure.

It was good to know that he had been there for a good reason. She must not let herself get suspicious while at the Praying Castle.

Swift Thunder saw that Moon Song was comfortable with the explanation about the cloaked figure, even though he did not feel the same relief. That same person had watched Swift Thunder from the shadows when he had been at the castle earlier. There had to be a reason behind it.

He decided to question Father John about this man after they left Moon Song in the room. Once and for all he would know why the mysterious Father Jacob seemed more interested in Swift Thunder than the other priests were.

But for now he was content to see that Moon Song was relaxed and comfortable and felt safe. He watched her as she gazed out the window. He knew what she was looking at, and he smiled.

This castle was not surrounded and protected by a palisade fence, but instead a body of water the priests called a moat.

He could remember how amazed he had been at the large bridge that came up and down on clanging chains to give one entrance.

He went and stood beside Moon Song,

placing a gentle arm around her waist. He started to talk to her about the moat, but stopped and stared at a canoe coming swiftly down the river toward the castle.

As the canoe approached, Swift Thunder recognized who was manning it. It was Winter Rain.

He was confused as to why Winter Rain would be there, when he had been left to see to Dove Woman's burial.

The only reason Winter Rain would neglect his duties would be because he had something of dire importance to tell Swift Thunder.

"Piercing Eyes," Swift Thunder whispered.

Moon Song also recognized Winter Rain as he left his beached canoe.

She gave Swift Thunder a questioning look.

Swift Thunder turned to Father John, then brushed past him as he ran from the room and down the steep flight of stairs.

As he got to the outer door, he could already hear the creaking of the bridge lowering to allow Winter Rain's entrance.

Winter Rain hurried across the lowered bridge, and Swift Thunder met him halfway.

"What brings you here?" Swift Thunder

asked, placing his hands on Winter Rain's shoulders.

His heart skipped a beat when he saw deep pain in his warrior's eyes.

Breathless from running, Moon Song ran up to Swift Thunder, with Father John following shortly behind her.

"Your grandfather, Fire Wolf, is no more," Winter Rain said softly.

Moon Song saw Swift Thunder flinch as though he had been shot. He jerked his hands from Winter Rain's shoulders.

"I was with him," Winter Rain said somberly. "He grabbed at his heart and then closed his eyes as though he were asleep. He did not open his eyes again. Nor did he take another breath."

Feeling as though someone had sent a volley of arrows into his belly, Swift Thunder turned from everyone and bowed his head.

Feeling his pain, Moon Song twined her arms around Swift Thunder's neck, drew him next to her, and held him.

Knowing that he had to gather the courage to return to his castle, where his grandfather no longer smiled or laughed, Swift Thunder eased from Moon Song's arms.

"I wish I could go with you, to be with

you during your sadness," Moon Song murmured.

"It is best that you stay here until there is no threat to you at my castle," Swift Thunder said tightly.

"But will you be all right?" Moon Song murmured.

"I have won many battles inside my heart, as I shall this," Swift Thunder said, then wrapped his arms around her and clung to her a moment longer. "I will miss you so, my love. But soon we will be together forever."

"I shall pray for you, my mother, and your grandfather, and also myself, and this will soon all be behind us," Moon Song whispered into his ear.

"Go to your room now, and I shall tend to the things that await me," Swift Thunder said thickly.

They kissed and embraced one last time; then Swift Thunder left with Winter Rain.

"I will accompany you back to your room," Father John said, gently taking Moon Song by an elbow and ushering her toward the staircase.

"I feel I should be with Swift Thunder," Moon Song said as they began walking up the stairs.

"You are where he wants you to be," Father John said. "Time will heal all sorrows."

Moon Song nodded. When they reached her room and the door was closed behind her, she looked out the window and found that Swift Thunder's canoe was already out of sight.

Tears spilled from her eyes. She missed him and her mother so much! She crawled up on the bed, curled up on the soft feather mattress, and allowed her prayers of mourning for her mother to begin.

She also said prayers for Swift Thunder's grandfather, hoping that she was not, in part, responsible for his death.

"Let this time of my solitude and sorrow pass quickly," she prayed to *Tharon-hiawakon*. "Please help Swift Thunder in his."

A soft knock on the door drew Moon Song from her prayers. She left the bed and opened the door.

Her eyes widened when she found Father John there holding a beautiful cat.

"I have brought you special company," Father John said, holding the cat out toward Moon Song. "Her name is Josephine. She can stay the night, if you wish."

"Oh, truly?" Moon Song said, gently taking the long-haired cat. It so reminded her of Blue!

"But one thing," Father John said, chuckling. "If Josephine goes sniffing at the door, let her out. She is good at sniffing out our resident mice."

"Mice?" Moon Song said, shuddering.

"Never fear mice while living here, for Josephine is skilled at catching them," Father John said. He reached over and gave his cat a slow stroke, then turned toward the staircase, humming.

Pleased to have the cat with her for company, Moon Song held it next to her, closed the door, then went and lay down on the bed with the cat snuggled beside her. "Cat, oh, beautiful cat," Moon Song murmured, stroking the gently purring animal. "I wonder if you might somehow be related to Blue."

She giggled. "I doubt it," she whispered, then gazed toward the window and wondered where Blue was at this moment.

She hoped he was all right and would return home one day.

She knew that if Swift Thunder had Blue with him now, the sadness he was experiencing over his grandfather's death would be lightened by his pet's presence.

"Come home, Blue," she whispered. "You . . . are . . . needed."

Chapter Twenty

His heart was pure and sweet and kind,
He was always there upon her mind.
He told her he loved her, she wondered
    if he knew
She loved him with all her heart, too.

In awe of the many shelves of books in the priests' library, Moon Song walked around the large room with Father John as he pointed out various volumes, explaining what they were about.

Josephine was content on a pillow beside the slow burning embers on the hearth of the massive stone fireplace at one end of the library.

Father John stopped and pulled a book from the shelf, opening it for Moon Song to see. He told her the book was about his homeland, England.

When he showed her a map and pointed out where England was, she became confused; how could a country be in two places at once, across the wide stretch of ocean, and also on the pages of a book?

Father John explained, but she could not

focus on the conversation. Her mind constantly strayed to Swift Thunder. A number of days had passed since he had brought her to the Praying Castle, and she had not heard anything from him since.

She wondered if it might be because he had not yet been able to accept his grandfather's death.

Or . . . had Piercing Eyes caused problems at the Castle of the Bear?

"And this is our people's Bible," Father John said as he replaced the book about England, then picked up a black book from a table and slowly opened its pages to show Moon Song God's written word.

"I have heard of the white man's holy 'talking leaves,' " Moon Song said, trying to look interested. But even as she spoke she could not get her mind off Swift Thunder's continued absence.

Where was he?

Why hadn't he come for her by now?

Surely under these circumstances, with her welfare to consider, he would not take the normal time required for mourning.

She had denied herself such a mourning period for her mother.

Moon Song's life lay in the balance. She had been forced to make safety her first priority. And she knew that Swift Thunder felt the same way.

She could not deny that she felt safe enough at the Praying Castle, yet she would feel much better if she were with Swift Thunder.

"You call the pages of books 'talking leaves,'" Father John said, smiling. "I find that quite dear, Moon Song."

He closed the Bible and offered it to her. "I see that you are tired," he said softly. "Why don't you retire to your room and rest?"

He held the Bible closer when he saw that she shied away from taking it. "This book will give you much comfort," he softly urged. "Take it. Hold it next to your heart. See if you don't feel comforted by it."

Hating to disappoint Father John, or chance hurting his feelings, Moon Song started to take the Bible, but eased her hand away again when she recalled her mother's teachings about the Black Robes.

Moon Song's mother had told her that the black-robed holy men would convert all red men and women to their religion if they possibly could.

And Moon Song's mother had also said that Moon Song should not be fooled by what the priests had said about moving to this area . . . that they had only done so to be available to the white people who had come to this land from England.

Anyone could see that the Black Robes had settled in the midst of Indian territory, which surely meant they planned to try to convert the native inhabitants.

"I cannot read it, so it will be useless to take it to my room with me," Moon Song carefully explained, glad that her refusal to take the Bible did not cause a wounded look in the gentle priest's eyes.

But she felt wrong at having lied to Father John. She *could* read.

The white prisoner at her castle long ago had taught her enough about his alphabet that she knew she could read this Bible if she wanted to.

In truth, she did not want to chance finding good in what she read, for she did not want to offend *Tharonhiawakon*. Without the guidance of *Tharonhiawakon*, she would be lost.

Father John smiled as he laid the Bible back on the table, then took Moon Song gently by an elbow and walked her from the library to the staircase that led to the upper floors.

"Swift Thunder will come soon," Father John said reassuringly, drawing Moon

Song into his gentle embrace. "His grand-father's death and burial have made life difficult and sad at this time for my friend Swift Thunder. I am sure that his prayers have delayed him."

"Yes, his prayers," Moon Song said, then stepped gently away from Father John. "I will go now and say my own prayers."

She placed a hand to her lips and stifled a sob behind it. "I not only miss Swift Thunder, but also my mother," she said, her voice catching. "Life can be so cruel."

"No, my dear, *people* can be so cruel," Father John said. "But in time, the warrior who took your mother's life will see the wrong in his deed. It will then be *he* who will go to his prayers. He must ask for for-giveness, or forever be lost."

"He has been a lost soul for so long now," Moon Song said, trying not to hate Piercing Eyes so much that she became as wicked at heart as he.

She had been taught by her precious mother that hate was a sickness, that if it was allowed inside one's soul, it would fester until there was no turning back into being a caring person.

"I know enough about him to know that is true, my dear," Father John said, patting her arm. He nodded toward the stairs.

"Now you go and get your rest. I shall send for you when the evening meal is placed on our dining table. I am glad that you have chosen to eat with us, instead of alone. Companionship is the best thing for you now. Not solitude."

"Yes, I have felt better since I began joining you at meal time," Moon Song said, smiling at him. He did have a way of making her feel calm just when she felt as though she might explode from her need of Swift Thunder's comforting arms around her.

Yes, she had to believe that Swift Thunder would come soon.

If not, she would leave the Praying Castle on her own and go to the Castle of the Bear to see what was keeping him there.

She had not expected to be separated from him for so long.

It had been seven whole days now since she had said her sad good-bye to him.

"Rest well, little one," Father John said as Moon Song went up the steep steps.

She turned and smiled at him over her shoulder. "I shall," she murmured. "Thank you."

"You need not thank me for everything I do in kindness toward you," Father John said. "Do you not know that your being here has bought this Praying Castle much sunshine?"

She stopped and turned to gaze down at him.

"With you here, the dark shadows of our home are no longer as dark," Father John said, gesturing toward the darkest corners. He dropped his hand slowly to his side. "When you are gone, you will be missed."

Touched by his words, she almost said thank you again, but stopped and only smiled. "Your kindness has warmed me through and through," she murmured.

Remembering something she had wanted to ask him since she had first arrived, Moon Song added, "Father John, I have never slept on a mattress like the one on the bed in my room here. It is as soft as the clouds in the heavens. Can you explain to me how such a mattress is made? I would like to have one for my own bed."

Smiling at her, he proceeded to tell Moon Song about the feather mattress and how it was made.

"But do not bother finding feathers, yourself, for a mattress," he concluded. "When you leave, I shall make sure the mattress is brought to your home for your bed. From this day forth, Moon

Song, the mattress is yours."

Moon Song squealed with delight at the prospect of having the mattress as her very own forever. "Thank you, oh, thank you," she murmured, clasping her hands excitedly before her.

She thought of something she could not say to Father John but could not help thinking. She blushed and lowered her eyes as she envisioned sharing such a bed with the man she loved. As they lay together, heartbeat to heartbeat, in the softness of the feathers, they would be transported to the stars and back while making unbelievable love.

"Moon Song?" Father John said, raising an eyebrow as he saw her blush. "What are you thinking about?"

His question made her blush deepen.

She gave him a shy smile, then turned and hurried on up the stairs until she reached the fourth floor where the privacy of her room, and the plush feather bed, awaited her.

She giggled as she thought of being with Swift Thunder on this mattress, and how it might enhance their lovemaking.

"If that is possible," she whispered, for surely nothing could be better than what they had already found in one another's arms.

As she started to walk down the corridor to her room, she heard a noise.

She turned with a start, then sighed with relief when she saw the cloaked priest whom she now knew by the name Jacob . . . Father Jacob. He was at the far end of the corridor, just leaving his room. She watched him as he closed his door and turned to walk slowly toward the staircase.

Yes, she did know this priest's name, yet he still remained a mystery to her. He never joined the others at the dinner table. He took his meals alone in his room.

And she had never seen Jacob mingle with the others at the Praying Castle. He was a loner, who might not even know how to speak, for never had she heard him utter one word.

He would appear suddenly in the shadows, and then would be gone again almost as quickly as she could blink her eyes.

Frequently he seemed to be watching her from beneath that hood he always wore low over his brow. But his face was always too shadowed to see his features.

She had assumed that his interest in her was because she was Indian. She was accustomed to getting second glances from whites whenever she was away from her castle to visit a trading post.

The stares were not pleasant, but she had grown used to them. She made it a point not to stare back, for she felt that it was rude.

Nonetheless, she did watch Father Jacob, expecting him to make a turn toward the staircase. When he didn't, and his cougar-light footsteps brought him in Moon Song's direction, she felt a sense of panic rise in her throat.

Although this priest had never given her any cause to fear him, she had never been alone in his presence either.

Even if she rushed into her room and closed the door, she would not be totally protected. There were no locks on any doors. Not even the main door of the Praying Castle.

She was all alone with a hooded, mysterious stranger who seemed intent now on accosting her in some way.

Not wanting to appear cowardly, and knowing she couldn't get past this cloaked figure, Moon Song straightened her shoulders, lifted her chin valiantly, and faced the danger head-on, as Father Jacob stopped only a few inches from her.

She breathlessly waited to see what reason he had for coming to her in such a way, when all other times he had only observed her from the shadows.

When he reached inside the folds of his black robe, Moon Song gasped, for if this man had a knife, would not that be where he would hide it? Had he been waiting for the right moment to kill her?

Terrified now, believing she might be breathing her last breath, Moon Song felt frozen to the spot as she watched his hand pull something from inside his robe.

If it was a knife, she hoped she could wrestle it away from him. He did not seem to be a strong individual. Surely she could get the best of him before he could kill her.

When she finally saw what he had taken from an inside pocket of his robe, she felt everything within her relax.

Shame swept through her for having suspected this man of plotting against her, when in truth he had approached only to offer her a book.

It was not the holy book the white priests called a Bible. Instead, it looked exactly like the small book the white prisoner had read to her when he was imprisoned in the stockade.

He had managed to hide the book when he was taken captive by the Oneida. And he had only brought it out when Moon Song was there to give him food and a moment or two of company.

Yet this could not be the same book, nor could this be the same man. She had watched Piercing Eyes burn the book when he had found it among the white man's belongings.

She had seen the prisoner hanging from the stakes, bloody and still!

As Father Jacob held the small book out toward Moon Song, she wasn't sure what to do.

She waited for him to explain, but he said nothing, only held the book out closer to her.

"Do you wish for me to take the book?" Moon Song murmured.

Still he did not respond, except to reach for one of Moon Song's hands and place the book firmly in it.

"This is for Moon Song?" she asked, staring down at the book.

The hooded figure nodded, then turned and walked quietly away toward the staircase.

Stunned, Moon Song watched Father Jacob until he disappeared down the steps.

Then she gazed at the book in wonder. "A gift for Moon Song?" she whispered. "Why?"

Anxious to see what sort of book it was,

Moon Song hurried into her room and closed the door behind her. Going to her bed, she plopped down on the feather mattress, and as she sat there, her legs dangling over the side of the bed, she slowly opened the book to the first page.

Her eyes widened in wonder when she turned to the next page, and then the next. There were more pictures than words, and the illustrations made her gasp with delight.

Here was the likeness of the knight the white prisoner had described to her. And the knight was on a horse that she remembered the white man calling a "charger." Each page showed the knight and his charger above the printed words.

She began reading the familiar story and became caught up in another time, another place, when the prisoner had read the same story to her.

It made her feel sad for the man who had given her a part of his life by teaching her to read and write. Yet she was happy to have this book that brought back those pleasant moments with the white man she had grown so close to. She would value this book forever.

She read until she grew tired, then closed the book and clutched it to her heart as she stretched out on the wonderfully soft mattress.

Smiling, she floated off into a sweet dream. She dreamed of knights. She dreamed of white chargers that seemed to take wing and fly across the wide blue space of heaven.

And then in the dream . . . the face of the knight became clear to Moon Song. It was Swift Thunder! He was riding proud and tall on the white steed, his body encased by a knight's armor.

As he rode his white charger across the sky, his eyes were filled with pride. He turned toward Moon Song, who was suddenly beside him on her own white steed!

But she was not dressed in armor. She wore a thin, sheer, white robe that rippled around her in the wind.

But suddenly she was aware of someone else in the dream.

Piercing Eyes!

He was no longer without an arm. He was a complete man again, and he wore no armor, only a breechclout, with a quiver of arrows at his back.

In his hand was a powerful bow. He shouted angrily at Swift Thunder as he quickly drew an arrow from his quiver, fitted it to his bow string, then let it fly through the air toward Moon Song.

Moon Song awakened from the dream in a cold sweat. She found that she had dropped the book on the bed beside her.

Shivering, Moon Song left the bed and went to gaze from the window down at the river where she had watched for many hours for Swift Thunder's approaching canoe.

"Swift Thunder, I am suddenly afraid," she whispered. "The dream. Was it an omen of some sort?"

If so, what had it meant?

Wunett, good?

Or *mannitto,* bad?

Surely bad, or why else would she dream that she was going to die . . . ?

Chapter Twenty-one

Tharonhiawakon above works wonders,
  you see,
He knows what we want — you and me.
He sees how we try to do what is right.
As a reward He sends love into the night.

A knock on the door made Moon Song cringe. Somehow she no longer felt safe.

She knew that dreams could foretell the future, and in her dream she had been about to die. She was afraid even to speak up and ask who was at the door.

But when a voice, oh, so wonderfully familiar to her came through the door, her smile was like sunshine after a storm.

It was Swift Thunder's voice! He had finally returned.

She could hardly get to the door quickly enough to seek comfort in Swift Thunder's arms. Tears spilling from her eyes, she yanked the door open.

Without speaking a word, she flung herself into his arms and clung to him.

Stunned to see Moon Song in such a state, knowing that something must have happened to frighten her, Swift Thunder held her for a moment, then eased her away from him.

He gazed into her tear-filled eyes. With his thumb he smoothed the tears from her soft flesh.

"Why are you crying?" he asked. "And I see fear in your eyes. What caused it?"

"It was a dream," she sobbed out. "At first the dream was wonderful. But then . . . then . . . it turned into something terrible."

"Do you wish to tell me about it?" he asked, seeing how she kept glancing over her shoulder at something on the bed. It was a small book.

At first he thought it might be a Bible that the priests had encouraged her to read. But then he saw that it was not a holy book.

He gave Moon Song a puzzled look as she once again gazed into his eyes.

"I want to show you a book that the mysterious cloaked man gave to me," Moon Song murmured. "But first, Swift Thunder, please tell me what has delayed your return to the Praying Castle. It has been seven days now. I had hoped not to be parted from you for so long."

"I wanted to come sooner, but word arrived that Piercing Eyes was contemplating coming to the Castle of the Bear to war with us over you," Swift Thunder said thickly, entering the room with Moon Song.

They stopped and stood beside the bed.

Swift Thunder's eyes were on the book as he continued talking. "But it was only a rumor. Four Toes is responsible for it. He purposely made up the rumor in order to make me and my warriors go to the trouble of preparing for an attack that would never come."

He sighed heavily. "I was tempted to go to their . . . to your . . . castle and show them what happens to those who start wrongful rumors," he said, his voice tight. "But I decided that keeping harmony in the area is best now. My people are mourning the loss of my grandfather. And I have *your* welfare to consider. I want to take you home to a safe haven, not to a place that might be the target of attack by my longtime enemy. If I ignore rumors of war, then Piercing Eyes may find other things to occupy his mind. He must realize that he has lost you forever, and that there are other things to do with his life."

"Yes, you would think that would be the logical thing for him to do, yet it is

Piercing Eyes we are talking about," Moon Song said bitterly. "He is not just any ordinary man. He is a heartless demon who truly values only one life — *his*. He would not even defend his own father if someone should come and threaten his life."

She reached a gentle hand to Swift Thunder's cheek. "Let us talk no more about the man we both despise," she said softly. "We have our future to plan. Let us think of today as the beginning of our lives."

Then she swallowed hard and a look of pain came into her eyes. "But I have to know, before I can put my past behind me. Is my mother resting peacefully among your ancestors . . . among ours?" she asked, her voice breaking.

"My people honored her as though she were one of them," Swift Thunder said warmly. "That is the way of my Bear Clan. They, we, are a people of good heart. During your mother's burial rites, no one acted as though she was born an enemy to the Mohawk people."

"I hope they will look past the fact that I, also, was born an enemy to your people," Moon Song murmured. "Can they, Swift Thunder? Will they truly tolerate my becoming the wife of their revered chief?"

"I made certain that they are ready. Even now, our wedding ceremony is being planned by the women," Swift Thunder said, gently enfolding her within his arms.

"I feel so blessed," Moon Song murmured, relishing his arms, his smell, his muscled presence.

"I am the one who is blessed," Swift Thunder said as she eased from his arms. "For I have *you*."

He reached past her and picked up the book. "Now tell me about this book — how it is you have it, who gave it to you, and what it is about," he said, gingerly opening it to the first page. His eyebrows lifted when he saw a man in armor on a brilliant white horse.

"The mysterious priest gave this to me," Moon Song said as Swift Thunder turned the pages.

"The hooded man gave this to you?" Swift Thunder asked, glancing at Moon Song. "Why?"

"I am not certain why," Moon Song said, softly shrugging. "But I do know more about him."

"What do you know?"

"Father Jacob never takes meals with the others," Moon Song said. "He eats alone in his room. And he never mingles with the others. I know not why, and I did not feel it was my business to ask Father John."

"Did not this priest, this Father Jacob, say anything to you when he gave you the book?" Swift Thunder asked, softly closing the book and laying it down on the bed.

"No, he just gave it to me, then left," Moon Song said. She took up the book and opened it. "Do you see the subject matter of this book?"

Swift Thunder again gazed at the picture of the man on the horse, then nodded.

"This book is about knights in armor," Moon Song softly explained.

Impressed, Swift Thunder smiled at her. "You know this by looking at the pictures?" he asked.

"No, not only by looking, but also by reading," Moon Song murmured. "You see, long ago there was a white prisoner . . ."

She explained to him all about the prisoner and how he had taught her to read, write, and count numbers.

"And now I have a book like the one the prisoner read to me so long ago, and taught me to read from," Moon Song murmured. "I am beginning to believe that there are many good white people, more than I had originally thought, for there was the kindness of that prisoner so long ago, and now Father John, and also this hooded priest who gave me a book to keep."

"Why would he single you out?" Swift Thunder asked, scratching his brow.

"I do not know, and I doubt I ever shall, yet I am touched deeply that he showed me such kindness," Moon Song said. She drew the book to her heart and hugged it. "I shall treasure it forever."

She lowered the book and gazed at it. "I wish I knew what to do to thank the man," she murmured.

Then she looked up at Swift Thunder. "Yet I doubt that he wants anything in return, for what could I give him?" she said.

"I imagine your presence at the Praying Castle was enough," Swift Thunder said, reaching for her hand and holding it. "He, as well as the others, surely enjoyed your company. Who could not? Your sweetness is contagious."

"I was not all that sweet," Moon Song said, sighing. "I did not join the priests at their dining table as often as I was invited. I needed time alone to pray for Mother, for you, and for us."

"Have your prayers been answered?" Swift Thunder asked, placing his hands at her waist and drawing her close to him.

"Since you are here now, yes," Moon

Song said, laughing softly. "Can we go? I am so anxious to begin our life together. And . . . and . . . I am anxious to visit my mother's grave."

"Yes, we can go," Swift Thunder said softly.

"I will treasure this book as a reminder of my time here," she said. "I do so love stories about knights."

"I am glad. Did you know I was honored with a knighthood myself? The King of England knighted me because I helped the English triumph over the French in the recent war," Swift Thunder said, chuckling when he saw that this news made Moon Song gasp in wonder.

"You . . . are . . . a knight?" she gasped out. "A true . . . knight?"

"Yes, well, in a sense I am," Swift Thunder said. "That is the way the English chose to honor me."

"I knew that you received some sort of special recognition for your deeds, but you never said what sort," Moon Song said, questioning him with her eyes.

"That is because I did not want you to think I was bragging about achieving such honors, especially since it was because of winning the battle against not only the French, but also your people," Swift

Thunder said. "It is not my way to say things that bring hurt to those I love. It is not a good thing to remind you time and again that I was the one who brought your warriors to their knees."

"Never hesitate to tell me anything about the war, for I understand the wrong that my people did by siding with the French," Moon Song said, swallowing hard. "Now let me say something to *you* that I will probably say over and over again. I am so proud of you I could burst. I am so proud that you are my *knight!*"

"Your knight," Swift Thunder said, chuckling. He took her hand. "Let us go and say good-bye to Father John and the others. Soon we will be home, Moon Song, *our* home. Soon we will live there as man and wife."

Chapter Twenty-two

As Swift Thunder and Moon Song left the room hand in hand, a door creaked slowly open.

Father Jacob stepped gingerly out into the corridor and watched them disappear down the steps. He moved quickly to the head of the stairs and watched them until they were gathered into the shadows at the foot of the staircase.

Then he went to the window and watched for the bridge to be lowered, so that he could see Moon Song and Swift Thunder walk toward the canoe. He would follow them with his eyes until they made the turn in the river.

He didn't understand why, but from the first moment he'd laid eyes on Swift Thunder, he had been strongly drawn to him. It was the same when he was around Moon Song.

Yet he could not remember how he knew either one of them. He rubbed his brow, wishing that his memory would return.

When he looked at Swift Thunder, his heart felt a powerful longing. That truly confused Father Jacob, for how could he have known *him?*

He walked from the window and went into the quiet of his room. There, he eased into a rocker and began slowly rocking back and forth.

His hands went to his hood and shoved it back so that it fell around his shoulders. A trembling hand went to his face. He shuddered as he ran his fingers across the scars. He didn't even remember how he had gotten them!

His whole life before he'd come to live with the priests was a mystery to him . . . a huge question mark.

But was it finally coming back to him?

Was that why he felt a need to study Swift Thunder and Moon Song? Would he truly ever know?

Surely, if he had known Moon Song and Swift Thunder in the past, they would remember him. If he had the courage, the next time they came to the monastery, he would remove the hood and allow them to see his face.

He hoped the scars would not hide his true identity from them if they had known him sometime in the past.

Chapter Twenty-three

*When two hearts are joined together as one,
There is no obstacle that cannot be
overcome.*

Swift Thunder's arms were around Moon Song, holding her close in his bed upon soft, thick pelts. Moon Song took strength from Swift Thunder's presence. She had just visited her mother's grave and said prayers over it, as Swift Thunder knelt beside his grandfather's, murmuring his own prayers.

It still did not seem real to Moon Song that her mother was gone from this earth; it was especially hard to remember that she died in such a horrible way.

She clenched her eyes closed to try to keep back the tears that burned in their depths, for she had cried so much now, she felt drained.

"I can feel your sorrow inside my soul," Swift Thunder said as Moon Song was unable to hold back a sob. "I, too, am burdened with my own sorrow. Let us together find our way back to a place where there are smiles and happiness."

"I am finding it already in your arms," Moon Song murmured, snuggling closer to him.

She was grateful for so many things that Swift Thunder and his people had done for her. Tonight she wore a soft doeskin gown that had been brought for her, along with other clothes her size, by the women of the castle.

She felt refreshed and clean after a moonlit bath with Swift Thunder in the river.

The fire was burning high and bright in the fireplace in the outer room, sending its glow down the corridor into Swift Thunder's bedroom.

Moon Song was so in awe of his home. It was vastly different from the longhouse she had shared with her mother at the Oneida castle.

But Swift Thunder was chief of his people. His status required a large longhouse.

He enjoyed the luxury of warm wooden floors, as well as a magnificent stone fireplace in his outer room, whereas most longhouses had earthen floors and firepits.

He also had furniture, which had astounded her the first time she had seen the pieces. And the rich furs that hung on his walls! They were so beautiful they even now stole her breath away.

Yes, his house of many rooms was a paradise compared to hers and most others she had ever been in.

She would take such pride in caring for this house, and especially this man she would share it with.

She loved how the moon was shining brightly down from the heavens and sending its beautiful glow through the window beside the bed, revealing the expensive pelts and colorful blankets beneath her.

The moonlight also shone on her husband-to-be's naked, muscled body as he stretched out on his side facing her.

That was the most wonderful of the gifts that had come to her from the love they had found together.

His elbow was propped against the mattress, his chin resting in a hand as he gazed back at Moon Song, his eyes filled with adoration. For this precious moment, she was able to forget everything but him.

"Marriage is the center of my thoughts at this moment," Swift Thunder said, smiling.

"Tomorrow?" Moon Song said, her eyes brightening.

She sat up quickly, her robe falling away and revealing the soft cleavage of her breasts to Swift Thunder's eyes.

"Can we truly be married tomorrow?" she said, clasping her hands together on her lap.

Suddenly her smile faded. She lowered her eyes.

"It is too soon," she said, her voice breaking. "I am not certain it would be right for us to marry so soon after . . ."

Swift Thunder reached up and slid a hand gently over Moon Song's mouth to keep her from saying the difficult words.

"Under any other circumstances, yes, it would be too soon," he said.

He slid his hand away and twined his fingers through her long hair as she moved down and lay beside him again.

"But none of the circumstances these past several days have been anything akin to normal," he said thickly. "It is best that you and I become man and wife soon, even as soon as tomorrow. Then let Piercing Eyes try his schemes to get you. No man of honor meddles with another man's wife."

"But do you not see?" Moon Song said. She visibly shuddered when she thought of Piercing Eyes, his leering smile causing her insides to grow cold with loathing.

"Piercing Eyes is not a man of honor. He never has been."

"Let us not talk about him anymore, or the sadness or hate that comes with his name," Swift Thunder said, his voice drawn. "Let us put everything from our minds tonight but you and me. Tomorrow, my woman. Tomorrow we will be man and wife. Then there will be children. We will have our own family. We will cherish our children, and then their children when we become grandparents."

Moon Song laughed softly. "Please do not go that far into the future," she said. She leaned on an elbow and gazed into his sparkling eyes. "I do not wish to think of myself as gray, wrinkled, and stoop-shouldered. I want to be beautiful as you see me now, forever and ever."

"And do you not know that even when you are gray and wrinkled you will be beautiful to me?" Swift Thunder said. He placed a hand gently behind her neck and brought her face down close to his. "You will always be this beautiful to me inside my heart, even when *I* am gray and stooped and can barely walk. When I close my eyes I will see you as I see you tonight. Ah, so beautiful you make my heart soar."

"I am that beautiful to you?" Moon

Song murmured.

She closed her eyes in ecstasy when Swift Thunder swept her beneath him and opened her gown to his searching fingers.

"Yes, so beautiful and so sweet," Swift Thunder said huskily as he slid the gown away from her shoulders.

His lips went to one of her breasts.

She sucked in a breath of pleasure and writhed in response as his tongue swept over her nipple, and then his teeth gently nipped at it.

He swept his arms around her.

His mouth moved up to her lips and he kissed her with a lazy warmth that left her weak and filled with longing.

It was so easy for her now to forget those moments when she could not stop grieving. Ah, yes, her lover was cradling her in his arms. He was kissing her. And she could feel the heat of his sex as he lifted himself up so that his body was scarcely touching hers.

Wanting him inside her so badly, knowing his body would truly fill the ache she felt tonight, Moon Song reached a hand to his manhood and gently wrapped her fingers around him.

When she heard his quick, quivering intake of breath, and felt his kiss deepen, she moved her hand on him, then guided his shaft to where she knew it belonged.

Swift Thunder needed no more coaxing. He reached down and gently lifted her hand away from his throbbing sex, then held her hand as he shoved himself gently into her.

Moon Song felt sweet currents of warmth spreading through her as Swift Thunder's sinewy buttocks moved, filling her so magnificently with his heat with each thrust.

She moaned as he again kissed her with easy sureness while his body moved slowly, then faster.

As his steel arms enfolded her, she felt his hunger deepening. She wrapped her arms around his neck and brought her legs around his waist.

Then she rode with him, movement by movement, heart to heart, soul to soul.

Swift Thunder felt ablaze with passion. He could feel the way Moon Song's body quivered with the ecstasy that he was evoking within her.

His lips parted and he searched with his tongue inside her mouth, trembling when her tongue met his in a passionate dance.

His hands reached beneath her and clasped her buttocks and lifted her more closely to him, molding her slender, sweet body against his.

How fiercely he wanted her. To him it was like a dream that she was there, again finding that pulsing crest of passion with him.

"I love you so," Moon Song whispered as his lips slid down and again he tasted the sweetness of her breasts.

She twined her fingers through his thick black hair. Groaning with pleasure, she tossed her head slowly back and forth.

Then she reached for his face and brought his lips to hers again.

They kissed deeply and hotly, their bodies straining together hungrily; they trembled with delicious shivers of desire as they found the wondrous joy of release.

Overwhelmed by the passion they found in one another's arms, never having imagined anything could be so wonderfully sweet and at the same time so explosively rapturous, Moon Song moved to lie beside Swift Thunder.

She could not keep her hands off his magnificent muscled body. As she slowly ran her fingers over him, she smiled into his eyes.

And when she came to the most sensitive places on his body and saw him quiver, she felt warm inside herself, for she adored giving him pleasure.

She adored receiving it, as well, and as he began moving his own fingers over her body, touching her sensitive places, she sighed.

When his hand went between her legs and began caressing her where she still throbbed from their lovemaking, Moon Song stretched out on her back and closed her eyes in building ecstasy as he stroked her.

When she found herself reaching a sudden, mind-numbing climax, she trembled and floated for a moment, then opened her eyes and gave him a look of wonder.

"That was wonderful," she gasped out. "How . . . ?"

"My fingers, tongue, and lips can bring you joy, as well as my body fitting into yours," Swift Thunder said huskily. "You can, as well, bring me the same magic with your own hands, tongue, and lips."

"Show me how," Moon Song said. She moved to her knees. "I wish to watch your face as you receive the same sort of pleasure that you gave to me."

"I would rather not take pleasure like that tonight," Swift Thunder said huskily.

He reached up and placed his hands at her waist.

He gently lowered her beside him.

"I am still enjoying remembering those moments when we came together with our bodies," he said thickly. "But there will be times when I will need quick release. Then I will request that pleasure of you, if you will not mind giving it to me."

"I shall always be ready to give you whatever you ask of me," Moon Song murmured. She giggled. "Especially pleasure."

"Hear the wind?" Swift Thunder said.

He looked toward the window.

"Hear how it is suddenly singing?" he said, turning his eyes back to her and watching her as she looked outside.

"Yes, it has become more than a breeze," Moon Song said. "I hope a storm does not follow. I . . . I . . . dread the first storm with my mother in the ground."

Swift Thunder turned to her. He placed a gentle hand on her cheek. "My woman, you know that only your mother's body lies in that grave," he said. "Her spirit is elsewhere. She would not even be aware of the rain hitting the earth above her grave."

"I know, but I hate to think of her body in the cold and wet," she gulped out. "Although her body was changed by the knife in it, she was . . . she was . . . still beautiful and will always be so in my mind's eye."

"In the spirit world, she is even more beautiful," Swift Thunder said, trying to reassure her. "I can see her now. She is glowing. She is smiling. She is with her loved ones."

"Yes, I know that is true," Moon Song said, sighing. "And it makes Moon Song so happy to envision it."

"Then when it rains, keep that beautiful picture in your mind, not one that disturbs you," Swift Thunder said. "Just think of her smiling and holding hands with your father. And think of how she will be looking down from the heavens and will see your smile tomorrow when you become my wife. Think of how she will sigh with pride when she sees her grandchildren from the clouds above."

"You know how to say things that make me feel so relaxed and wonderful," Moon Song said.

She snuggled closer.

"That is because I love you so much," Swift Thunder said, embracing her.

"The wind?" he then said. "Do you know the myth about the wind?"

"Long ago my father told it to me but I do not remember it very well," Moon Song said, enjoying this moment with Swift Thunder. It might be one of those moments that she would remember on a day when she needed to be reminded of the blessings in her life.

Swift Thunder.

He was a blessing she had never thought she would have, not when she had been forced to leave the area shortly after meeting him.

But she should have known then that destiny would not cheat them . . . would not keep them apart.

They were meant to be together. From the moment they were tiny seeds in their mothers' wombs, it was written in the stars that they would one day wed and bring their own children into the world.

"This is how it is said it was done," Swift Thunder began, finding it hard to concentrate on the story when she lay so close. He loved the feel of her sweet body pressed against his, her softness, her lilac scent.

The heaven of just having her was what made him feel so blessed.

"*Tharonhiawakon*, our Creator, decided that there must be wind. The wind would strengthen the people whom He had left on the earth. In the west, our Creator made the thing that was sometimes covered by a veil. That was earth. Slowly it moved and revolved. There the wind was formed, and the Mohawk people were happy. It strengthened their breath. The wind *is* the strength that makes us Mohawk content and happy."

"I, who am Oneida now, who will soon be also Mohawk, am content and happy," Moon Song said, twining her arms around Swift Thunder's neck, drawing his lips to hers. "Never did I believe that I could be so happy.

"There is one link in our happiness that is missing, though," Moon Song added, sighing heavily.

Swift Thunder's eyebrows lifted. "What could be missing? I feel that everything is right here in my longhouse, except for the children that will be born to us one day, I hope soon," he said.

He swept his arms around her and drew her face close to his, their breaths mingling. "Tell me what is missing and I shall give it to you, for I do not want you ever to want for a thing," he then said.

"This is something that you cannot get for me," Moon Song said, her voice low and sad. "Blue, Swift Thunder. I miss *Blue*."

She saw a sudden pain enter his eyes.

He eased her from his arms and sat up on the bed as he gazed again through the window into the moonlight-splashed night.

It was at this moment that Swift Thunder realized just how much *he* missed his cougar.

Swift Thunder had been so preoccupied since Blue's disappearance, he had not had time to miss his pet.

"I miss him as well," he said. "I wonder now if I should have sent warriors out to search for him when I realized that he was gone."

"You did not do that because you thought he had gone to find a mate," Moon Song said, sitting up beside him. Her eyes lowered. "I would feel so bad if I knew he was unable to come home because he was hurt."

Swift Thunder turned to Moon Song and placed a finger beneath her chin and lifted it, bringing her eyes level with his. "He did leave to mate. We both have to believe that. One day he will return, perhaps with a kitten or two."

Moon Song smiled dreamily. "His kitten would steal my heart away," she murmured.

"*You* have stolen *my* heart," Swift Thunder said huskily as he wrapped his arms around her waist and slowly lowered her to the bed, then knelt down over her.

He enveloped her within his muscled arms and gave her an all-consuming kiss, his body awakening again to the needs that only his woman could fulfill.

He loved the way she trembled and moaned softly against his lips when he shoved himself into her and began the rhythmic strokes that would catapult them again into paradise.

Moon Song clung to him and moved her body with his, hoping that somewhere inside her even now lay a seed that would become their first child . . . a child born of devoted love!

Chapter Twenty-four

Laughter, sunshine, and rainbows, too,
This is what I promise you.
She held him tight, as he held her.
He was sure he could hear her purr.

Wearing a beaded doeskin dress, and beads woven into her shiny black hair, Moon Song stood beside Swift Thunder in the presence of all of his people in the courtyard of the Castle of the Bear.

Their marriage ceremony was already underway. Though it was more low key than was customary, to Moon Song, whose eyes showed her radiant happiness, it was perfect. She was being joined to the man she loved forevermore.

As Swift Thunder's shaman, Spirit Wind, blessed their union, Moon Song smiled. She would never forget how the castle had been prepared for her and Swift Thunder by the women of his village. The entrance to their wedding grounds was a bower of green and an assortment of flowers, leading as if into a garden.

And now the sun shone high above the crowd.

Birds filled the air with the rapture of song.

And a tantalizing aroma wafted through the air from the many outdoor cook fires and deep, open pits, where various foods had been prepared for the feast that followed the "joining of hearts."

As Spirit Wind continued to speak, Moon Song caught a glimpse of the many Mohawk girls crowded together as they watched their chief take a wife. They were vivid spots of color in their beautiful attire, their eyes wide and wondering as they gazed first at Moon Song and then at Swift Thunder.

Moon Song turned her own eyes to Swift Thunder. His handsomeness today almost drew her breath away. He wore a buckskin cloak lined with fur of the bear, and a unique headband of white coral.

Beneath the cloak he wore a full costume of fringed doeskin, which contrasted beautifully with his sun-darkened face and waist-length thick black hair.

As they stood hand in hand, the breeze fluttered Swift Thunder's hair against his straight, muscled back.

His moccasins were finely embroidered

with tiny shells from the Mohawk River. On his wrists he wore bands of embroidered doeskin; matching bands adorned his ankles.

It was a day for Moon Song to marvel over. If anyone had told her six sunrises ago that today she would be marrying her "knight," she would have scoffed at him and told him it was an impossible dream.

But today it was real!

And she loved every waking minute of knowing that she had won this particular battle over the terrible Piercing Eyes.

She wished he could see her at this moment. How right she had been to escape the life he wished to force on her.

The only thing that stung her heart was the loss of her mother. She tried not to think about that, for when she did, she felt, oh, so responsible.

But Swift Thunder kept reassuring her that she had had nothing at all to do with her mother's death. It was the fault of one evil man.

And Swift Thunder had vowed to her that one day, somehow, he would find a way to make Piercing Eyes pay.

For now, it was best to play a waiting game. Swift Thunder was not a man who entered into warring lightly. He was born a man of peace. He had said that he would die the same.

As Spirit Wind stepped away, his role in the ceremony finished, Swift Thunder took Moon Song's hands and turned her to stand before him, facing him.

Their eyes met and held and Moon Song tried hard not to cry. As the man she loved gazed so tenderly down at her, her intense joy overflowed.

"My *niu*, my wife, as you know, in our culture it is the custom that when a woman marries, her husband moves into *her* longhouse, and that except for a man's weapons, clothes, and personal possessions, all property becomes the woman's, even down to the farming tools," Swift Thunder said thickly. "But as your longhouse is located in the castle of your husband's enemy, I shall give my longhouse to *you*, including all of my possessions, except for my weapons. If Blue were here, even he would now be yours."

He gently squeezed her hands. "Today, my love, I proudly become your husband, to stand by your side through all trials and tribulations, and through moments of ecstasy. I love you, forever and ever, Moon Song. You are my princess, as well as my people's, for they are your people now, too."

Touched too deeply to speak right away, Moon Song swallowed hard, cleared her throat, then smiled again at her chieftain warrior.

"My *wachia*, my husband, today I wish to break with tradition," she murmured. "Everything that is yours, that you have given to me as a part of your wedding promise, I give back to you. But I am, oh, so happy to share it all with you as your wife. I love you, Swift Thunder. I proudly become your wife today. For now, and for always I give you my heart, my everything."

Before everyone, and beneath a sky so blue it seemed a reflection of the great river beyond, Swift Thunder drew Moon Song into his arms and gave her a deep, wondrous kiss.

She clung to him and returned the kiss, forgetting that she was being watched by a people who could have hated her for who she was, yet seemed content enough to accept her as their princess, because Swift Thunder had seen the good in her.

And when his lips slid away and he whispered something sweet and sensual in her ear, Moon Song blushed and giggled; then her breath was stolen away as he swept her up into his arms and carried her through the approving crowd.

Only when Moon Song and Swift Thunder were in the privacy of their lodge, with the closed door separating them from the outside world, did the drums begin to beat in the courtyard where the true celebration had begun. Now the earth and the air were filled with music from drums and rattles. The castle was alive with song and dancing.

Earlier today, while in council, Swift Thunder had encouraged his people to forget their sadness over the recent loss of their past chief. He had explained that his grandfather would not want any long faces and wailing over his achievement of the ultimate goal in life — entering that world above where there was no longer any pain or war. There was only peace and love!

"I am so glad that my people listened to my plea to enjoy themselves today, to dance, to feast, to sing," Swift Thunder said as he carried Moon Song past the large piles of food on wooden platters, which would be consumed after they had made love for the first time as man and wife.

"I am so glad they accepted me into their lives," Moon Song murmured as Swift Thunder laid her on his bed, which was now also hers. "If they had not . . ."

Swift Thunder knelt over her and kissed her words away.

Then as his eyes filled with hot passion, she sat up and let him undress her.

After her beautiful clothes were set aside, along with the beads from her hair, Moon Song moved to her knees and removed Swift Thunder's clothes.

When his clothes joined Moon Song's at the foot of the bed, and his wonderfully muscled body was bare for her hands to wander over, she moved closer to him and spread kisses across his breast, down across his flat stomach. She was aware of how he sucked in his breath when her lips came close to his manhood, which was tight and large with arousal.

When he twined his fingers through her hair and began urging her mouth toward him, she glanced up at him.

His eyes were closed with rapture. And when her fingers wrapped around his manhood and moved on him, she saw him flinch with even more heated passion. She sucked in a sharp breath when she realized what he now wanted, even needed, from her as she flicked her tongue over his sex, where his heartbeat seemed centered.

His hands in her hair urged her mouth

even closer to him, and she made love to him in this way until he groaned, "Stop . . ."

Moon Song's heart pounded like thunder as she moved gently away from Swift Thunder, his hands on her shoulders positioning her on her back.

Swift Thunder knelt down over her, his lips showering her body with intimate kisses.

Closing her eyes in her own moments of ecstasy, Moon Song moaned when she felt his lips and tongue moving lower over her body.

And when she felt his fingers parting the fronds of hair at the juncture of her thighs, she scarcely breathed, for she knew that he was now going to give her the same sort of pleasure as she had given him.

When his tongue swept down over her throbbing womanhood, and then he moved it on her in long, sensual strokes, Moon Song gasped out her pleasure and twined her fingers through his long, thick hair, urging him closer to her heat.

"Please . . . please . . ." she whispered, not even sure what she was begging for, except that what he was doing was sending exquisite sprays of warmth throughout her body.

When Swift Thunder bent lower and

thrust his tongue into her, Moon Song cried out in rapture and became lost to everything but the flashes of passion that were bursting forth inside her mind, the spinning sensation flooding her whole body.

And when she came down from that plateau of pleasure, and slowly opened her eyes, she was stunned that she had found such intense pleasure without him inside her.

Swift Thunder saw her look of puzzlement. "I told you there were many ways to make love," he said huskily. "We are man and wife now, and I will now feel free to teach you all ways to find the passion that you just enjoyed."

"But you did not allow me to give you that much pleasure by doing . . . that . . . to you," Moon Song murmured, questioning him with her eyes.

"A man does not need that much preparing for the true thing," Swift Thunder said, chuckling low. "A man's needs and a woman's differ."

"Will you one day let me take you all the way to paradise with this sort of lovemaking?" Moon Song asked, reaching over to stroke him. "I would love to know that I have given my all to you, as you just have for me."

"Yes, one day," he said, again chuckling. He moved over her and swept his arms around her and lowered his lips to her mouth. "But for now, my *niu*, I wish for only one way to make love."

"My body aches to have you inside me," Moon Song whispered, sucking in a wild breath of pleasure as he plunged inside her and began his rhythmic strokes.

As he moved and slid, she quietly groaned.

Only a few more strokes and they both went over the edge into total ecstasy.

Afterwards, after they came down from their wonderful place of bliss, Swift Thunder wrapped a soft pelt around Moon Song's shoulders, and then a blanket around his own.

Taking her hand, he led her out to the fireplace and sat with her on pelts before it.

After fixing her a platter of various meats and fruits and handing it to her, he fixed his own.

As they ate and laughed and talked, Moon Song felt a contentment she had never known possible.

"I want to share everything with you," Swift Thunder said, placing his empty platter on the floor beside him.

"What do you wish to share that you have not already?" Moon Song asked, putting her empty plate with his.

She moved on her knees before him, the pelt around her shoulders sliding down and resting around her waist.

She inhaled a quivering breath of pleasure as he placed his hands on her breasts and cupped them in his palms.

"My name," he said, softly stroking her breasts. "It has not always been Swift Thunder. I have another name."

"Truly?" Moon Song asked, her eyes widening. She was trying not to be enraptured again by his caresses, not yet anyhow, not this soon. She wanted to build up to their next intimate encounter. "What name have you not told me about?"

He gently shoved her pelt away, revealing her soft curves to his feasting eyes, and then he lifted her onto his lap, her legs straddling him as his own blanket fell away.

She twined her arms around his neck and trembled when he kissed her; then she drew away and questioned him with her eyes. "Is it a name you have decided not to share with me after all?" she asked.

"My father, who as I have told you was white, called me by another name when we

283

were alone," he said, lifting her now and carrying her again toward his bedroom. "My mother never knew the name. No one but me and my father knew it. But I shall now share it with you."

"It is a white man's name?" Moon Song asked as he laid her on the bed and moved over her, his body already thrusting against hers although he was not yet inside her.

Moon Song could feel the strength, the full length of his manhood, and knew that soon she would be transported again to the world that only lovers knew about.

"*Qua,* it was a white man's name, the name of a *pirate,* the man my father was before he became a trader," Swift Thunder said huskily as he bent low and nuzzled Moon Song's neck.

"Your . . . father . . . was a pirate?" Moon Song gasped out, recalling tales of pirates told to her by the white prisoner long ago. She had learned from him that some pirates wreaked havoc on land and sea. She had been told by the white prisoner, who confessed to her that *he* had been a pirate in *his* past, that loot was taken which was sometimes called "bounty."

She had found it hard to envision that white man as a pirate, for he had been too gentle. When he had explained that he was a good pirate who took from the rich to give to the poor, then she understood.

"Yes. My father, whose true name was Patrick Fitzgerald, was a pirate when he was young and wild," Swift Thunder said.

He leaned away from her and smiled down at her. "And his pirate name was Bryce," he said. "That was the secret name he gave me when we were away from my mother."

"Bryce?" Moon Song said, as though testing the name on her lips. She giggled. "What a funny name."

Swift Thunder blushed, then laughed. "*Qua,* I now see it as strange, yet when I was a young brave wanting to know the ways of the world, I thought it special, for you see, anything that my father did, or gave me, was very special to me. When he was gone from my life, there was such a void, even more so than when Mother was taken from me."

He swallowed hard, then continued. "Without my father, his strength, his guidance, I felt a strange sort of detachment from the world," he said solemnly. "It took a long time for me not to feel that detachment. But, finally, after the years passed and I grew to accept the loss of someone so special to me, I no longer felt it."

"Yes, I know what you are saying, and how you felt," Moon Song said. "I recently felt that way when Mother died and I was suddenly aware of not having a mother or father for guidance."

She reached a gentle hand to Swift Thunder's face. "Then I reminded myself that I had *you*," she said softly. "You filled that terrible emptiness inside me." She softly stroked his cheek. "I wish your father were still alive, for I truly believe I would adore him. You see, anyone who fathered someone like you had to be special and someone easily loved."

Swift Thunder nodded. "Yes, that was my father," he said.

"Bryce, please make love to me, over and over again?" Moon Song whispered against his lips as he lowered his mouth to kiss her.

"Bryce?" he said, laughing softly. "And so now I am Bryce to you?"

"Only when we are alone," Moon Song whispered back. "I think I could grow to like the name Bryce, especially since it was a name you enjoyed as a child. Do you care if I refer to you sometimes in that way when we are alone?"

"Whatever you wish, you do," Swift Thunder said huskily as she lowered her hand from his face and he felt her other hand guiding his swollen sex inside her.

He gathered her into his arms and filled her with his heat.

He held her close as they made love, this time slow and filled with the wonder that came from loving one another so much.

"Bryce?" Moon Song whispered, clinging.

"Yes?" Swift Thunder whispered back.

"I am so lucky to have found you," she murmured. "Without you, I —"

"Shh," Swift Thunder said, interrupting her. "We are together. We are man and wife. Let us not think of how it might have been. This is now. Think of nothing but now."

Sighing, Moon Song nodded, yet there was something else that she could not help wishing for.

Children!

Each time they made love there was a chance they were making a child. She desperately wanted to be a mother. She knew how. She had had the best teacher.

Her own mother.

"Did not your mother ever discover that your name was sometimes Bryce?" Moon Song asked, momentarily interrupting their lovemaking.

"No, she never knew," Swift Thunder

said, stopping long enough to gaze into her eyes. "But mainly because it was the arrangement between my mother and father that I would be called by an Indian name. My father did not want it to look like he was breaking a promise by calling me something else. Until his dying day, and hers, it remained a secret."

"Until now," Moon Song said, gasping with delight when Swift Thunder swept his hands beneath her and lifted her closer to his heat.

"Until now," Swift Thunder said, then kissed her long and hard, banishing all thoughts of anything but their lovemaking from her mind . . . and his.

She clung.

He dipped.

She sighed.

Chapter Twenty-five

The winter winds blew hard and cold.
It brought a chill, complaints from the old.
Even in the dead of the ice and snow,
Tharonhiawakon *above does not forget*
  — he will know.

Many moons had passed since the wondrous day of Swift Thunder and Moon Song's marriage. It was now winter and laughter rang through trees whose limbs were beautifully white with snow.

When the cold weather and its attendant snows settled upon the land of the Mohawk, the tribesmen gathered to play their favorite sport called "snowsnakes."

Now in her second month of pregnancy, and thrilled to be with child, Moon Song sat on a platform covered with thick, warm pelts in a heavy coat made of many rabbit pelts.

The fur was worn inside out, next to her body, and kept her cozy and warm while a hood sheltered her head from the winds that blew incessantly from the north.

She also wore fur mittens which warmed

her long, slender fingers, and knee-high boots of thick buckskin that warmed her feet.

She glanced around at the crowd of Mohawk who stood on two sides of the area where the game was soon to start.

The women wore various winter attire, but most had wrapped thick blankets around their shoulders.

The elderly as well clutched blankets.

But the children, who did not wish to be kept from the fun of racing around, wore no cumbersome blankets, but instead wore hooded fur coats and mittens.

For the most part, the warriors would be participating in this game of snowsnakes today; only a few were standing and watching with their wives.

And then there were those who stood at the sentry posts to keep watch for any signs of an enemy who might take advantage of the games to attack today.

There was no need to watch for canoes in the river. It was frozen over with ice and impassable. The only way anyone could make a surprise attack was by land, and even then they would have a difficult time traveling by foot because of the treacherous deep snow.

And if they came with dog sleds, the

dogs could not be kept quiet as they tugged and pulled on their sleds manned by thick-muscled warriors.

"Let the games begin!" Swift Thunder shouted, breaking into Moon Song's thoughts.

She sat up straighter and strained to see her husband amid the many warriors who stood around him. Although it was cold, Swift Thunder and his warriors wore no robes, blankets, or coats, which would impede their skill at the game of snowsnakes.

Moon Song was anxious to see how well Swift Thunder's team did today, for she knew he had eagerly anticipated winning.

If he did not win, she wondered how he would take defeat. He did not seem the sort to lose at anything.

She smiled, certain that he and those on his team would be the victors today.

Moon Song's pulse raced when she saw Swift Thunder and knew that he had been chosen to begin the game today. She watched him with an anxious heart as he grabbed up his snowsnake and poised it for release, then made a running approach to the trough that had been readied for the game.

She giggled behind a hand as she watched her husband try to maintain his concentration in the face of heckling by members of the opposing team, who hoped to ruin his aim.

If any player missed the trough, or if his shaft hit at an angle, he would be the target of a stream of good-natured abuse from the opposition.

Moon Song was familiar with the game. It was not only popular in the Mohawk castle, but in the Oneida, as well. The game itself was deceptively simple, the goal being to slide a long, smooth stick along a trough in the snow farther than one's opponents.

But expertise required not just strong muscles to start the stick on its course, but also an accurate eye and great skill in placing the shaft properly in the trough so that it would travel the maximum distance.

The game got its name from the flexible sticks that undulated in a snakelike fashion as they sped along the trough.

Moon Song had learned long ago, as a child excitedly awaiting the first snowsnake game of the winter, that snowsnake sticks might be as long as nine feet or as short as five, and were made of hickory, maple, or walnut.

They were designed for speed and, if skillfully handled, traveled their icy course with the velocity of a loosed arrow.

To give a stick sufficient weight, its conical head was tipped with lead. Each shaft was about an inch wide at the crown and tapered off to less than half an inch at the tail.

To make the trough that was being used today, the warriors had dragged a series of smooth-barked logs through the snow and placed them end to end to create a trench about fifteen hundred feet long and a foot deep. Its bottom and sides were packed down into a smooth, icy surface.

Any number of men could play the snowsnake game, either as individual competitors or as members of teams.

Today there were teams.

In addition to active participants, each side had snowsnake "doctors" who cared for the sticks, rubbing them with "medicine" — beeswax, or animal oils — to reduce their friction.

Contests were refereed by umpires who made certain that the rules were strictly observed.

The game ended when every contestant had had his turn, and the distances were all tallied. Winners then collected whatever had been bet on the outcome.

Today many lustrous, thick, rich pelts

had been wagered.

Moon Song was shaken from her thoughts when a loud voice filled the air, announcing that someone was coming through the snow, and that that someone was a black-robed priest!

Hearing that news made Swift Thunder stop abruptly and lower his stick to his side.

He whirled around and gazed up at the sentry high on the wall.

"Is there only one?" he shouted. "And how is he traveling?"

He had heard no dogs barking, as he would have if there were a sled.

Had the priest come this far from his castle, on foot? Why would he do such a thing? Had Father John died? Or had the Oneida found a way to attack them? Was this one priest who approached his castle today the only Black Robe survivor in the Praying Castle?

"The priest who approaches walks alone," the sentry responded.

Swift Thunder didn't stop to ask what the priest's condition might be. He dropped his stick and broke into a run toward the closed gate.

"Open the gate!" he shouted. "Let the priest enter!"

Moon Song rushed from the platform, then made herself slow down when her feet almost slid from beneath her. She placed a quick hand on her abdomen, for she had to do everything possible to ensure the safety of her unborn child. She had waited too long to be a mother to do anything that might take this baby from her.

But she had to know why the priest had come. Anyone who braved this cold temperature, and walked as far as the priest had to have walked, could easily get frostbite.

Moon Song was reminded that winter had many moods. A fun side, and an evil side with claws like a bear.

This day had begun lightheartedly with the anticipation of games and then a celebration including dancing, singing, and eating in the large council house. But now everything had stopped. The smiles had faded. The games had ended.

And the Mohawk people were following behind Moon Song, seeming to hold their breath as Swift Thunder stood at the gate while it was opened.

And then she felt the color rush from her cheeks and her heart skip a beat when she caught sight of the priest. It was not Father John. She should have known that no one his age, or so thin, would make the voyage in this bitter cold.

The priest who had arrived, who was one of the youngest among the many at the Praying Castle, almost fell into Swift Thunder's arms.

Moon Song had seen the blueness of the man's face and lips. She had seen ice actually frozen in his nostrils. His black robe was frozen almost stiff on his body.

She hated to think about the condition of his feet, for surely he wore nothing as warm as the Mohawk's winter footwear.

When Moon Song ran up and stood next to Swift Thunder, she placed a hand over her mouth to stifle a gasp. She feared that the priest might have traveled his last journey anywhere, for he seemed only half alive.

Not waiting to hear why the priest had come to the Mohawk castle on such a dangerously cold day, Swift Thunder used every muscle he had to lift the priest up into his arms.

"Clear the way!" Swift Thunder shouted as he hurriedly carried the almost lifeless man through the gawking crowd.

Moon Song hurried along beside Swift Thunder, yet still making sure that her feet were steady on the mashed-down snow.

And when they were almost at Swift Thunder's longhouse, she went ahead and opened the door for her husband.

Everyone stood outside, watching and wondering, as Swift Thunder carried the priest into his longhouse and placed him on the floor on thick pelts before the fire.

Moon Song hurriedly closed the door, then went and stood over Swift Thunder, who was trying to revive the man by briskly rubbing his cheeks, and then his hands, and then his cheeks again.

"Get me more blankets and one of my warmest robes," Swift Thunder said to Moon Song without looking up at her. He was quickly undressing the man, who remained unconscious.

Moon Song gathered everything up in her arms and took it back to Swift Thunder.

"Now warm me a cloth and bring a bowl of soup from your cookfire," Swift Thunder said, struggling to place his warm robe on the body that was so stiff with cold.

Moon Song nodded.

She took the time to remove her own outdoor clothes, as well as her boots, then ladled some stew into a wooden bowl. She poured water from the pot she kept warming over the fire into a wooden basin and took these things, as well as a cloth, and set them down beside the priest, who was still in a lethargic sleep.

"Will he live?" Moon Song asked, kneeling down beside her husband. "This is Father Peter. He is such a kind, young priest. He was so polite to me while I was at the Praying Castle."

"I believe he will survive, yet I fear he may suffer for some time from the cold that ate away at his toes," Swift Thunder said, folding a blanket away from Father Peter's feet long enough for Moon Song to take a look.

"I have seen this before when warriors of my castle stayed too long on the hunt in the wintertime," she said, shuddering at the thought. "He may lose his toes."

Swift Thunder nodded, replaced the blanket over the priest's feet, then dipped the cloth in the warm water and began slowly caressing the priest's cheeks and forehead with it, sighing when the color began returning to his flesh.

And then he and Moon Song jumped as Father Peter awakened and suddenly grabbed Swift Thunder's free hand.

"I have come to seek your help," he choked out, his tongue sounding as though it might still be half frozen. "Our supplies, especially food, are gone. The river is frozen. No one can get to us with the supplies we need . . . to . . . make it through the winter."

"Has anyone suffered so much they . . . ?" Moon Song began, but couldn't say the word "died." She didn't have to. He looked at her with sad eyes, and she knew that someone among the priests had died.

The priest grasped Swift Thunder's hand harder. "Care not for me," he begged. "Go. Please take food to my companions."

Swift Thunder gazed at Moon Song and knew that she probably wanted to ask the same question as he. Had Father John come through this alive? Or . . . ?

"Father John sent me to you because I am the youngest and strongest," Father Peter said. "I will be all right. If I can stay beside your fire and have some nourishment, I am certain I will survive."

"You will be well taken care of," Swift Thunder said, rushing to his feet.

"I want to go with you," Moon Song said, also rising. "Swift Thunder, I can get another maiden to come and sit with Father Peter. She can see to his needs. But I wish to go and see who is and who is not all right at the Praying Castle."

She did not admit to worrying about Father Jacob, the generous priest who had given her the book that she had read so much that the pages were worn thin. But now that she knew Father John was all right, Father Jacob was next in her heart. All of them had shown her much kindness, but she felt closer to those two.

"Our child," Swift Thunder said, glancing down at her belly. "Perhaps it is not best that you travel in the cold because of the child."

"I will be dressed warmly and I will travel on the sled beneath many blankets and pelts," Moon Song quickly said. "Please, Swift Thunder? What can it truly hurt if I go with you? It would do me more harm staying behind and worrying and wondering about things instead of being able to discover firsthand whether those I care about are well."

Swift Thunder placed a gentle hand at her cheek. "Your time there became special to you, did it not?" he asked.

"Those who were there made it special," she said, then followed him when he started going around the longhouse gathering up supplies and equipment to take with him on his dogsled.

"Very well, you may go with me, but only if you take more blankets and pelts than you normally wear on our dogsled outings," he said bluntly.

Smiling ear to ear, Moon Song began helping Swift Thunder gather up more things, then packed them in buckskin bags as he left to ask others to donate some of their supplies to those who needed them more.

"Food stored for later on must be shared now with those who might die without it," Swift Thunder announced as his people crowded around him.

Then, being the kindhearted people they were, everyone began bringing bundles from the longhouses. Before long, Swift Thunder and Moon Song, accompanied by many warriors, were on dogsleds racing across the land, where the snow was so bright it could almost blind you.

Moon Song huddled warmly beneath her pile of blankets and pelts as the sled flew over the icy packed snow, the dogs yelping almost every inch of the way.

When finally the Praying Castle came into view, and only the river remained to be crossed, Moon Song gripped the sides of the sled and readied herself for the dangerous trek across the ice. If any of it was not frozen hard enough, the weight of the dogs and sleds could break through in an instant.

When they reached the river, the dogs and sleds went across one at a time.

Finally, without mishap, they journeyed onward.

Moon Song watched the bridge being lowered at the castle.

She could hardly wait to get inside and help those who had so generously helped her in her time of need.

Chapter Twenty-six

*It is like a blessing sweet and honest
from above,
When two hearts are blessed and joyful
with love.*

Moon Song was glad to see that only two priests had died due to the cold and lack of food; she was especially happy that Father John was all right — weak and more gaunt, yet very much alive. She went from room to room to take food to the priests who were not strong enough to come to the dining hall for the sudden, wonderful feast.

When she stopped just outside the door that she knew was Father Jacob's, Moon Song hesitated before knocking on the door.

She felt she was intruding on this man's privacy by going into his room, even though she knew he needed food. She sensed that he would not relish anyone, especially a woman, entering his room.

Surely he did not go to bed with the hooded robe. That meant that when she entered the room and walked over to his bed, she would get a full view of his face for the first time.

But perhaps he would shadow it with his blanket. Would he be that determined not to allow her to see his face?

It was still a mystery why he shied away from everyone; he had not taken meals with the others even when he was well.

Seeing that the door was slightly ajar made her even more curious. Always before, the door had been closed.

Determined to do as she saw best, to get some nourishment into this weakened man, Moon Song used the toe of her moccasin to nudge the door open so she could edge her way in sideways with the tray of warm broth, bread, and meat.

As she entered the room, her cheeks flushed with the excitement of finally seeing the man's face, Moon Song saw that the blind was pulled on the one window.

The only light in the room was from a candle that had burned down almost to its wick; the flame was swimming and sputtering in the melted wax.

But it was enough light to see by, and she could see a bed across the room against the stone wall, and on that bed was a figure covered up to his face with a blanket, his back to her.

"Who is there?" Father Jacob asked, causing Moon Song's heart to skip a beat; she had never heard his voice.

She had even begun to believe that he had lost the ability to speak. Now that he had, and she could hear his pleasant voice, she breathed more easily. He had not immediately ordered her from his premises.

She frowned in concentration, for there was something familiar about the voice. Yet how could that be? He had never said one word to her.

Still, there was something about it that was familiar.

"It is I, Moon Song," she murmured.

Warily she edged closer to the bed.

"Do you remember me?" she asked softly. "I am the Oneida maiden who came and sought safety at this Praying Castle some months ago. I . . . I . . . have since married Swift Thunder."

"Swift Thunder?" Father Jacob said, slowly turning.

Scarcely breathing, knowing that he was going to reveal his face to her, Moon Song stopped short. Her eyes were wide and her pulse raced anxiously when he made the final turn that made his face visible to her wondering eyes.

When she did finally see his face, she

305

gasped and took a shaky step away from him, for in the candle's soft glow she saw an image that threw her back in time.

Even though he was scarred and older, she knew this was the white man who had been held prisoner at her castle, the one who had been so kind to her.

He had not died after all!

He was there!

And his voice. She now knew why it was familiar to her. Who could forget a man's voice when it had told so many fascinating tales?

"It . . . is . . . you . . ." she gasped out, taking slow steps closer to the bed.

She gazed intently at his face, grief filling her at how scarred it was. The last time she saw him, his face had been covered with blood. Now there were scars that would last a lifetime.

She understood now why he had kept his face hidden by the hood.

He was ashamed of a face that had at one time been handsome and intriguing, and oh, so friendly. She still remembered how he smiled and laughed with a young maiden who'd been captivated by him.

She moved beside the bed and set the tray of food on the table next to it.

"You recognize me?" Father Jacob asked,

searching her face. He had earlier recognized something about her, yet had never been able to remember where he might have known her in his past life.

"Yes, I knew you long ago," Moon Song murmured. "But let us not talk about that just yet. I have brought you food and drink. Let me help you eat if you are too weak to feed yourself."

"Yes, I would appreciate your help," Father Jacob said as he eased his back up against the headboard.

When the blanket fell away from him, Moon Song felt even more sick at heart, for his chest was as scarred as his face.

Moon Song drew his blanket up to rest just beneath his armpits, then began spooning broth into his mouth. She watched him struggle to swallow at first, and was relieved when it became easier for him — so easy, in fact, that he pointed to a piece of meat.

"Did your husband bring this meat home from the hunt?" Father Jacob asked as Moon Song handed him a chunk of venison.

"Yes, and the stew I have on the tray was also made of the meat from my husband's hunt," Moon Song murmured. "I cannot say that I made it especially for you, for when I was making it I had no idea that anyone but me and my husband would be eating it. But it is now yours, and I am so glad I was the one to have made it for you. You were so kind to me years ago at my castle, and then when I was here, seeking shelter."

"You speak of another time," Father Jacob said, pausing before taking a bite of the meat. "When was that? How did we meet? My memory of the past has been stolen from me."

"You seemed to know me when I was staying here," Moon Song murmured, glad when he took the meat into his mouth and was able to chew and swallow it. "I saw you watching me. You were watching Swift Thunder, too."

"I watched you, Moon Song, because I was intrigued by your loveliness, and I had a feeling of having known you in my past," he said, coughing as he swallowed the meat. "I watched the man you call Swift Thunder because I see in him someone I feel I should know. Yet I do not know why I should know him. I am white. He is Indian."

"I will tell you what I know about you, as well as Swift Thunder, and by doing so, perhaps something will come to you that will help begin your journey back to who you were, and are," Moon Song murmured.

"Yes, please tell me what you know," he said, then put a hand between her and the food she was about to feed him. "I have had enough for now. I cannot take too much into my stomach at once. I am afraid I might become ill."

"I understand," Moon Song said, placing the food back on the tray.

She scooted a chair over beside the bed and sat down on it, where he could see her face as she talked, and she could see his.

She was thrilled to be with him again, and felt, oh, so happy that he had not died as she had thought.

When he had been taken out of her castle, he had not been dead, after all. Piercing Eyes must have known that the white man could not live long without help, but apparently he had not known that the priests were close enough to take the injured man in and make him well again.

Moon Song began her tale of a white man being brought into her castle and placed in the stockade, and continued by telling Father Jacob how kind he had been to her — reading to her, as well as teaching her to read and write and do numbers.

She explained about the wonderful stories he had told her about knights in shining armor, and about the book he had shown her.

She then told him all about Swift Thunder, and how Swift Thunder's father had been white and his mother Mohawk.

"He was born a half-breed?" Father Jacob said, trying hard to remember. "There is much about him that proves he is of a mixed marriage."

"Yes. His father's name was Patrick Fitzgerald, and his mother's name was White Wind," Moon Song said, raising an eyebrow when she saw him flinch at hearing these names.

Then she smiled and tried to lighten his mood. "I know a secret that was kept from Swift Thunder's mother," she said, laughing softly. "I shall share it with you if you do not tell Swift Thunder."

"A secret?" Father Jacob said, leaning toward her. "If it is a secret shared between you and your husband, should you tell me?"

"It has to do with names, so I thought you might enjoy knowing the name that Swift Thunder's father called him when they were alone," she murmured. "For you see, it is a white name, not Indian."

He leaned closer. "Tell me."

"His father gave him a pirate name," she said, remembering the moment Swift Thunder had told her this, and now thinking that perhaps she was wrong to divulge the secret. Yet she had already begun; she could not stop now. "Bryce. That was what Swift Thunder's father nicknamed him."

When Father Jacob winced and gasped and fell back down onto his bed, Moon Song rushed from the chair, afraid that he was suddenly worsening.

"What can I do?" she asked, her eyes wild. "Did I cause this? Oh, please do not be ill because of my rambling on and on. I did not mean to make a nuisance of myself."

He breathed hard. He closed his eyes as tears rushed from them. "Bryce," he said, choking on a sob. "My Bryce."

"Your . . . Bryce . . . ?" Moon Song gasped out, her eyes even wider. "What do you mean?"

His eyes flew open and through the tears he gave her a look that she did not understand.

She jumped with alarm when he suddenly reached a hand out and grabbed her arm.

311

"Go for Swift Thunder," he said, his voice breaking. "Please. Quickly. It's important."

She didn't have to. Swift Thunder had just entered the room. Concerned about her safety, he had come looking for her.

When he saw Father Jacob grasping Moon Song's arm in desperation, he was not sure what had happened. From where he stood, Moon Song blocked his view of Father Jacob so Swift Thunder could not see the man's face.

But as Moon Song turned and he caught a glimpse of Father Jacob's face, Swift Thunder froze. Beneath the scars and lines was a face that was somehow familiar to him.

"Swift Thunder?" Moon Song said, feeling that the mystery was about to be cleared up.

Swift Thunder came into the room and stood beside her.

As he gazed down at the elderly, scarred man, he was flooded with memories. Yet he could not place the face.

"Bryce?" Father Jacob said, causing Swift Thunder to flinch and gasp as though someone had slapped him.

Only one person besides Moon Song and Swift Thunder knew that he was called Bryce.

Moon Song broke away from Father Jacob and flung herself into Swift Thunder's arms. "I am so sorry," she cried. "I did not mean to tell him your nickname. It . . . just . . . seemed the right thing to do when I was telling him about you. I thought telling him the name might lighten his mood."

"I did not speak the name Bryce to you, my son, because Moon Song told me the name," Father Jacob said.

"You called me *son*," Swift Thunder said. He stepped closer to the bed to get a better look at the man's face. "Why?"

"Because I am remembering everything now, son," Father Jacob said. He reached a hand out for Swift Thunder. "The name Bryce seemed somehow to jar my memory. Bryce . . . Swift Thunder . . . oh, how long has it been?"

Father Jacob swallowed hard. "When I was taken away, on the day of your mother's death, you were just a boy," he said. "I knew she had hidden you well. That was all that saved you from the fate your mother met that day. I . . . I . . . was dealt with severely, as you can tell by my scarred face and body. But my memory was also lost, or I would have come looking for you long ago."

Then Father Jacob closed his eyes and drew in a deep breath. "Talking . . . talking . . . has weakened me," he said, barely audible. He opened his eyes and gestured with a hand toward Swift Thunder. "Come to me, my son. Let me hold you. Let me know the miracle of having you with me again."

"Papa, is it truly you?" Swift Thunder choked out.

Swift Thunder saw how his father's old, tired eyes lit up, and how a smile quivered across his lips as Swift Thunder bent over him, then returned his embrace.

"Son," Father Jacob said, clinging to him. "Bryce, oh, Bryce. Swift Thunder, my son, Swift Thunder."

Moon Song was frozen still and silent as understanding dawned. It was a father and son being reunited. And it was obvious to her now who had caused them to be apart. Her Oneida people!

They had abducted this man and killed his Mohawk wife. They had brought Swift Thunder's father to her castle, and she had thought that he had died there.

After hugging his father for several moments, Swift Thunder sat down in the chair that Moon Song had pulled up to the bed as she pulled another chair up and sat down beside him.

Swift Thunder was afraid that talking would tire his father too much, yet his father seemed to need to talk about what had happened to him.

He was remembering everything now. He said that his captors had thought that he was dead when they took him down from the stake and threw him into the forest to be food for the forest animals.

He couldn't remember coming to, or crawling to a cabin where white holy men were living. All he could remember was what the Black Robes had told him. They had taken him in and clothed and fed him and doctored his wounds. He was scarred terribly from beatings and knives slashing at him while he was a captive of the Oneida.

At that time, though, no one was sure who was responsible for the sins against him, because he couldn't remember. He couldn't remember his family, either, or even why he was in the area.

Until recently, when his memory began coming back to him in bits and pieces, he could remember only back to that day when he'd awakened in the priests' cabin. He had been with them ever since.

Yes, only recently did things start

coming back to him. Seeing Swift Thunder and Moon Song had caused the first stirrings of his memory. Although Swift Thunder was a grown man now, there was still some of the boy in his son's features.

Father Jacob explained that when Moon Song started talking of knights, of having been told stories about them when she was a little girl, by a white man who had been imprisoned by her people, memories flooded back to him.

Father Jacob reached up to his face and shuddered, then said that was why he wore the hood low over his face, and why he never ate with the other priests. Although he had become a priest himself, he had not wanted to disturb their meals by having a man with a hideous face at the table.

Listening to all that his father had suffered, Swift Thunder was overwhelmed by conflicting emotions. Knowing that it was Moon Song's people who had done this to his father, who broke his family apart so many long years ago, made his blood boil.

For Moon Song's sake, Swift Thunder knew he had to keep that anger hidden now.

Later, he would decide what to do about the Oneida's worst offense against him. Because of them, he had been wrenched from his family at a young age.

He put it from his mind for now. It was just too wonderful to be reunited with his father, to know that he had not died that day, as Swift Thunder had always thought.

"Father, oh, Father," Swift Thunder said, standing and leaning over to embrace his father again, an embrace that had been denied them for far too many years.

"Come with us to our home," Moon Song blurted out. "I will take care of you. I will make you well."

Swift Thunder moved from his father's arms. "Yes, come with us," he said thickly. "Our home is your home. It is only right that you should live there with us."

"I am not well enough yet to leave my bed," Father Jacob said, reaching both hands out for them. Moon Song took one of his hands. Swift Thunder took the other.

"But when I am stronger, I would like to come from time to time for visits," he said softly. "But this is my home now. I have joined the priesthood. I feel strongly about the religion."

He sighed, then said, "And I have made another decision," he said. "I shall never wear the hood again. It has not been fair to my friends at the monastery. They should

317

know me as I am today. And . . . I . . . will join them now at the dinner table. Today my life has begun again, so I must make certain I begin it without shame about how I look."

"I am so glad to know you feel that way, for you have isolated yourself for too long," Swift Thunder said. "And if you would rather stay and live with the priests, then I will just make it my habit to come and visit you. My wife and I, and the baby that will be born to us soon, will visit you often."

Father Jacob's eyes lit up. "You are with child?" he said as he gazed at Moon Song's flat tummy.

"Only barely," Moon Song said, laughing softly as she took her hand from his and slid it over her belly. "But time passes quickly. When the hot months of summer are upon us, our child, your grandchild, will be born."

"I have always wanted a grandchild," Father Jacob said, tears filling his eyes again.

"I have always wanted my father, and now I have him," Swift Thunder said, feeling as though his father had risen from the dead.

Chapter Twenty-seven

The air was heavy with the scents of love,
Stars rolled across the sky above.
Lost in love the whole night long,
Two hearts beating to love's sweet song.

Swaddled in warm blankets, the moon creating a white path of light as it streamed through the window beside them, Moon Song snuggled closer to Swift Thunder's muscled naked body.

They had just finished making love, but his body was tight and tense, not relaxed as she had thought it should be.

She would have thought he would be soaring with happiness to know that his father was alive.

But even while they were making love, it had not been the same as their other times. Although he was wonderfully sweet and tender, she could feel some reserve on his part.

Moon Song leaned on an elbow and spoke Swift Thunder's name to get his attention. When he turned his head and his eyes met hers, she saw something akin to torment in them.

"Why are you this way tonight?" she blurted out. "My *wachia,* why are you not happy? I know you well. There is much about you tonight that tells me something terrible is bothering you. Would it not help you to tell me about whatever it is that makes you foreign even to yourself tonight?"

"*Niu,* my wife, all of my life I wondered who it was who altered the course of my life," he said thickly. "As you know, I was hidden beneath the floors of our cabin while my mother was murdered and my father was taken captive."

She saw him shudder and reached out a hand to gently stroke his chest. "Go on," she murmured. "It will help you to get it all said tonight. Then perhaps you can put it from your mind forever. And having your father to love and hold should be enough now, *wachia,* to help get you past the agony of that day."

"It is as though I am that little boy again, reliving it as it is played over and over again in my mind," Swift Thunder said, his voice breaking. He ran his fingers through his long hair. "It all happened so fast. When my mother swept me into her arms and carried me to the trap door that led down below our cabin, tears fell from her eyes. As she lifted the door and told me to stay hidden, I knew then that I would never see my mother again."

He paused, closed his eyes, and gritted his teeth.

"Go on, get it all said this time; then perhaps you will never need to say it again," Moon Song encouraged.

"I felt like a coward down in that crawl space," Swift Thunder said. "I cried out to my mother not to close the door, and I pushed hard against it to stop her. But I was only a little boy. She was an adult. She got the door closed, and I heard her moving furniture so that the door would be hidden from the intruders. Also, the weight of the table made it impossible for me to open the door so that . . . so that . . . I could go to my mother's rescue."

He hung his head in his hand. "I felt that my father was already dead," he said, swallowing hard. "And then I heard my mother scream. Afterward there was silence except for the heavy footsteps of those who had wrongly come into our home. I knew then that my mother had joined my father in death."

"But your father did not die," Moon Song murmured. "He is alive, Swift

Thunder. Please focus only on that and let the torment of that day be gone from your heart forever."

He pushed himself up and sat on the bed, his gaze moving past her to stare out the window. "But do you not see, Moon Song?" he said tightly. "*All* of my life I wondered who did these things to my family . . . who took my parents from me."

He turned his eyes to her as she sat up beside him.

He smiled at her as she lovingly placed a blanket around his shoulders, and then drew one around her own shoulders.

Then his eyes became haunted again and his smile was gone.

"*Nui,* all of my life I've dreamed of vengeance, but I never knew against whom," he said thickly. "Now that I know who is responsible, what do I do? It is your people who took so much from me."

He reached for her hands. "These people, *your* people, take and take," he said, his voice breaking. "You would think the war, and their defeat, would be enough to make them stop and think before wreaking havoc again."

He reached a hand to her cheek. "But what they did to you . . . what they did to your mother . . . prove that is not so," he said tightly.

"But do you not see, my husband?" Moon Song said softly. "It is not my people as a whole who are responsible. It never *has* been my people who tormented others. These evil deeds have been perpetrated by Chief Charging Crow and his evil son."

"And so you are saying that no one but they should be held accountable," Swift Thunder said. "That you want me to again put my need of vengeance aside. You believe that if my warriors, under my lead, attack your people's castle to avenge the acts of one evil chief and his son, too many innocent people would die."

"It would hurt my heart to know that those I love might die for the sins of someone else," Moon Song said, lowering her eyes. Slowly she lifted her eyes to Swift Thunder. "But I know the hunger of vengeance, myself, and understand how it can be strong within your heart. I feel it myself. My mother lies in the ground now. You know who is the cause, as well as I, yet I urge you, husband, not to act on this need for vengeance that you and I share."

She shoved her blanket from around her shoulders, revealing her nakedness beneath the shine of the moon. Her eyes pleading with Swift Thunder, she reached for his hand and gently laid it on her belly. "Husband, please do nothing that would jeopardize our child's future," she said, a sob lodging in her throat. "If you go to war and you are downed by an arrow or war club, our child will be fatherless, as I was. I know how empty my life seemed at times without a father. You should also know. You were denied *your* father, as well. I do not want that for *our* child."

She crawled up next to him, and as his blanket fell away she moved into his embrace and clung to him. "And, oh, how my mother mourned for her husband," she said. "For so long I would hear her crying into the wee hours of morning. She never regained her spirit, her love of life, once her husband was taken from her. Nor would I, were you taken from me."

She clung harder. "I could not stand losing you," she said, suddenly sobbing. "Please, oh, please let this thing go. Let it die now, or it will forever plague you."

"It is so hard," Swift Thunder said. He felt how her body was trembling, heard the sobs coming from deep within her.

She came first now, in all things. And knowing how distraught it made her even to think that he might go to war out of vengeance, he knew he could not do such a thing to her.

Or their child.

He had no choice but to let the hunger for vengeance rest now inside his heart. In a sense, had he not achieved it already by taking the woman who had always been meant for the evil chief's son?

Already he had all the vengeance he needed. And he was so happy to know that he would be a father, and so happy to have found his father again.

"I will forget vengeance," he said aloud.

Moon Song's gasp of joy proved just how right he was to take this stance. He eased her away from him and gazed into her misty eyes. "I do not want to take away from the miracles I have been blessed with of late by spilling blood in the name of vengeance."

"Not even though the man who has wronged you still has his life?" Moon Song asked warily.

"He might still be walking, eating, and breathing, but in many ways he is not truly living," Swift Thunder said, smiling. "He lost much in the war, and worst of all, he has lost you to his worst enemy. Can you not see that I have won many victories over

Piercing Eyes, and even his father?"

He inhaled deeply, then drew her into his embrace again. "Yes, I have everything they want," he said softly. "So in that sense, I *have* achieved vengeance."

"And you have your father again," Moon Song said, snuggling more closely.

"And so do you," Swift Thunder said. "My father is now your father."

"I already feel a closeness with him," Moon Song said, smiling. "I truly believe he feels the same with me."

"I wish he would change his mind about living at the Praying Castle," Swift Thunder said.

"Perhaps in time he will change his mind and will come and live among our people at the Castle of the Bear," Moon Song said, then yawned and moved from Swift Thunder's arms. She stretched her arms above her head, her yawn changing into a slight giggle. "Husband, it seems your pregnant wife needs some sleep."

Swift Thunder reached his hands to her waist and easily lowered her to the pelts, then gently covered her with two blankets. "Sleep, my love, but when you awaken I probably will be gone," he said, stretching out beside her in the blankets.

She leaned on an elbow. "Where will you

be?" she asked. "We usually make love upon first awakening, and then enjoy a leisurely morning meal before you go into council with your warriors."

"I doubt that you know just how much of our food supply we took to the Praying Castle," Swift Thunder said, reaching a hand to sweep fallen strands of hair back from her eyes. "Tomorrow I must scare out some rabbits from hiding. Perhaps something even larger. I did see tracks of a big buck today in the snow. I need to bring home enough meat to last until the thaw, which should come soon."

He smiled. "Also, if you must know, I feel the call of the forest," he said. "I need to be there, to breathe in the scent of nature, to feel the wonder of it all around me."

Moon Song sat up quickly. Her eyes were bright and beaming. "I want to go with you," she said. "I, too, enjoy the forest. I would enjoy joining you on the hunt."

"Women do not join hunts," Swift Thunder said in a growl. Hunting *was* a man's job. A woman would not only jinx the hunt, but get in the way.

Moon Song straightened her back and folded her arms against her chest. "But, husband, I am not just any woman," she said, lifting her chin proudly. "I am the wife of a wonderful chief. I am my chief's princess." She smiled slowly. "And I can handle a bow and arrow as well as any man. After Father died, I had to help put food on my mother's table. I took my father's bow and arrow. I taught myself how to use them."

She frowned. "But even though I brought meat home to my mother, she accepted meat from the warriors of our castle, as well," she said. "I always wondered if it was because she felt ashamed of a daughter who did the work of a man, when all other girls my age concentrated only on beadwork and such as that."

"I am certain your mother just wanted to be sure that you had food enough to last the winter, for I doubt she allowed you to hunt when snow covered the ground and the rivers were covered with ice," Swift Thunder said.

"Well, yes, you are right about that," Moon Song said, shrugging. Then she moved on her knees before Swift Thunder and framed his face with her hands. "But that does not mean that I must stay behind now because of the snow, or false taboos about wives joining husbands on the hunt."

"I do not usually let taboos keep me from anything I desire to do," Swift Thunder said, feeling foolish now for allowing his fear of being jinxed to enter his mind.

"Yes, come with me," he blurted out. "But we must make sure you dress warmly enough."

He placed his hands on her tummy and smiled down at it as she covered his fingers with her own. "You are watching out for the welfare of two people now, not just one," he murmured.

She moved away from him and bounced down onto the pelts and snuggled into them. She grabbed a blanket and drew it up over herself. "I must get to sleep if I am to be worth anything to you tomorrow," she said, glad when he moved down beside her, snaked his arm around her waist, and drew her back up against the front of him. The warmth of his body melted into hers, making her sigh.

"Sleep, sweet *nui*," Swift Thunder said, reaching around her to cup a breast in his hand. His other hand lowered and stroked her tummy. "Sleep, little one, for your mother has talked your father into letting her go on an adventure with him tomorrow."

Loving Swift Thunder so much, Moon Song sighed joyously, then closed her eyes. "Good night, precious *wachia*," she murmured.

"Good night, adorable *niu*," Swift Thunder returned.

Moon Song did not go to sleep right away. She was relieved that Swift Thunder was allowing her to go with him tomorrow, yet she felt guilty for having told him a false tale about hunting for her mother's dinner table after her father was no longer there.

Except for one time when she had trapped a rabbit and then killed it with her mother's knife — the rabbit she had brought for Blue — she had never hunted. She had never even lifted her father's bow and arrow. But she had to convince Swift Thunder that she was capable of these things in order to convince him she would be all right on the hunt.

She had only told this white lie because she had felt a strong need to go with him tomorrow. She wondered if *he* had uttered a falsehood to *her* by saying that he was leaving for the hunt when he was really planning to go elsewhere.

Although he had said he would not seek vengeance, she could not believe he would let go of it so easily. Perhaps tomorrow he might be planning to go find Piercing Eyes and Chief Charging Crow. Perhaps he had thought it all out and knew of a way to kill those two men without beginning a war between the two clans.

She did not want to take a chance. Going with him tomorrow was a guarantee that he could not go through with such a plan.

But what of the next day, and the next? she suddenly thought, her heart sinking.

Vengeance was a thing that ate away at one's insides. She knew that. Because she had felt it so deeply inside her heart since her mother's death, she was afraid of her own feelings.

She had decided to let it go, or forever be tormented by something beyond her control.

Now she must make sure her husband had truly forsaken vengeance, as well!

Chapter Twenty-eight

The winds are cold,
We feel the chill deep in our soul.
Happiness was ours for a while,
You, my sweet woman, taught
my heart to smile.

Having left the dogs and sled behind, Moon Song was trudging through the snow beside Swift Thunder in search of the first kill of the day. He was hunting with his bow and arrow, a weapon that was light, but accurate.

The sunshine was actually hot on Moon Song's face where her skin was exposed beneath the hood that surrounded her face with soft, fluffy white fur. She even felt uncomfortably warm in her fur-lined coat.

She gazed up at the sky. If she did not see snow all around her, she could think she was experiencing a beautiful day in spring. The day before had been bitterly cold, but today it felt as though the spring flowers might pop up through the snow at any moment and show their rosy, smiling faces to the heavens.

Moon Song was glad for this quick

change, for she had not let on to Swift Thunder how she had dreaded accompanying him today on the hunt. Through the night, as she was comfortably snuggled in her bed beside Swift Thunder, she had hardly been able to get the half-frozen face of Father Peter off her mind. When the north winds of winter blew, one's face could get frostbite quite quickly.

No matter how the weather was today, Moon Song had still felt it was best to join Swift Thunder on the hunt, for she had not been able to rid herself of the suspicion that he might set off for the Oneida castle.

When she had awoken this morning and found Swift Thunder's hunting gear loaded on the sled, and the dogs harnessed to it, she had felt that she had been wrong to think Swift Thunder was going to do anything but hunt today. He seemed too intent on leaving for the hunt to have anything else on his mind.

"Are you warm enough?" Swift Thunder asked, breaking into Moon Song's thoughts.

She glanced quickly at him, hoping he could not tell from her expression that he had caught her thinking things she knew would hurt his feelings. A wife should never lack trust in her husband, especially a husband like Swift Thunder who had truly never given her cause to doubt him.

She felt ashamed now, and vowed never to doubt him again.

"I might say that I am *hot*," Moon Song said.

She glanced up at the brightness of the sun and sky, then smiled at Swift Thunder, who was sweating in his own fur coat, hood, and thick buckskin boots.

The only difference in his attire was that his hands were bare so that he could fire his bow and arrow once he spied game.

"*Tharonhiawakon* smiles down at us today by giving us pleasant weather so your wife's nose will not freeze off her face," she added, giggling softly.

"*Tharonhiawakon* has smiled down upon us since that first day we met, even though He delayed our ultimate joining for reasons only the Creator will ever know," Swift Thunder said. "But we are together now forever. That is all that matters."

"And our child," Moon Song murmured. "*Tharonhiawakon* has blessed us in that way, as well."

As Swift Thunder trudged steadily through the snow, which was quickly softening and melting from the hot rays of the sun, he gazed down at Moon Song's stomach. When he thought of how she would soon be looking, her tummy growing into a round ball, he could not help laughing softly with joy.

"What do you find amusing?" Moon Song asked.

"It was not a mocking laugh, but a laugh that spills forth from deep inside me at the joy I feel to think that soon I will see the growth of our child by the swell of your stomach," he said. "I shall lay my ear on your tummy each morning and say hello to our child. I shall even tell it myths of our people as it lies there, listening. I might even sing to the child."

"You will sing?" Moon Song said, laughing softly. "I will anxiously await that moment, for never have I heard you sing." She stepped closer to his side and gazed up at him flirtatiously.

"Sing to me?" she teased, her eyes dancing. "Now? Will you sing to your wife?"

He felt trapped, for no one, not even their unborn child, would truly want to hear him sing. He had never been able to carry a tune, and had only been teasing his wife when he had said that he would sing to their child.

Swift Thunder was not sure how to get out of this, for he did not want his wife to hear his meager attempts at singing. It would not only scare away whatever forest animals might be lurking in the bushes, it might even send his wife back to the sled to get away from him.

"Swift Thunder, I truly wish to hear —"

Moon Song didn't get the chance to prod her husband any more about his musical abilities, for she had heard the muffled sound of hoofs pounding the ground.

Moon Song looked away from Swift Thunder just in time to see a buck coming full tilt toward them.

"Swift Thunder!" Moon Song screamed, taking an unsteady step backwards.

Swift Thunder quickly notched his bowstring with an arrow and let it fly.

Moon Song's eyes widened and she swallowed a gasp behind her mittened hand as the arrow found its mark low on the buck's neck, bringing him to the ground with a loud, echoing whack.

When Moon Song and Swift Thunder reached the fallen animal, the buck's body quivered one last time, then went still, its large brown eyes locked in a death stare.

Moon Song loved animals so much, it pained her deeply to see such a lovely, valiant creature lying so still on the ground, its life's blood pouring from the wound and staining the ground and melted snow red.

But her father had told her long ago that in order for Moon Song's people to carry on, to survive into the next century, such kills would always be necessary.

As she was lost in grieving for this lovely creature, Swift Thunder was on his haunches beside the buck giving thanks, and sprinkling tobacco on the ground where the buck had died.

She was shaken from her reverie when Swift Thunder rose to his feet, handed her his bow for safekeeping, then yanked his thick-bladed, sharp knife from the sheath at his right side.

"The animal is too heavy for me to pack or drag to the sled, so I must butcher it here," Swift Thunder said solemnly. His eyes searched hers. "You know what comes next. You know it is not a pleasant task, or sight. Being with child, will you be able to stand watching? Know now, wife, that I plan never to ask of you the chore of butchering kill that I bring home from the hunt. Not even when you are no longer with child. You are my princess, my *people's* princess. Those sorts of chores will be done without you."

"I never want to be put above the other women in any way," Moon Song said, proudly squaring her shoulders. "No one will ever be able to say that I am behaving as though I am too good to do chores other women do. Never will I put myself above anyone, not even if I am the wife of a chief, the princess of our people. You must understand that is not the sort of person I am. Please do not ask that of me."

Swift Thunder smiled broadly. "You are proving to your husband exactly the sort of woman you are, and always will be," he said, nodding. "I will be sure not to ask you again to put yourself above anyone else. But know this . . . I will, myself, treat you as more special than anyone else I have ever known. Even . . . even . . . my mother, who was everything to a little boy who idolized her."

"I know you will," Moon Song said, smiling sweetly at him. Then she gazed down at the animal again. "Proceed. I will stand here and help you in whatever way I can. I never want to be useless. I want to help you in all ways possible."

"Just being with me, being my pregnant wife whom I adore, is all I ask of you," Swift Thunder said, then knelt down beside the buck, resting one knee in the small patch of snow beside the animal. He proceeded by first breaking off the arrow shaft that stuck halfway into the buck's body. He laid the shaft aside and began opening the buck with his knife and ridding him of his entrails.

Knowing that the animal was still too heavy to pack, Swift Thunder waited until the blood stopped dripping from the wounds, then scraped the blood from the animal's coat, and cut off his head as near his ears as possible.

As Moon Song watched, determined not to feel sick at her stomach from the sight, Swift Thunder cut through the second joints of the front feet to the muscles, then slipped his knife down between the bone and muscles to the hoof joint. By inserting these bones through the thin part of the hind legs, Swift Thunder was able to swing the animal over his shoulder.

Carrying Swift Thunder's bow for him, Moon Song turned and walked beside him back in the direction of their dogs and sled. Almost all of the snow was melted now, leaving a half-frozen, half-soggy ground upon which to walk.

When they reached the sled, Swift Thunder placed the prepared animal on the second sled which he had attached to the one on which he and Moon Song traveled.

Just as Moon Song handed swift Thunder his bow, a sound echoed through the forest that took them both off guard.

They gave each other a quiet, wondering stare.

When the same sound came to them again, like a baby crying from somewhere in the forest, Swift Thunder grabbed up his bow, fitted an arrow to it, and walked guardedly in the direction of the sound. Moon Song crept along beside him, her eyes searching for whatever might have cried out.

Again they heard the sound, nearer this time. It was close enough for Swift Thunder to recognize the cry.

It was the sound a cougar made when it was in pain.

"Blue," he whispered agonizingly.

Moon Song gave Swift Thunder a startled look. "You do not believe the animal that is crying out for help is . . . is . . . Blue, do you?" she gasped out, her heart skipping a beat at the thought of that precious animal being harmed in any way.

She understood Swift Thunder's look of pain. He was hoping that this *wasn't* Blue, but it very well could be, for he had not seen Blue for many months.

When the sound came again through the forest, Moon Song almost stopped with fear of what she was soon to see. If it was Blue, and he was dying, she was not sure she could stand it.

Moments later, they caught sight of an animal through a break in the trees a short distance away. Moon Song reached over quickly to grab Swift Thunder's hand.

She flinched when she heard Swift Thunder's mournful outcry. It was Blue. He lay stretched out on his side, where snow had melted long ago from the heat of his body.

Moon Song swallowed back sobs when she saw how lifeless Blue was, his eyes only half open as she and Swift Thunder ran and knelt beside him.

Clearly the cougar was unable to move. There were no visible wounds. But there was a long, thin leather thong tied around the animal's neck, the thong's other end fixed to the base of a tree.

"Oh, Blue," Swift Thunder gasped out, the pain of seeing his friend like this so deep he could hardly stand it. He reached for his knife and quickly cut the thong from the tree, then carefully sliced through

341

the leather binding his pet's neck.

Then Swift Thunder sat down on the ground and pulled Blue onto his lap.

Sobbing, Moon Song sat down beside Swift Thunder. "Who could have done this to Blue?" she said between sobs. "Someone purposely captured him, then left him here in the cold, to die."

Her heart almost broke when Blue's lethargic eyes gazed at her and he managed a soft mewing sound, then closed his eyes and fell into unconsciousness.

"Is he dying?" Moon Song asked, her voice catching.

Swift Thunder ran his trembling hand over Blue's body. He could tell that Blue had not gone long without food. His body was well filled out. And his body was still warm.

But it was obvious that he had been tied up in the cold long enough to cause harm. He did not want to think about his pet having spent even one night tied up out in the cold.

"We must get him home and beside the fire," Swift Thunder said, grunting as he pushed up from the ground with his muscled legs while holding Blue steady in his arms.

"You did not say," Moon Song said,

rising beside him. "Will . . . he . . . live?"

Swift Thunder began walking in the direction of his sled, the weight of the animal keeping him from running.

He glared down at Moon Song.

She saw now that anger had replaced Swift Thunder's pain at having discovered his beloved animal in such a condition. She had not ever seen him so angry, his eyes like two points of fire.

"For the sake of whoever did this, my pet had better not die," Swift Thunder said. "I am already planning ways to make the man pay. The manner of Piercing Eyes' death will depend on whether Blue lives or dies."

"You believe Piercing Eyes is responsible for this cowardly crime?" Moon Song said, keeping up with Swift Thunder, step by step.

"Who else would do something like this to an innocent animal?" Swift Thunder growled out. "Surely Piercing Eyes found out somehow about my love for Blue and he, or his warriors, searched until they found him."

"But they could not be certain this cougar was Blue," Moon Song said, hating to think that the warriors she knew as young boys could be so cold-hearted.

"No, they could not be certain. Perhaps

they just chanced upon Blue and tied him in hopes of my finding his carcass in the spring, dead and rotted," Swift Thunder said, shuddering at the thought.

When they reached the sled, Swift Thunder laid Blue among warm pelts and blankets and wrapped him in them.

Moon Song positioned herself in the sled beside Blue, close enough so that she could place an arm around him.

As Swift Thunder boarded the sled and shouted at his dogs, Moon Song talked softly to Blue and stroked his head lovingly.

"I promise we will make you well again," she murmured, a sob lodging in her throat. She sighed with relief when Blue's eyes opened and he gazed up at her. "Blue, we love you so. We . . . we . . . have missed you."

A slight noise proved to Moon Song that he was fighting hard for his life, and that he might even remember her.

As Swift Thunder shouted at his dogs and the sled careened over the half-melted snow, he swore to himself that he had had enough! He could take no more from Piercing Eyes, for he *knew* that it was he who had done this thing.

Although Swift Thunder had been given

many reasons to go after Piercing Eyes, he had held back for the sake of peace and harmony. But how could he be expected to let this feud go on and on without fighting back?

This was the last straw!

When Swift Thunder returned home he would get Blue comfortable and warm beside his lodge fire, and then he would go to his shaman, Spirit Wind, for guidance.

He hoped Spirit Wind would agree to Swift Thunder's plan to attack the Castle of the Turtle tomorrow.

He looked quickly around. Piercing Eyes and his warriors might even now be hiding and waiting to ambush Swift Thunder and his wife before they reached the safety of their castle.

He rarely used a whip on his dogs. But now, worrying about his wife's safety, he had no other choice. He grabbed up the whip, cracked it over the dogs' backs, and sent the sled racing over the patches of snow and half-frozen ground.

When he saw his castle's walls a short distance away, he breathed more easily.

Then there was a sudden loud cracking sound like that which came from a cannon!

Swift Thunder jumped and looked hurriedly over his shoulder at his wife.

Chapter Twenty-nine

The wind rushed through the trees,
She knelt there on her knees.
He watched her silent as she prayed,
He cried at the sacrifice she made.

Her hand trembling, Moon Song slowly opened the door of her longhouse and gazed out at the activity that she had hoped would have been discouraged by Spirit Wind.

But after Swift Thunder had gone and met with the shaman, Spirit Wind had said that it might be time to take action. Otherwise Piercing Eyes would begin to feel that he could do anything and get away with it.

Ignoring the cold air on her face, and knowing that Blue was comfortably warm beside the lodge fire, Moon Song clutched her shawl more closely around her shoulders and continued to watch the frantic activity around the fire.

One thing she was thankful for. The noise that had sounded like cannon fire had proved only to be ice cracking on the river.

After the initial shock, they had gone on

to their castle and gotten Blue warm by the fire.

Blue had eaten now, and it was wonderful to know that he was not going to die.

But the act that had brought him close to death aroused both fear and guilt in Moon Song's heart. She felt responsible for what was happening today, and what might happen in the next few hours.

Lives would be taken. Even her husband might die while attacking the Castle of the Turtle.

And she felt, oh, so torn. She loved her Oneida people except for Piercing Eyes and his chieftain father.

She had prayed all night for guidance, for a way that Piercing Eyes' madness might be stopped without lives being lost.

But nothing had come to her.

A battle seemed inevitable. She longed to rush outside and beg Swift Thunder not to begin a war that would spill blood on both sides of the Mohawk River.

But it was too late.

His plans were already set in motion.

And even if she had spoken up earlier, she knew that it would have been a useless thing. And she understood. She knew that Swift Thunder could no longer just stand by and watch the evil that Piercing Eyes spread wherever he went. He was beginning to feel as responsible for these deeds as though he had done them.

In the name of peace he had tried every means to avoid battle with the Castle of the Turtle.

After today, the old blood feud would begin anew, and who could know where it would end this time?

She shivered as she watched the sparks hissing from the large outdoor fire, as the frantic figures of the Mohawk warriors leapt into the air, twisting themselves into a ceremonial war dance. Rattles clapped a weird accompaniment to shrieks and howls as the warriors continued their ominous dances around the fire.

Tears filled Moon Song's eyes as she found her husband among the dancers. His face was streaked with war paint.

And even though it was fiercely cold today, the sun hidden behind black, rolling clouds, the warriors only wore brief breechclouts so that their painted bodies could spell out the intensity of their hatred for their enemy.

In all of the longhouses, mothers and sisters were preparing battle rations — bearskin bags of dried corn flour mixed with maple sugar.

Moon Song's own prepared bearskin bag lay just inside the door for her husband to take when he was through with the preliminaries of war.

She knew what came next. She had witnessed it time and again at her own castle.

When the dancing was done, and the men had reached the fever pitch of their anxiousness for war, the military expedition would begin with the thud of a hatchet in the village war post.

That would mean a warrior had a score to settle somewhere and that all who wished to follow him might do so.

Today, all but those who would be left behind to protect the women, children, and elderly, were accompanying their chief on the war path.

She could see it in their eyes, the hunger they had for war.

If she had never left her castle and met Swift Thunder, if she had married Piercing Eyes as her chief had demanded, perhaps none of this would be happening.

The castle of the Mohawk would be peaceful, with their children laughing and playing, the warriors hunting game for their wives' cooking pots, and the wives sewing, cooking, or nursing their children with contented smiles on their faces.

The people of the Castle of the Turtle would not be living their own last moments of joy.

Tears were now spilling from her eyes. Unable to watch the throwing of the hatchet, Moon Song hurriedly closed the door and leaned her back against it.

Hanging her face in her hands, she cried until her whole body ached from it.

When she felt something rubbing back and forth against her legs, Moon Song raised her face from her hands, her eyes wide as she gazed down at Blue. His strength was back, and he was showing his love for Moon Song by rubbing against her, his blue-green eyes lifting to hold hers.

For a moment she was able to forget everything that was transpiring outside her longhouse.

"Blue, oh, Blue," she cried.

Her shawl slipped away from her shoulders and fluttered to the floor as Moon Song fell to her knees and drew the cougar into her arms.

When Blue began stroking her cheek with his thick, rough tongue, licking her tears away, Moon Song giggled. "You are such a loving animal," she murmured. "I love you, Blue."

For the moment forgetting that her husband was painted for war, and that he was not in the longhouse, Moon Song shouted out his name, expecting him to come to her quickly from another room.

Then, like a knife stab in her heart, the frenzied war cries penetrating her closed door reminded Moon Song that Swift Thunder was not in their longhouse, ready to celebrate Blue's recovery.

As it was, Swift Thunder might never even know.

He was not planning to return to their lodge before departing for battle.

Moon Song was going to carry his battle rations to him when she knew he was ready to leave. Then she would die inside as she watched him walk through the wide gate and disappear from her sight.

"Oh, Blue, we may never see him after today, except . . . except . . . to prepare him for his burial rites," she whispered, still clinging to Blue as though in truth he were Swift Thunder.

Then she was aware of a different commotion outside her lodge.

Tense, eyes wide, she moved away from Blue as she heard loud voices, and then a strange sort of silence.

Someone had arrived, and whoever it

was had caused the war dance to stop.

The rattles no longer made their loud rhythmic clacking.

There was absolute silence now except for a voice that reached Moon Song's ears as a low drone through the closed door.

Moon Song opened the door and saw Swift Thunder talking with Winter Rain, who had gone ahead in his war paint to scout the area before the whole war party left for the Castle of the Turtle.

"What . . . ?" she began, but did not get the chance to say anything further before her husband ushered her back inside the longhouse, closing the door behind them.

His dark eyes searched Moon Song's face. Then he placed gentle hands on her shoulders and nervously cleared his throat.

"There will be no war party leaving our castle after all," he said. Sudden joy filled her eyes and she wriggled free of his grip and flung herself into his arms, sobbing with happiness.

"I am so glad!" she cried. "I did not want you to go. And not only because my people were in danger. If anything should happen to you —"

"Shh, Moon Song," Swift Thunder said, easing her away from him. "It is not what you think."

"What do you mean?" Moon Song asked, his demeanor puzzling her. "Why should I not be happy that you changed your mind? Both castles will be better off because of it."

"You did not want war, I know," Swift Thunder said, sighing heavily. "Nor did I. But you knew that the time had come for it, or . . ."

Blue came then to Swift Thunder, his blue-green eyes gazing up at him, bright and alert, proving to Swift Thunder that his pet was not going to die.

Swift Thunder knelt down and drew Blue into his arms. "Blue, it is good to have you back," he said, his voice breaking.

Moon Song knelt beside Swift Thunder and wrapped an arm around his neck. "We are now happy again, are we not?" she asked, her eyes smiling into Swift Thunder's. "Can I get water and wash the war paint from your face and body?"

Swift Thunder swallowed hard.

He released Blue.

Then he took Moon Song into his arms. "I have something to tell you," he said, holding her tightly, for he knew what he was going to tell her was going to momentarily tear her world apart.

"Winter Rain brings harsh news. Many

353

of your people at the Castle of the Turtle are dead."

He hurried on without waiting for her reaction. "We know who did the killing. They left their mark on the gate of the castle, a flag with a drawing of their Raven Crest. It was a neighboring Algonquian tribe. I know they have warred with the Castle of the Turtle in the past.

"Apparently someone at the Castle of the Turtle must have antagonized the Algonquian tribe again, and they have retaliated in the worst way possible.

"Many of your people died in the attack. Even innocent women and children now lie sprawled on the ground, their blood spilled.

"Winter Rain saw it with his own eyes. He came close enough to see that no sentries were guarding the castle, and that the gate had been left wide open.

"When Winter Rain saw the death and destruction inside, and realized that no one was going to stop him, he went on inside to check on what had happened. He discovered that among those who died early this morning were Chief Charging Crow and his son Piercing Eyes. The warriors who had not been slain were injured too badly to fight off any more aggressors."

Stunned speechless, aching for those she loved at the Castle of the Turtle, Moon Song could say nothing.

Swift Thunder felt a terrible guilt. It was hard now to think that he could have caused such deaths himself if he had followed through with his plan of attack.

He also knew now that if he had brought down women and children with his arrows, doing so would not only have harmed his wife's feelings for her husband, but also his own for himself.

Moon Song sighed heavily and tried to keep her sense of balance about what had happened. She would not allow herself to think of how this might have been her husband bringing news of the destruction he had caused. As it was, it was another enemy tribe that had caused such death and mayhem at her castle.

"Husband, how do you feel now about a people who have been stripped of everything, even their loved ones?" Moon Song asked, searching her husband's eyes. "I know you well. Surely you are feeling a deep empathy for those who lost so much today."

"Yes, I feel it in my soul, and I am glad that it is not I who am to blame," Swift Thunder said. He released her hands and wiped a smudge of war paint from his brow. He spread out his fingers before his eyes and stared at them. "Warring has never been my way. It has never been a fever in my blood. It is a shameful thing . . . warring, killing, maiming."

"I am so sad for my people," Moon Song said, staring into the dancing flames of the fireplace.

She then turned on a heel and gazed at her husband as he went to a basin of water and hung his head over it, splashing his face with water and cleansing it of the war paint.

"Husband, we must help my people," she said warily. "They *are* my people. I know them all. The women, the children —"

Her voice broke and tears fell from her eyes. "My husband, I feel their loss so deeply," she sobbed.

His face clean now, Swift Thunder went to Moon Song and drew her into his embrace.

As she clung to him, he stroked her back with gentle caresses.

"What do you want of your husband, the man whose life was changed as a child because of the Turtle Clan of Oneida?" he asked, his voice drawn.

"Those who are responsible are now

dead," Moon Song said, leaning away from him so that she could look into his eyes. "I . . . want . . . to go . . . and help my people. Will you allow it?"

"You will not be alone in this mission of mercy," Swift Thunder said thickly. "The river ice has split wide apart enough for canoes to travel in the river. Canoes of both men and women of this castle will go to yours and offer help," Swift Thunder said, seeing how his offer brought new warmth and joy to her eyes. "I will not even call council to get other opinions. Mine is all that matters. And I will see that everything that can be done for the survivors will be done."

"Thank you, thank you," Moon Song cried as she flung herself into his arms.

"Hate leads men to do things they would not ordinarily do," Swift Thunder said, his voice breaking. "Love mends those things that have been done because of hate. Why must there be death before there can be love?"

"Because people like Piercing Eyes and his father are born with hate in their hearts and spread it wherever they go," Moon Song said softly. "But now they are both gone. Perhaps, oh, just perhaps, those who are left since the attack will finally be able to live in peace and harmony. Perhaps they can love freely now that their evil chief and his son are no longer there."

Chapter Thirty

The wind blew the sunshine hither and yon,
She wondered —
Would she survive until another morn?

Moon Song's heart beat rapidly as she approached the Castle of the Turtle in her canoe. She had encouraged Swift Thunder to let her go on ahead, alone, to speak with her people about Swift Thunder's generous suggestions.

At first he had been adamantly against her traveling alone when a slaughter had only today occurred at the Castle of the Turtle. Although he had no quarrel with the Algonquian tribe that had attacked the Oneida, the Algonquian knew not of Moon Song's marriage to him, and if they saw her, she might be in danger.

Moon Song had told him that those who had done this ghastly deed were long gone. They had done what they had come for. They surely had no need of further vengeance.

And she had told him that she *must* do her part today, and in her own way, in order to quell the guilt she was feeling over having so much now, when her people had so little.

Seeing her determination to do what she felt was right, yet scolding her for feeling guilty about her happiness, Swift Thunder had told her to follow her heart.

He would not be far behind her in the river.

He would give her just enough time to arrive at the Castle of the Turtle and explain why she was there; then he would arrive with the other canoes of women and warriors who would assist the Oneida, if they allowed it.

Moon Song edged her way to the left, away from a jagged piece of ice, then steered her way into the center again.

She was glad that the sun was melting the remaining ice so that soon the river would no longer be impeded by it.

Today, the dead would be seen to. She hoped those who had survived the attack would willingly leave the Castle of the Turtle and travel down the river to the Mohawk stronghold.

They would find warmth, food, and shelter at the Castle of the Bear. There they could make plans for the rest of their tomorrows.

A quivering sigh breathed across Moon Song's lips as she got her first look at her people's castle past the bend in the river that she knew so well.

Oh, how often had she played along the banks of the river there? How often had she built sand castles with friends? How often had she skipped rocks across the river with the boys, proudly outdoing most of them?

Now no more children would play there.

All of the innocence of childhood had been destroyed today when the enemy had proven how cruel life could be.

Fighting back tears that threatened to spill from her eyes, Moon Song hurried her pace now, her arms aching from the continued paddling.

Soon she had her canoe beached. She forced herself to go inside the open gate to see the devastation firsthand.

As she took her first step inside the gate, she stopped, gasped, and covered her mouth with a hand to hold back a scream, for the sight she saw was almost too unbearable to stand.

But she had to be strong. She had much to do to help her people.

Above all else, she had to find a way to convince them that the best thing to do was to leave this place.

Let it be a memorial to what their lives had once been. Let it be a reminder of what evil leaders could bring to a people. As she stared at the bodies that lay on the ground, she placed the blame for this disaster on Chief Charging Crow and Piercing Eyes.

They had made enemies everywhere they went. This time they had made an enemy who was not ruled by a desire for peace.

She wondered what horrible deed had been done to cause the Algonquians to retaliate in such a venomous, heartless way.

"Moon Song?"

A voice at her left side made Moon Song turn with a start.

Four Toes!

He had survived the attack!

His head was bandaged and one arm hung limply at his side, while blood covered his fringed buckskin attire, but he was alive.

"Four Toes, oh, Four Toes, tell me what happened?" Moon Song said, rushing to him.

She would not allow herself to remember how he had followed Piercing Eyes' instructions when he had been ordered to guard Moon Song. And she would not believe that Four Toes could have had anything to do with Dove Woman's death. Surely, he would not kill an innocent Oneida woman only because his chief's son gave him the order to do it.

No, she would not believe he was guilty of that. She would think of him as he had been long years ago when they were children, playing, laughing, and just enjoying life.

She would never forget the day, though, that she had beaten him by skipping rocks farther than him many times in one day. The look on his face had made her wish she had not bested him. It was the look of a wounded animal. He had even cried like a baby!

"Our people were taken off guard," Four Toes said, his voice quivering. "The gate of our castle was wide open. There were no sentries. It was a day of celebration, for there was to have been a wedding. Piercing Eyes was marrying Star Shine. They were sitting on a flower-covered platform in the middle of the courtyard as our people sang and danced around them. Much food was being prepared for the feast that would be held after the wedding ceremony." He ducked his head. "It was I who was supposed to be watching from the main sentry post. But my friend was getting married. I . . . I . . . wanted to be there and enjoy it as much as everyone else."

"Piercing Eyes was getting married?" Moon Song gasped out. "And it was Star Shine? Star Shine of the Algonquian tribe who came and killed today?"

"Yes, it was that Star Shine," Four Toes said, slowly lifting his eyes. He gazed with silent pain into Moon Song's eyes. "Piercing Eyes sent many warriors to steal her away. I was among them."

He shook his head slowly back and forth. "I do not know how the Algonquians knew that it was the Oneida who abducted one of their women," he said, his voice drawn. "All I can conclude is that it was the tracks in the snow that led them to our castle. We left with the woman in such haste."

Moon Song was incredulous. "You, who know so much about tracking, allowed yourself to be careless on the day you abducted a chief's daughter?" she said mockingly. She stepped closer and glared into his eyes. "You are responsible for all of these deaths at our castle. You, alone, because you are undependable and ignorant!"

"But it was not I who gave the order to

abduct her," Four Toes said defensively. "Everything bad that has happened is because of Piercing Eyes." He lowered his eyes again. "If it had not been the Algonquian tribe, it would have soon been Swift Thunder, for I know that Swift Thunder had more than one reason to come to our castle for vengeance. Piercing Eyes even gave the order to find Swift Thunder's pet cougar. He gave the order to tie the animal and leave him to die."

"Did you, personally, follow that order?" Moon Song hissed, her anger raging inside her the more she heard this cowardly warrior reveal.

Four Toes swallowed hard, lifted his eyes, and nodded.

Unable to hold back her rage any longer, Moon Song yanked the glove from her right hand, then smacked Four Toes across the face with her bare hand.

"You coward, you *fool*," Moon Song cried. "You are even more responsible for all that has happened than Piercing Eyes, for you were too cowardly to stand up to the madman and refuse to follow orders that you knew were wrong."

Four Toes' eyes filled with tears. As he caressed his stinging flesh, where Moon Song's hand had left an imprint, he backed slowly away from her, then ran through the open gate.

Trying to get control of her anger, Moon Song closed her eyes and counted to five, then sighed heavily and turned. She was not surprised to find the survivors of the attack standing there, gazing sadly at her.

Moon Song's heart ached as she looked from one woman to another, from child to child, and from wounded warrior to wounded warrior.

"I have come to offer you help," Moon Song finally said.

When she heard footsteps behind her, she turned and found Swift Thunder and several warriors and women coming through the gate.

Then she turned toward her people again and explained what the Mohawk had to offer them. They were invited to go and stay at the Castle of the Bear until they could establish themselves at another Oneida castle. While they were at the Castle of the Bear, the wounded would be seen to, and everyone would be given lodging, food, clothes, and friendship.

When she finished telling them her husband's generous offer, no one responded at first.

Moon Song understood. In their eyes,

Swift Thunder was still an enemy. Moon Song, too, was part enemy, because she was married to one.

But as they thought things through, they realized that Swift Thunder's goodwill was genuine. As one, they accepted his generous offer.

Since the castle was going to be totally abandoned, the courtyard was used for burials.

One by one, the bodies were laid in the earth. One by one, words were spoken over their graves, so that the dead might depart for the hereafter in the sky.

Then, one by one, the women loaded up their most precious belongings in the many waiting canoes.

Moon Song wandered almost listlessly to the longhouse that had been hers and her mother's. Since her mother's death, no one had claimed the lodge. What remained there were reminders of Moon Song's life with her mother.

She went through the lodge, touching things that were precious to her, things that her mother had made with her own loving hands.

"Let us fill a bag with the belongings that mean much to you," Swift Thunder said as he stepped beside Moon Song.

"Then you will at least have a part of your mother with you."

"Yes, it would mean a lot to me to have these things," Moon Song murmured.

She tried hard not to remember that terrible moment when she had seen her mother sitting lifeless in the canoe.

She had not told her people how her mother had died, nor by whose hands. They had been so preoccupied with grieving over their own losses, they had not even thought to ask about Dove Woman.

She saw no need to reveal to them the tragic way her mother had died. It was something best left unsaid, for every time she told of the tragedy, it made her relive it all over again.

She walked around the longhouse, picking up her mother's embroidery work and material that had been left for her next sewing chore. Strings of beads, beautiful shells, painted porcupine quills, and even an occasional river pearl lay in her mother's sewing basket.

That was the most prized possession of all to Moon Song, for all of her mother's sewing supplies were there.

As Moon Song used them, she would feel close to her mother. Then she found something else loved by her mother . . . an onyx and liquid silver necklace. She proudly placed it among the other things, to keep forever.

Finally everyone was loaded in the many canoes.

Swift Thunder looked from canoe to canoe as he stepped into his own after helping Moon Song into her small, individual canoe. He was touched deeply by the eager faces of the Oneida people as, one by one, the canoes were shoved off and headed in the direction of his castle.

He now saw hope in their eyes that had been extinguished until they realized what Swift Thunder was offering them.

He felt good that he had given these people a second chance at life, when he could have hardened his heart against them and left them stranded, hungry, and afraid.

Smiling, he sat down in his canoe, which held ten of the Oneida women and children and the meager belongings they had chosen to take with them to their new life. He shoved away from the riverbank and guided his canoe down the river.

Moon Song had left only moments ago, so Swift Thunder was following her. Behind him, all of the other canoes were now following in single file.

Moon Song felt many things at this moment, most of all pride in her husband who could so courageously help a people who had been his enemy since the day he was born. By helping the Oneida, he had confirmed to her, and everyone who knew him, what a generous, kindhearted, peace-loving man he was.

Even if he had gone on the war path, painted with war colors, she now doubted that he would have actually attacked her people, killing women and children.

No, she would not believe that he could do that, not after seeing his love for the Oneida children today, the way he carried so many of them to the canoes and placed them lovingly in the arms of their mothers.

She would *never* believe that he would aimlessly kill the innocent to take vengeance on two heartless men.

"Men who are now cold in the ground," Moon Song said. She had felt victorious the moment they had been placed in their shallow graves, the dirt still too frozen to get anyone buried very far beneath the surface.

"Their reign of terror is finally over," she added, sighing gratefully.

Suddenly something caught her attention at the edge of the riverbank, where ice still clung to it.

She strained her neck and paused momentarily, then gasped, for she was looking at a dead body.

It was Four Toes! And there was a knife in his chest!

Surely he had taken his own life, tormented by the wrongful deeds he had done.

Now the last of the evildoers was gone. When Moon Song thought of what he had done to Blue, she began to believe that he could have even been the one who'd thrust the knife into her mother's chest.

Perhaps the very knife that he had used to take his own life?

Yes, finally the end had come to all of those who had made life miserable for so many.

Chapter Thirty-one

Confusion began to smooth itself out,
What seemed hard to give was now
easier to take!

The ceremonial fire in the center of the vast Mohawk council house sent flames leaping upward, the smoke spiraling lazily through the opening in the roof above.

The crowd assembled inside the council house was double the usual number, for added to the Mohawk people were the survivors from the Oneida castle.

Swift Thunder had asked everyone to meet in the council house to foster the peace that he hoped to seal today by offering a Two-Row Wampum to the Oneida chief who had been named by his people this morning.

Forked Lightning, the strongest of the male Oneida survivors, and a distant cousin of their former chief, had humbly accepted the title of *sachem* from his Oneida people. Henceforth he would be their spokesperson.

Several days had passed since the

tragedy at the Oneida's castle. The survivors were now temporarily established in longhouses at the Castle of the Bear, the largest of them holding several families.

The pain and anguish that had been struck into the hearts of the Oneida that day were still worn on the faces of the men, women, and children. But the wounded were proving they were strong enough to survive.

Sitting beside Swift Thunder in the council house, Moon Song felt fortunate that she still had him. So many women had lost their husbands during the attack. Had she never met Swift Thunder, she would have been one of those who had witnessed the horror of the raid. She might even have died. . . .

Her thoughts grew still when Swift Thunder, dressed in fringed and beaded buckskin, stood up. Everyone's eyes were drawn to him.

The silence in the large longhouse was overwhelming. All that could be heard was the popping and crackling of the council fire.

There was a pleasant aroma of food which had been prepared earlier and was warming at the edges of the fire, to be eaten after the meeting.

But it would not be the usual celebration. No dancing or music accompanied this solemn occasion. Too many were still in mourning to do any of those things.

Today the council was for another reason: to seal a new bond of friendship between those who had only known hate and resentment toward one another before.

Friendship was needed now, for it might be some time before the Oneida people could travel north to join others of their tribe. The cold weather and their injuries would hold them back.

Perhaps when spring came in its full glory and promise, Swift Thunder could help lead the Clan of the Turtle northward, to find those of their own people who would take them in out of kindness and love.

Swift Thunder had already told them they did not have to leave at all . . . that they were welcome among his people. He reminded them that Moon Song was there, and would be there always.

Thus far, the people of the Turtle Clan had not said what they wished to do. They could hardly think past the horror of seeing their loved ones downed by hatchet blows, knives, and arrows. They were not yet ready to make definite plans for the future. But they repeated over and over their gratitude toward the Mohawk.

"Today, as we are all a part of the Iroquois League, both Oneida and Mohawk, allow me to open council by offering thanks to the earth where men dwell, to the streams of water, to the maize and the fruits, to the medicinal herbs and the trees, to the animals that serve as food and who offer their pelts as clothing, to the great winds, and the lesser winds, to the Thunderers, and the sun, to the moon, to the messengers of the Great Spirit who dwells in the skies above, who gives all things useful to men, who is the source and the ruler of health and life. Then shall I now declare this council open."

All of the warriors of both clans moved forward and sat in a half circle around the fire with Swift Thunder.

A young brave brought a calumet pipe to Swift Thunder, and a flaming twig to light it. Then Swift Thunder began the ritual of the pipe.

Toward the east he blew the smoke, then to the west, to the north, and finally toward the sky. He lowered the pipe and rested the bowl upon one of his knees where his legs were crossed before him.

"To the world and to its master, *Tharonhiawakon,* the smoke of the Mohawk rises," he intoned.

He then handed the lit pipe to Chief Forked Lightning. The Oneida could hardly hold it with his injured hand, which along with his other arm had been half crushed beneath a war club.

His injured hand trembling, Chief Forked Lightning held the pipe before him, drew smoke into his mouth from the long stem, inhaled it and then let the smoke spiral forth into the silent air.

"To the world and to its master, *Tharonhiawakon,* the smoke of the Oneida rises," he said, his voice breaking.

As rings of smoke circled peacefully from the calumet, Forked Lightning envisioned those who lay dead in their graves back at his castle. He was glad when Swift Thunder's voice broke into his thoughts.

"Our two clans come together today, smoking the pipe together, to signify the rebirth of our role in the Iroquois Federation," Swift Thunder said.

He nodded to the young brave to come and take the pipe away.

When that was done, Swift Thunder stood up, then reached down beside Moon Song and lifted a buckskin bag into his arms.

As everyone watched, he took something from the bag and held it up for the people to see.

It was a *Kahswenhtha,* a Two-Row Wampum Belt, which was seen as good medicine. The first such belt had been introduced when a special agreement was needed to restore peace between the Dutch and the Indians many moons ago.

This belt was soon recognized as an agreement of peace and respect for each other's way of life. It had since been used in the tribal and intertribal affairs of all Iroquois.

It was being introduced today by Swift Thunder as a way to seal the agreement of peace and respect between the Turtle Clan of the Oneida and the Bear Clan of the Mohawk.

Moon Song gazed in awe at the belt her husband held up. It was made with a background of white wampum beads, with two rows of purple beads from one end of the belt to the other. The white and purple disk-shaped beads had been painstakingly fashioned from clam shells strung together.

She looked again at her husband, proud of how he was bringing her people and his together today. Everyone had known of

Swift Thunder's quest for peace. There would be no more talk about blood feuds between the Oneida and the Mohawk. Her husband would not allow it.

And she knew Forked Lightning. He was a man of good heart. She could see him and her husband becoming good friends. It was clear that they were beginning to admire one another.

Smiling, Moon Song listened now to her husband. His words were bringing looks of peace and love to the faces of those who listened.

Even those of the Turtle Clan who had never had the chance to see him before were looking at him with admiration.

"As the Dutch laid particular emphasis on this 'Belt Of the Treaty Of Peace and Friendship,' so do I today," Swift Thunder said. "This Wampum Belt, which symbolizes our six nations, has the power to make a good mind . . . a warm heart . . . and continued peace."

He gazed down at Forked Lightning and smiled, then nodded at him. "Come, Chief Forked Lightning," he said. "Come and stand before me."

Everyone followed Forked Lightning's movements as he rose and then stood before Swift Thunder.

"Chief Forked Lightning, I want to present you and your people with this Two-Row Wampum Belt so that you and I can be like brothers, and our people can be as though born of the same woman's womb," he said proudly.

He offered the belt to Forked Lightning, smiling when the Oneida took it in his maimed hands and shakily held it out before him for everyone to witness this kindness toward a fallen people.

"Chief Forked Lightning, the two rows of beads symbolize two paths, or two vessels, traveling down the same river side by side," Swift Thunder said. "One is a birch bark canoe of the Oneida, the other a birch bark canoe of the Mohawk. We shall travel the river together now, side by side, as friends."

Swift Thunder reached out and gently touched the outstretched belt. "The background of the white beads represents the Mohawk River, and the two parallel rows of purple beads represent our people's two vessels traveling the river. It is recognized that the river is large enough for the two vessels, for us two clans, to travel down together. It is the responsibility of the people in each vessel to steer a straight course. Such is the symbolism of this gift to you today. It is an emblem of mutual respect."

Touched by her husband's gesture of friendship toward people who were only recently his avowed enemy, tears fell from Moon Song's eyes. She could never love him any more than at this moment.

She would proudly, lovingly tell their sons and daughters about their father's big heart and love for all humanity. They would learn from his example and be as good as he.

She wiped her tears away and listened to Forked Lightning's response to Swift Thunder's offer. Tears welled in the Oneida chief's eyes as he began a speech of gratitude that brought tears to almost all who were gathered there.

Chapter Thirty-two

Our love is blessed with magic it seems,
Love fills all our dreams.
You are forever in my heart.
Look, my woman, we will never part!

The moon was high and bright in the sky. Several days had passed and the people of the two clans were more comfortable now in the presence of each other.

The children were helping in this respect, for they were creating bonds where before there had only been thoughts of hate and vengeance.

Tonight, as the darkness and cold deepened at the Castle of the Bear, the fire at the center of the council house burned bright and warm.

Around it sat as many as could fit into the longhouse, for tonight, Long Moon, the Turtle Clan's beloved storyteller, sat beside Eagle Flying, the Bear Clan's master storyteller. Each would spin tales that were known to leave people spellbound.

A sudden bout of sickness brought on by

her pregnancy had delayed Moon Song and Swift Thunder's arrival at the council house.

Moon Song lay with her head resting on Swift Thunder's lap as they sat on blankets before their lodge fire. Swift Thunder lovingly caressed her brow with a cool, damp buckskin cloth.

"You should be with your people at the council house, sitting beside Chief Forked Lightning," Moon Song murmured. "This is a good opportunity to show camaraderie with my people's chief. With you and Forked Lightning there, smiling, even laughing at an amusing tale or two, our people will forget their pain. Seeing both chiefs so carefree will bring sunshine and peace to the hearts of those who have not yet accepted how their worlds have been changed."

"Yes, I know the importance of this, but you are of primary importance to me," Swift Thunder said. He laid the cloth aside, then drew Moon Song up into his arms. "My beautiful, pregnant wife. Soon the time will pass, and then you will no longer be ill from pregnancy. You will blossom more and more each day. You will be radiant. It will be such a wondrous thing to see. I will beam from happiness and pride."

"I am so happy I am with child," Moon Song said, sighing contentedly. "And do not be afraid that being ill with this child will make me reconsider having many. Everything I go through, good or bad, while pregnant will be well worth it in the end. Seeing the joy the child will bring you will be my joy. I love you so, Swift Thunder."

He drew her onto his lap and cradled her close as his lips went to hers, gentle and sweet.

When they heard laughter wafting through the air from the council house, Moon Song leaned quickly away from Swift Thunder and rose to her feet.

Standing over him, she reached a hand out for him. "Come," she said softly. "Let us join our people now. Let us join in the laughter. Let us be mesmerized by tales told by our storytellers."

Swift Thunder took her hand and rose to his feet.

He looked down where he had last seen Blue. The impression of the cougar's body was all that remained in the blankets that had been Blue's bed.

"I cannot believe that Blue is gone again," he said, his voice drawn. He threw his free hand into the air in frustration. "First he is here, and then he is gone again."

"I am sure it is because he has loved ones out there somewhere who are longing for him, as he was longing for them," Moon Song said, feeling her own sadness over Blue's absence. "In time he will return to us again. How could he not? He received such loving care from both of us."

"It is apparent that it is not our sort of love that sustains Blue," Swift Thunder said, reaching for a fur-lined cloak and placing it around Moon Song's shoulders.

He then slipped into his own fur coat and walked with Moon Song from the longhouse, leaving the door ajar in case Blue chose to return home.

"When I left the door open for Blue to take his usual morning walk, I did not even think about him not returning again," Swift Thunder said. "I thought he was home for good. He seemed content enough."

He slid an arm around Moon Song's waist and held her steady against him as they walked over the freshly fallen snow that had turned the world all white and glistening again.

"We both should have known that he missed his freedom, as well as his mate," Moon Song murmured. "When I saw some restlessness, I should have warned you about it. But my thoughts were filled with so many other things, I just did not remember to tell you."

"I saw him pacing the longhouse myself but did not think much of it, because Blue has always been a pacer," Swift Thunder said. He paused when he thought he saw a movement out of the corner of his left eye.

"What is it?" Moon Song asked, stopping when Swift Thunder stopped. She followed his steady gaze, then gasped when she saw a sudden streak of tawny fur, then two more.

Suddenly three cougar kittens rushed out of the shadows, with Blue proudly following them.

"Blue, you have returned, and oh, look at your kittens!" Moon Song cried.

She bent to her knees in the snow and laughed softly as the kittens began mewing and playing with one another.

Swift Thunder was all smiles; then he sucked in a deep breath when he saw another set of green eyes peering out of the brush toward him. It could be nothing but Blue's mate! He had brought his entire family to Swift Thunder and Moon Song!

Swift Thunder knelt down beside Moon Song and leaned close to her. "Moon Song, we have another visitor," he whispered. "Over there. You can see the eyes. It is Blue's mate. She has accompanied him and the kittens, but it is apparent that she is too skittish to come near us. She cannot trust her husband's judgment that easily, for it is not a natural thing for cougars to ally themselves with people."

"Unless it is done when the cougar is a kitten, like Blue, and now *his* kittens," Moon Song whispered back. She could see the eyes herself, and wished the female cougar would come out of the darkness so that Moon Song could at least see her.

"We must not do anything that will frighten her away," Swift Thunder whispered. "She will not want to leave her children or her mate with people. But if she feels threatened, she will abandon both Blue and her kittens and never be seen again."

"Then I shall be careful how I behave with her kittens and mate," Moon Song said, only daring to stroke one of the beautiful little things as it came to her.

Blue paced back and forth, his chin lifted proudly, his eyes watching as the humans made much of his kittens. And then he carried first one kitten and then another to its mother. He gave Swift Thunder and Moon Song each a loving lick on the hand,

and slipped into the darkness with his family.

Swift Thunder rose to his feet and helped Moon Song up. Arm in arm they stared for a moment longer at the spot where Blue and his family had disappeared into the darkness.

"I feel this is the last time we shall see Blue," Swift Thunder said, his voice breaking. "It is best for him to live in the wild, away from hunters who might want his pelt."

Moon Song reached a gentle hand to her husband's face. "We would not want such a fate for our beloved Blue, nor any of his family," she murmured. "It is enough for me that I have had the time I had with Blue. And the kittens? Oh, how adorable they are. I hope they are safe forever and ever."

"When you want to hold a cat, we can go to Father's Praying Castle and you can hold Josephine," Swift Thunder said, smiling. "She enjoys your company. You are probably the only woman she has ever known."

"Do you still feel sad about your father's choice to stay at the Praying Castle instead of coming to live with us?" Moon Song asked softly.

"I want my father to be happy," Swift Thunder said. "He and Father John are good friends. They are good for one another."

Moon Song could hear the voice of the storyteller that she had listened to as a child. She smiled. "Let us go into the council house," she said. "I so love the stories. Come inside and hear my storyteller's skills. I love Long Moon so much and I am so grateful to *Tharonhiawakon* that He saved our storyteller from the recent tragedy. He will soon be ninety winters of age! Is not that incredible?"

Swift Thunder's eyes widened in wonder. "His age matches that of my people's storyteller," he said. "Surely it was the destiny of these two storytellers to live to this age so they could meet and combine their stories."

"Two master storytellers under one roof," Moon Song said, sighing.

"Let us go and listen and marvel together at what we hear," Swift Thunder said, quietly opening the door so that he would not disturb the one telling the story, nor those who were being transported beyond themselves by the wondrous tale.

They did not work their way to the front of the crowd where a platform sat awaiting their arrival beside the platform where Chief Forked Lightning and his wife Yellow Daisy sat.

Before Moon Song sat down beside Swift Thunder on the matted floor of the council house, she smiled at the empty bowls and cups beside both of the storytellers. Before their tales had begun, they had been given corn soup and pine-needle tea and places close to the warm fire.

She gazed then at Long Moon and smiled when she recognized the pipe he held and occasionally puffed on. It was a pipe given to him by her very own father long ago, one that her father had made specifically for Long Moon as a way to thank the storyteller for the tales that he had heard as a child from this very same man.

She had sat and watched her father make the pipe. The bowl was made of clay. The bowl depicted a face that her father said he had seen in a dream, a face that now looked at the elderly storyteller each time he held the long stem between his lips.

Even now Long Moon paused to take a few puffs, then gazed slowly around at the crowd.

When Moon Song saw the elderly man's right eye twitch, she thrilled inside, for her father had explained to her that when anyone saw that happen as a storyteller sat weaving his tales, it was a good omen!

Moon Song sat down beside Swift Thunder just as Long Moon spoke up.

"*Onen-tsi-ne-i-nakkara?*" Long Moon said. "This now is my next story. Do you all wish to hear it told to you?"

He held up the pipe in a gesture that commanded attention.

As though one entity, the people responded at once.

"Yes!" they all chimed in, the women, children, and men alike leaning forward eagerly to hear. "Tell us! Tell us your next story!"

When he began his story, Moon Song smiled brightly, for she recognized this story to be the very oldest of his tales, and the most prized. He had shared it with Moon Song when she was a child of three winters and he was already growing into an old man.

"Listen well, my children," Long Moon said, resting the bowl of his pipe on his robed knee, for he wore a long, plain buckskin robe, and his hair, so white it seemed to be the reflection of the snow that covered the earth outside the lodge, hung in thin wisps upon his frail, lean shoulders.

His face was a crater of wrinkles. His eyes were sunken almost into their sockets, yet when he talked, they beamed and lit up the room.

Everyone seemed to have stopped breathing as they listened.

"The woman in Skyland dreamed that the great sky tree was uprooted," he said in a voice that was smooth and hypnotizing. "The woman looked through the hole left by its roots and saw the earth far below her. It was unlike the earth today. There was no land. There was only water."

He paused, drew in a long, quivering breath, then continued. "As the woman looked in wonder down below her, she slipped. She desperately clutched at a tree branch that lay near the hole. But she only stripped away a handful of seeds. Then she fell."

Again he paused, but this time he lifted his pipe to his lips and sucked leisurely on the stem.

Everyone watched the lazy swirls of smoke rising from the pipe, then looked at Long Moon again as he rested his pipe and resumed talking.

"Animals and birds of the water looked up and saw the woman falling toward them," he said, his old eyes looking slowly around to see if everyone still listened attentively, or if some of the elderly were drifting off to sleep.

When he saw the heads of two old women nodding and their eyes beginning to close, he stopped his tale.

"Are you all awake and listening?" he said, chuckling when that brought the women's heads up and again they watched and listened.

"The animals and birds decided among themselves to help the falling woman," he continued. "The geese flew up and caught her between their wings. The other birds and animals saw that she needed a place to stand, so they dove down to bring up earth from the bottom of the huge body of water, but failed. Only the muskrat could finally bring up the earth. Then the Great Turtle offered its back as a place to spread the earth the muskrat brought up. The woman from the sky stepped onto this new moist earth. She then dropped the seeds from the sky-tree into her footprints. From these seeds grew the first plants. And when her child was born, who was the first on the new earth, the child was a girl. This girl child would grow up to marry the west wind. . . ."

The story went on and on and no one

tired of hearing it, for everyone was captivated.

Moon Song reached over and took Swift Thunder's hand in hers. He turned and smiled at her, for both knew that one day their children, too, would be spellbound by the storyteller's tale, and both seemed to believe it would still be Long Moon who would be doing the telling. Or perhaps it would be High Cloud, the Mohawk storyteller, who smiled along with everyone as he listened as attentively as if he had never heard the tale, when in truth Swift Thunder had heard him tell it many times when Swift Thunder was a small child.

"It is a good night," Moon Song whispered to Swift Thunder.

"Every night, every moment with you is good," Swift Thunder whispered back.

Content that everything seemed to be working out for everyone, and that her world was falling into place again, Moon Song silently gave thanks to her husband, who had made it all possible for everyone.

She hoped that both peoples, the Oneida and the Mohawk, understood this, and would make every effort to keep the peace Swift Thunder had begun.

She slipped a hand over her tummy. She smiled, for now she knew that she was free to concentrate on the child that grew within her. She would be counting off the days, weeks, and months until that precious day when she could nurse her child the first time at her breast.

Chapter Thirty-three

Their children were perfect in every way!
Swift Thunder and Moon Song's
   love was great!
Every day they thanked Tharonhiawakon
   above for their many blessings!

Many years had passed now, in peace. The Oneida Clan of the Turtle had joined another Oneida clan further north, but before they had left for the journey to their new home, Chief Forked Lightning had vowed continued peace with the Mohawk Clan of the Bear.

In the valley of the Mohawk, it was now late summer and it was time to celebrate the gift of corn with the Green Corn Festival.

The first crop of corn was always a beautiful sight to the Mohawk because it meant that the earth's fertility had not failed them.

In fact, the three sister goddesses, the corn, the bean, and the squash, had been generous. The spirits of these plants were deified and known as *De-o-ha-ko*, the "life supporters."

The three plants were referred to as "three sisters" because they were envisioned as three beautiful women clothed in the vines of their respective plants.

With the people seated on rich, soft pelts on both sides of the council longhouse, Swift Thunder was standing tall and proud before them, ready to express the gratitude of his people to their Great Creator, *Tharonhiawakon,* while Moon Song watched from her nearby platform.

Moon Song's eyes were brimming with tears as her own pride welled within her over the accomplishments of her chieftain husband.

Their four-year-old son, Red Eagle, was sitting nearby now with his grandfather, Father Jacob. He had come to join the celebration, but he would return soon to his duties at the Praying Castle.

Father John had died two moons ago and Father Jacob was now the monastery's acting head priest.

Moon Song was big with child again.

She was doubly thankful for this pregnancy, for she had begun to think that she might not have any more children since so much time had passed since her first pregnancy.

But today her family was not only celebrating the Green Corn Festival, they were also giving thanks to *Tharonhiawakon* for having blessed them with a healthy son, and perhaps soon a healthy daughter.

Content now to sit and watch her husband in his role of chief, Moon Song reveled in the sound of his deep, friendly voice as he began reciting a Mohawk prayer of thanksgiving.

"We return thanks to our mother, the earth, which sustains us, to the wind, which moves the air and banishes diseases, to our grandfather *He-no*, that he has protected his grandchildren and has given to us the rain, to the sun, that he has looked upon the earth with a beneficent eye!"

Moon Song glanced over at her son, whose eyes had not left his father since Swift Thunder had begun speaking.

Red Eagle listened intently as Swift Thunder expanded on his prayer of thanksgiving, saying more about *He-no*, the Thunderers.

Moon Song turned her eyes back to her husband. His name had been taken from his people's pride in their Thunderers, even though at times the Thunderers could be savage.

"And now this is what *Tharonhiawakon* decided," Swift Thunder said, his eyes proud as he recited something that always came with ceremonies that were celebrated when their land had been blessed with the thunder and rain.

"*Tharonhiawakon* said, 'I shall have helpers who will live in the west. They will come from that direction and will move about among the clouds, carrying fresh water. They will sprinkle all the gardens which grow of their own accord on the earth. There will be a relationship when people want to refer to them: they will call them grandparents, *he-no*, the Thunderers.' He left them in the west. They always come from that direction. They are performing their obligation, moving about all through the summer among the clouds, making fresh water, rivers, ponds, and lakes. We now give thanks for them, our grandparents, *he-no*, the Thunderers."

With this everyone chanted, "*Wi-munai*," meaning, "It is true, indeed."

Swift Thunder then smiled and reached his hands out toward his people. "Now it is time for feasting on rich, thick stews of meats and vegetables, hot corn dumplings, ash-baked apples, and mushrooms!" he shouted.

The screams of laughter and the singing of many voices echoed through the air as they rose and hurried from the council house. Outside a feast had been spread, and later there would be dancing which would continue into the night.

Moon Song sat still on her platform until everyone was gone from the council house except for her husband, son, and father-in-law . . . and a kitten on Red Eagle's lap that Father Jacob had brought from the Praying Castle.

It seemed that Josephine had disappeared for a while and had returned heavy with kittens.

This one was now Red Eagle's.

Blue had also recently returned for a brief visit. The cougar had been gone for some time, but he was still alive, scarred somewhat from his battles, but alive.

Swift Thunder held a hand out for Moon Song. "Do you hear the laughter?" he said, smiling. "Do you hear the music? *Niu,* do you feel like joining the fun? Or do you require rest for a while on the softness of our feather mattress?"

The mention of the feather mattress sent Moon Song's eyes to Father Jacob, who had accompanied two other priests the day they had delivered the mattress that Father John had promised.

It was a gift she cherished, and not only

because of the comfort of it, but because it had been given to her by Father John, whom she had grown to love like a father.

She rose slowly to her feet and grabbed at the small of her back with both hands when a quick, sharp pain shot through it.

When Swift Thunder saw Moon Song wince and grab her back, he was concerned. She had tried so hard to get pregnant after Red Eagle's birth, but something had kept the seeds he sent into her womb from developing into children.

Now that she was pregnant with their second child, *very* pregnant, everyone had been watching Moon Song, hoping that nothing would stop this pregnancy from going full-term.

"I think I should go to our longhouse, but I would rather not lie down on our beloved feather mattress," Moon Song said, trying to hide the pains that were now coming at steady intervals, with time only to take a deep breath between them.

"But your face is so flushed and I see pain in your eyes," Swift Thunder said, taking her hand and helping her down from the platform. "Bed rest is surely what you need."

Moon Song gave him a soft, sweet smile as she placed her moccasined feet on the floor. "*Wachia,* I do not want to soil our mattress in childbirth," she said, laughing softly when she saw the sudden look of panic in her husband's eyes.

"You are soon to have the child?" he gasped out.

"Perhaps even here in the council house if you do not get me quickly home," Moon Song said.

She gave Red Eagle a soft smile as he came and clutched at her skirt, his wide green eyes gazing up at her.

"Yes, my son, you soon will have a brother or sister," she said, reaching a hand to run her fingers lovingly through his thick black hair.

Red Eagle was Indian in every respect but one. His kinship with his white grandfather was proved by his eyes, which were so green they seemed the color of the beautiful grass of spring.

"Come now, Red Eagle," Father Jacob said, whisking the long skirt of his black robe around his legs as he came hurriedly to take his grandson's hand. "We must step aside so that your father can help your mother to your longhouse."

"I want to go and watch," Red Eagle said, holding the kitten gently in his arms. He then begged with his eyes as he gazed up at his grandfather. "Can I? Please?"

"It is not your place, or mine, to get in the way of those who will be helping your mother during her time of labor, and then giving birth," Father Jacob murmured. "Do you hear the laughter? The music? There is also much food, Red Eagle. Let us go and be a part of the celebration. That will make the time go much more quickly, and then before you know it, you will be holding your brother or sister in your arms."

The entire castle and every longhouse echoed now to the rhythm of dancing feet.

Moon Song gave her father-in-law a smile of gratitude as Red Eagle handed his kitten over to his grandfather, then ran on ahead of them outdoors where she heard his squeal of laughter as he joined the other children at play.

"Thank you," Moon Song murmured, then gritted her teeth and closed her eyes as another pain sent her almost to the floor.

Swift Thunder placed a firm arm around her waist and helped her home, and soon, before there were many more pains to grab at her insides, the child was born.

Everyone came to see the beautiful daughter, whose eyes were as dark as midnight and whose skin was as white as winter snow.

But it was the thick bunch of red hair on her head that caused everyone to stop, stare, and wonder.

Father Jacob had an explanation for everyone as he stood beside the bed where his daughter-in-law was now comfortably lying on her feather mattress, her face radiant with happiness.

"My granddaughter is as beautiful as my mother was, for it was my mother whose hair was as red as the rising sun," Father Jacob said, proud of his Irish heritage.

"And that is why we call our daughter Rising Sun," Moon Song said, gazing at the baby's hair and running her fingers slowly through it.

"Rising Sun is as beautiful as her mother," Swift Thunder said, kneeling down beside the bed to place a gentle hand on Moon Song's flushed cheek. "*Niu*, your husband has never seen you more beautiful than now."

"I have never been as *happy* as now," Moon Song murmured, then giggled when Red Eagle climbed onto the bed and crawled over and snuggled against her, claiming his rights as a son who did not want to be forgotten despite the newborn in his parents' lives.

"And so are you beautiful, my son," Moon Song said, smiling at Red Eagle as he smiled at her.

"No, he is not beautiful," Swift Thunder said, gathering his son up into his arms and holding him. "He is *wiktcu*, handsome!"

"Yes, handsome . . . handsome like his father," Moon Song murmured.

When Rising Sun began crying, everyone grew quiet and watched as Moon Song placed her child's lips to her breast.

When the child began suckling, her tiny fingers contentedly kneading her mother's breast, it seemed that the entire world was centered there in that one room.

Moon Song gazed up at her husband and smiled him a quiet thank you, for he was like the Thunderers. He was a man of strength and courage. As he went from place to place he spread contentment and peace.

His name was well known now, far and wide across the countryside. Even in England his name was still spoken in awe.

And so it would be until the end of time, Moon Song thought proudly to herself as Swift Thunder handed their son to Father Jacob, then bent to a knee beside the bed and brushed a sweet, warm kiss across Moon Song's brow.

When a rumbling of thunder came to them from the west, Moon Song and Swift Thunder smiled into each other's eyes, for they knew that their second-born child had just been blessed by *Tharonhiawakon* from high above!